A Bit On T

C000002189

by

MARGARET COOK

To Jim and Mary

Love

from

Margaret

MKRY
PUBLISHING

Published in 2014 by MKRY Publishing

ISBN eBook: 978-0-9931698-1-6
ISBN Paperback: 978-0-9931698-0-9

A CIP catalogue copy of this book can be found in the
British Library.

Published with the help of Indie Authors World

Acknowledgements

I am very grateful to Kim and Sinclair Macleod of Indie Authors World for making this publication possible and guiding me through the process; to Christine McPherson for her patience, tact and insight as my editor, and to Steven Parry Donald for the photograph.

I should also like to thank all my friends in the horse world with whom I have spent many happy hours and from whom I have learned so much.

Chapter 1

"What is she like, standing there? Is she freaking out?"

"Scared bloody stiff, d'you reckon?"

"She looks like she's seen a ghost!"

Gail pushed the stable girls aside to peer through the office doorway at the person prompting their remarks. A solitary figure was standing stock still in the middle of the yard. "Are you okay out there, Mrs Fraser?" she called.

Megan turned round, smiling self-consciously, probably aware that her behaviour looked odd. "Yes, I'm just drinking in the atmosphere," she replied. "I know I'm a bit early for my lesson."

Gail, the stable manager, was tall and skinny, with straight mousy hair, enormous spectacles and a cigarette dangling from her fingers. She nodded affably. "We've just got a little job to do, then I'll take your money and sort out who you're going to ride. We'll be another fifteen minutes, okay?"

Pushing her way back to her desk, she muttered, "Now you lot better be nice to her. She can be as weird as she likes; even see visions, if she wants. She's a VIP, didn't you know?"

"What, filthy rich like? She looks like a beginner to me. No fancy gear on her." One standard-issue stable lass – a teenager with thighs like hams straining at her filthy breeches – continued to stare brazenly at the lone figure. She and her friends gauged the status of a person purely on their success in the horse-world, or the price tags of their riding clothes.

"She's married to a famous telly personality. Didn't you see him here the other day? Dick Fraser?" Gail sighed as the girls shook their heads, looking blank. "He's not on Corrie or one of those soaps. Not an actor. He fronts some serious programmes, investigates dodgy deals, supports charities, challenges politicians, and all that. He was on *Question Time* a week ago."

The girls looked unimpressed.

"Still," said one, "must be exciting being married to him. You'd think they'd swan off to some fancy place abroad for holidays. Not this dump."

"I saw him here the other day," another one piped up. "He was really nice to me, not posh and putting on airs like you'd expect. And gorgeous with it. Like that sports commentator. Made me go weak at the knees."

"He *was* really nice," said Gail. "I don't think he'd been on a horse before. That young kid who works here on Tuesdays had to give him a stick to make Greywether stand up and stop rolling in the dust, taking the piss out of a spoonie. The guy took it all in good part, though, didn't seem to mind looking an ass. It was as if he was on one of those reality shows, playing to the crowds."

"*She* doesn't look anything special. What's she got that I haven't?" asked Frankie, she of the hefty thighs. They all laughed.

"She's got a lovely head of hair," said Gail wistfully. They peered round the doorway again, where Megan was now ambling round, looking inside the boxes. "And a good pair of pins in those leggings. Neat arse."

"Not a rider's backside," agreed Frankie. "Hmmm, I guess she's not bad-looking. One of those lucky women who have it all in spades."

"Have you seen their two kids? Two angelic little boys with red hair and freckles, straight out of a church choir. Probably little monsters."

***

Megan was aware of the chat and laughter going on in the background, but blissfully unaware that the conversation was about her.

The girls' analysis of her appearance hardly did her justice; she was graceful and well-proportioned, with bronze curls in profusion and green eyes her best features. Not pretty exactly, but she glowed with the bloom of her happy womanhood, her thirty-something years; what the Scots call "bonny". She was well used to being envied, but after ten years of wedded bliss, she knew that being married to a rising star had plenty of unforeseen snags. Since her two sons had arrived, Megan had discovered that parents had to work as a team. And teams can be de-stabilised when one of the members is a prima donna.

Living in the moment, though, she was feeling bliss-fully content. It was such a heady experience finding herself on her own like this. She was usually at the mercy of so many people making demands of her that her few moments of solitude were indescribably precious. This morning Dick had promised the boys they would go and do some male things down by the river, as he was going off to London next day on a work-related concern. It would keep him away for less than twenty-four hours, but it was against all the family rules for holidays, and Megan was hardly mollified by his offer to liberate her for a morning.

Still, she had felt her spirits rising as she walked over the fields, smelling the fresh morning scent on the wet grass, patting the donkey in his enclosure, hearing the Spring birdsong, and anticipating the joy of a two-hour ride in the New Forest countryside without having to keep an eye on Jeremy and Sam. By the time she'd reached the stable yard, she was in a bubble of happiness, almost like floating in the clouds and looking down on herself, and being aware that this was the start of something really good in her life.

Peering into the dark interiors of the horse-boxes, Megan found them mostly empty, neat and clean, smelling of sweet hay and straw. Most of the horses were outside at this time of day, working or grazing in the field. She looked at the few occupants, assessing how friendly they were before patting their necks, scratching behind the ears or caressing that delicious velvety knob beneath the chin. They snorted and flared their nostrils at her, eyeing her speculatively through enormous brown eyes fringed by long, thick, sexy eyelashes.

In the last box there was something happening. Two girls worked on a lovely skewbald horse. One held her by the head collar while the other lifted the tail and washed underneath with a sponge and water from a bucket. Intent upon their task, they ignored Megan.

She moved off and walked a little way down the track towards the open moorland, where she would shortly be riding. In her relaxed and dreamy mood, she didn't mind waiting; she would have been happy to stand and stare for hours in the dappled morning sunlight and gentle breeze.

Suddenly, sounds of urgent activity erupted in the yard, people running around and sounds of peremptory clapping.

"Look, the hack's nearly back and we haven't even started yet. Get cracking. Where's the mare? Is she ready?" bellowed Gail. "Okay, Penny, you going to hold her? She's very sensible, and she's well in heat. That's fine, good, good..."

Megan hastened back to the paddock, sensing some event was imminent, as the coloured mare she had seen being bathed was led in. The skewbald had bandages on her legs, while the tail was also bandaged and tied up in a loop.

"Just keep her walking around for now," Gail instructed her staff. "Frankie, you'll cope with the stallion, won't you? Just take care, he's not madly experienced. I'll give you a shout when we're ready."

In the paddock the mare was taken over to a corner, facing the fence, while Gail and another girl inspected her rear end. Megan could see the horse's soft moist parts below the tail writhing and vibrating as if in anticipation, exuding a few drops of urine. She leaned her elbows on the railing, aware of how the mare felt and conscious of feeling a bit tingly herself around the erogenous zones.

Gail stomped past on her way back to the yard, grinned, and shrugged at Megan. "It's Spring," she said in explanation.

Then Frankie came into the paddock leading an extremely uptight horse. His steps were springy and his eyes stood out as if on stalks. He caught sight of the mare, who stood quite still, her back legs braced and apart. He started to prance while he unfurled his member, which swung hugely between his back legs.

Megan couldn't take her eyes off it. It was enormous! Shaped just like a man's too, with a knobby end, and pink with dark patches.

Frankie – a large and muscular young woman with a big bosom well strapped down under her T-shirt – was barely able to hold the stallion as it leapt up in the air, fortunately well away from the mare. The stable hand crouched and scrambled out of the way, her hands over her head. Then, as the stallion came to earth, Frankie turned with remarkable agility and grabbed the rope again. She and Gail turned the stallion towards the mare, and inched him towards her.

His nostrils twitched and flared, and his head tossed, while the women murmured placatory noises at him. Then suddenly he seemed to twig what he was supposed to do, reared up, and heaved himself on the mare's back.

Megan watched entranced as his front legs bent at the knees, and he supported his weight on them with his front feet well out of the way to the sides. "How neat," she thought. "So she doesn't get kicked or scraped."

With Frankie still holding the rope, she and Gail were bending down, looking with prurient fixation as the engorged phallus swung to and fro, taking on a life of its own like a blind serpent. "In!" bellowed Frankie triumphantly, as it fumbled its way into the wet orifice.

A few moments later it was all over, the stallion subsiding from the mare with his member softening, dripping white goo. He was led triumphantly away, while Penny walked the mare around the paddock again.

One of the stable girls joined Megan at the fence, shaking her head with resigned amusement. "These guys just don't have a clue."

"Not much in the way of foreplay!" Megan laughed. She looked forward to relating the incident to Dick later, when the boys were in bed.

***

Megan was pleased but surprised to see Dick and the boys waiting to collect her when she arrived back at the stable after her hack. Jeremy and Sam were feeding carrots to a small Shetland pony, and being fussed over by a few of the stable girls.

"You must have been missing me!" she joked, and introduced them to Storm, her staunch companion for the past two hours.

"Errrr... there's been a change of plan, Mum," said Jeremy, looking a little glum. Megan's heart sank.

Dick was holding court, working his charm on a couple who had obviously recognised him. Eventually he extricated himself with brisk goodbyes, and shepherded his family into his sleek silver Jaguar. Although Jeremy hadn't said any more, Megan gathered that Dick wanted to go out for lunch, directly from the stable.

"I'm scruffy and sweaty," she protested. "I must go back to change first!"

But Dick was in dynamic mode and drove off in the other direction. "God, what a bore that fellow was," he grumbled. "And she was a toffee-nosed b–"

"Dick, please explain what's going on!"

Conscious of the boys listening in the back seats, and as usual driving in haste even along the narrow country lanes, he suggested they wait for explanations until they reached the café. Once they were ensconced at their table in the rustic village restaurant, having ordered steaming soup and salads, he dropped his bombshell.

He had received a call from the studio that morning and it was imperative for him to go to London that day, spending two nights away from them. Critically, because time was tight, he needed to take the car and barely had time to drop them all back at their holiday cottage after lunch.

Megan was aghast, as he'd known she would be. She put down her spoon and glared at him.

"You can't leave us here for two days without any transport!"

"Why not? Surely you've got all you need in the Forest? You'll get lots of riding, you lucky things."

"At the very least, I need the car to shop. Why can't you hire a car?" It seemed he didn't have time. "Well, we'll have to shop before you go. There's next to nothing to eat in the house. Do you think we can go native and support ourselves fishing or something?"

"Megan, I can't spare the time. I really have to be off." He looked at his watch. "In half an hour or so."

"And are we to starve?" Megan's natural instinct was to cast around for a solution, but for once she didn't see why she should let him off the hook. The boys were beginning to look round-eyed and alarmed at the prospect of two days with no food.

"I have a plan," Dick smiled reassuringly, taking out his mobile. He tapped in a number then spoke effusively on the phone. It soon became apparent that he was asking their landlady, who lived in a large mansion adjacent to their holiday cottage, if she could possibly take Megan and the boys into Fordingbridge.

"My wife needs to do her shopping," he explained, while outlining the reason for his emergency departure. He ended the phone call warmly, put the mobile down with an air of "Mission Accomplished", and turned to Megan with a winning smile.

"There we are. Easy. Ten tomorrow morning, she'll take you into town."

"Since when did we call Mrs Weston Wendy?" asked Megan. "Dick, I'm horrified at you asking her for favours like that. I hate to be dependent on people's charity. And it's not MY shopping, it's OURS. She may have been all over you today, but she won't be so charming to me tomorrow. I think I'd prefer to get her to take us to a garage and I'll hire a car. Or if she's very reluctant, I'll get a taxi to the garage."

"Well, suit yourself, but it's a needless expense."

Megan was quiet for a bit, feeling better that she had her own solution. She'd feel happier if they had their own wheels, but she'd call on Mrs Weston first and see what her reaction was.

Keen to change the subject, Dick – with a little prompting from Jeremy – began relating an incident at the stable when they had been waiting for her. Although he was a witty raconteur with a superb sense of timing and capacity to mimic, Megan was hardly concentrating. Her thoughts were on whether they needed milk before tomorrow, and whether there was something she could pick up there at the café-shop for their evening meal.

Picking up the threads of the story, she gathered they'd seen a pukka family of horse owners arrive in a Land Rover Discovery, dressed in immaculate riding wear, and talking loudly about the next point-to-point meeting. The tale involved the family's young boy, who had gone with his father to buy a riding hat but had bought the wrong colour.

"You ARE a muggings, daahling," his mother had said, while his sister taunted him publicly without pity. Sam had gone up to the boy, feeling sorry for him and trying to make friends, but the mother had pulled the child away.

"Was that who you were speaking to as I rode back?" Megan asked.

"Yes," said Dick. "The fellow knew who I was – he was a down-to-earth businessman – but *she* came from another planet. Talk about looking down your nose."

Megan divined that Dick had felt out of his social comfort zone, a situation he hated. Eventually he reached the moral of his tale, pondering on the chasm that would have to be crossed before they could aspire to ride elegant, spirited horses and wear immaculate, velvet helmets.

"We should get proper riding clothes," he said.

Biting back the comment that they should actually learn to ride first, Megan replied, "Do you remember that incredibly upmarket shop for all things horsey we saw in London years ago, when we were students? And the outrageous prices they charged for everything? Wonderful name – Swaine, Adeney and Briggs. Talk about Dickensian!" She laughed as she remembered. "We couldn't believe anyone would be daft enough – or rich enough – to shop there."

But Dick was looking at her in delighted amazement. "Megan, you are a genius! I can go there and get myself kitted out when I'm in London. Well remembered."

Megan's jaw dropped in horror. "Dick, you can't be serious. It would cost a mortgage. Those things are for the aristos, the folk with more money than sense – and most especially, the people at the top of the sport."

She realised with a sinking feeling in the pit of her stomach that he was at least half-serious. For Dick, his estimate of himself could only be measured through other people's eyes, and the price of his image could never be too high. What had started out as the high-spot of her holiday was becoming memorable for all the wrong reasons.

Megan was aware that other clients in the café were looking round at them in curiosity. Dick was a striking figure – tall, broad-shouldered, with patrician features and bearing. No doubt most of them recognised him.

Out of the corner of her eye, she saw a middle-aged lady get to her feet and begin to home in on them with serious intent. Megan glared and tried to put the woman off with unfriendly body language, but to no avail. The woman arrived and, leaning over Dick, began to gush about his latest television programme. She turned round to pull up a chair, saying, "May I join you?"

But this was a step too far for Megan. She brought the flat of her hand down on the table sharply, startling everyone. "NO! My husband is about to go, and we want some precious minutes with him. Please go away."

The woman jumped back as if stung, pushed the chair back into place, and retreated looking angry and flushed.

"That was incredibly rude, darling," said Dick, looking a little uneasy.

"It certainly was – rude on her part. I'll get some milk then pay the bill. See you in the car."

As they set off for the cottage, Dick lectured Megan about the need to keep his fan-base sweet and cautioned her against being rude to one of his admirers.

"It's not as if you're an MP and need votes to keep your job!" she observed.

"Nevertheless, my success depends on my popularity. You must just put up with occasional intrusions."

They drove the short distance to the cottage with a slight atmosphere then, dropping off the family with rushed goodbyes, Dick sped away as if on a mercy mission.

Megan immediately went next door and rang Mrs Weston's bell. The landlady did not look at all pleased to see her and was, as expected, decidedly frosty. Apologising on Dick's behalf, Megan cancelled the arrangement for a lift into town the following day, and Mrs Weston's demeanour visibly thawed.

"Just as well," she said. "I have a Women's Institute committee meeting here tomorrow afternoon, and I couldn't really spare the time. What has called your husband away to London so suddenly?"

Megan paused. "Do you know, I'm not sure. Something about an interview. We hardly had time to discuss…"

Mrs Weston's eyebrows flickered, and Megan could guess what the woman was thinking. "Well," she sniffed, "men must have their freedom, I suppose."

Megan didn't reply. Instead, she asked about car rental, and was directed to the information book in the cottage. "If there's any difficulty, just mention my name," Mrs Weston added.

When Megan telephoned the dealer, she was able to arrange a hire car that day. And when she mentioned her landlady's name, the garage man offered to drive it over to the cottage within the next hour. She heaved a sigh of relief; her life was organised and on track again.

Such organisational skills had won Megan a prestigious job in hospital management at an unusually young age. Unfortunately, the same qualities also enabled Dick to exploit her as carelessly as he had done today, she reflected. Why had she not interrogated him about the sudden need for his departure?

More importantly, though, she still had a little repair work to do with her boys.

"Why were you so unkind to that lady, Mummy?" asked Sam. "You were like the snooty woman at the stable who wouldn't let me speak to her boy. The one who got the wrong colour hat." Astonished at the curious logic of children, she had to think for a moment before replying.

"Well, Sam," she began eventually. "When you went to speak to the boy, you were sorry for him, right? You wanted to be friendly and make him feel better. He'd been made to feel stupid and was standing on his own. Now in a café, it isn't polite for a stranger to intrude on other people in their family groups. You would never do that, I hope, and nor would I. But because your dad is famous, people think they know him and can claim his attention. It's rude and selfish. They aren't doing it for nice or kind reasons. They just want to boast to their friends."

"Actually, I think you were quite right, Mum," said Jeremy.

Chapter 2

Since the catastrophe two weeks ago, Annabel had longed for solitude, only to find that when she was alone she needed someone around her. She was struggling to cope with these see-saw emotions. Alone, she sank into apathy and brooded. In company, she got on with things more or less as normal; on the surface, at least.

This morning, after the girls had gone to school and Ralph had departed for his psychotherapy session, Annabel knew she would find time to be alone and think. Eva, her housekeeper, was working around the house, but the young Polish woman could be kept at arm's length. Annabel knew Eva was well aware that the family were in crisis, and would make the most of what gossip came her way.

Leaving her to get on with tidying up, Annabel headed upstairs and sank down on her unmade bed. The bright, airy room was tastefully decorated with honey-coloured wood furniture, full length mirrors, walk-in wardrobes, heavy window drapes, all in a melange of pale apricot, mushroom and cream. But this morning it didn't delight her eye as it normally did. Strewn with the detritus of two troubled people – clothes and shoes everywhere, papers and magazines on the floor, bedside tables littered with packets of pills and dirty tumblers – it just looked depressing.

Annabel piled pillows up against the bedhead and sank back against them. No matter how often she replayed the sequence of events in her mind, she could not get the tragedy out of her thoughts. Poor Mimi. Annabel forced herself to think of her best moments with the beautiful mare (Mimi was short for Melting Moment): the triumphs in competition, the exhilaration of the hunt, the sheer joy of grooming that sleek, shiny, thoroughbred, mahogany-coloured body. They had been so in tune that the horse had instinctively known what Annabel wanted her to do almost before she knew herself. Her tears welled up and overflowed.

Annabel was the first to admit she led a privileged life, and had always accepted this as the norm. But now, with the series of terrible events that had happened of late, she couldn't help wondering if the fates had turned on her, and she was being punished for something.

First, there was her husband – a workaholic of the first order. They were both Edinburgh lawyers, but it was Ralph who took his career more seriously, working all hours at the office, becoming increasingly stressed and moody, but certainly successful and earning a staggeringly good income. She didn't interfere until the signs of stress became worrying: he couldn't take time off for their usual Easter holiday in Umbria; he always had a tumbler of whisky on his desk when he worked at home; he became distant, bad-tempered and non-communicative; and their love-life suffered.

Then there was their elder daughter, Lily – always a difficult, contrary girl, she was galloping headlong into a turbulent, tetchy adolescence. Annabel had even been invited to the school to discuss Lily's belligerence and rude confrontations with teachers. Thankfully, their younger child, Poppy, was sweet and biddable as ever.

Annabel had been coping reasonably well with the family issues –until the Mimi incident.

She could clearly recall that Saturday morning. Preparing to set off with her daughters to Hadley Riding Centre – all dressed in their boots, jodhpurs and fleeces – it was Annabel who had answered when the phone rang. The owner of the centre, Lady Miranda – most people called her Mandy – had sounded hesitant, her husky voice lacking its usual cheerfulness. A cold hand had gripped Annabel's heart and she knew almost before Mandy could get the words out that disaster had struck. Where had that dreadful premonition come from?

Mandy had explained that Mimi had been found that morning with a fractured leg. "I'm so-o-o-o sorry, my dear," she had sympathized. "The vet has been called. Can you please come straight away?"

Annabel found she continued doing the things set in train before the news reached her brain, as if it was programmed and could not be deflected. She bundled the girls into the Honda four-wheel drive, and set off; quite sensibly, not rushing and taking risks, or doing anything foolish. Lily and Poppy knew something was up. They were tense, snatching quick glances at each other with troubled faces. Annabel told them that Mimi had had an accident, but she didn't yet know how serious. She drove the rest of the journey in silence, then parked and told them curtly to wait in the car.

The vet, Tom Cormack, was standing at the edge of the field with Mandy and a stable hand. Joining them, Annabel looked into their faces which were heavy with gloom.

Tom said, "It's a fracture, I'm afraid. A spiral one." He shook his head. "She'll have to be put down."

Annabel broke. Tears streamed down her cheeks and she shuddered and choked with sobs, her hands over her face as if her sorrows were too terrible to be witnessed. "How did it happen? Was she kicked?" Inevitably her mind raced to avoidable causes, wanting to blame someone, to have a focus for her anguish, someone to scream blue murder at.

Tom turned, muttering about not leaving the mare suffering. He had only been waiting for her permission. Annabel wanted to see Mimi, wanted to say goodbye, yet could not bear to see her broken, damaged and in anguish.

"I suppose I'd better not see her?"

Mandy said gently, "No dear," and guided her back to the car. "Jill, you go with Annabel. Go back to the house and put the kettle on for coffee. I'll be along shortly."

For the rest of that day, the girls tiptoed round and talked quietly as if there had been a human death in the family. Annabel was touched at their tactful intuition. That afternoon, she took herself out for a long walk across the golf course adjacent to their house, and into a hilly nature reserve beyond, ruminating and weeping. She sat on a rock with a view towards the Firth of Forth, staring into the middle distance, wondering how she should be so unlucky. Then she sighed, gathered herself together, and walked back home; dinner and domestic obligations called.

She had been sitting in the kitchen, still sad and musing, wondering how she could ever have gloried in its walnut and silver, state-of-the-art cabinets and fittings, when Ralph burst in.

"What's the matter?" he demanded abruptly, knowing instantly from her expression that some catastrophe had occurred.

When she told him, he turned away, exhaled hugely, then went round the table and sat down opposite her. She looked at him with big, round eyes, wondering at his strange, unsympathetic response. For the second time that day, she had an intuition of something bad. Had they gone bankrupt? Had a war broken out? What? What!

"You're so miserable right now, I think it's right to tell you something else. I've been having an affair. But it's over now."

Annabel stared at him expressionless.

"What? Who with?"

"Oh, you've guessed before now. Claire, my PA. But we've had a bust-up. It's over. Happened today. Really is over, that's why I'm telling you."

She registered his naïve admission, but said nothing.

"Look. You and I, we've not been seeing enough of each other. We've drifted apart. Too busy, always too busy. We should make this a chance to get together again. Why don't we go away for a weekend? I'm sure my mother would look after the girls. The Lake District maybe. Wouldn't you like that?"

Annabel continued to stare at him with a fazed expression, her emotions a blank. She gave an incredulous, bitter little laugh.

"Just like that. I've had an affair. Sorry. It's over. Be nice to me. Let's go away together. For God's sake, Ralph!"

"We need time to heal our wounds. Rebuild our marriage. It's our duty to the girls, as well as ourselves. I'll give Mum a ring this evening."

Annabel noticed how deftly the blame and responsibility had been apportioned between them; how he was trying to rush her past the bit where she might be expected to explode in wrath.

But in the ensuing days, it became apparent that his confession had been a desperate response to the humiliation of being rejected by Claire, plain dumpy nonentity that she was. She had chucked him, and his ego – never very robust – had been crushed, felled like a tree. He admitted Claire had wanted him to make an honest woman of her and he had refused. Or so he said. There had, at any rate, been a quarrel which was beyond repair.

Annabel had the impression that she was expected to commiserate and support him in his traumas. But she had not blown up or even shown anger. Secretive and reserved as she was, even she was bewildered by how neutral she felt about his confession. Cynically, she realised that Ralph was crying out for her mothering and support, to nurture his battered self-esteem. He had not said a word of sympathy for her own loss. He had barely registered it. He just assumed her concern for him would swamp everything else. She had slipped into the role of carer without meaning to.

Annabel had examined her own feelings, finding she felt absolutely nothing for him; no anger or resentment over his affair. All her passionate sorrows were centred upon her lost mare, and the magnitude of that loss eclipsed any fury she might have felt towards him. She wondered if the timing of his confession made him crassly insensitive, or cunningly astute.

Passively, she had gone along with the Lake District plan. Ralph told the girls he was taking their mother away to cheer her up. While they were there, he regressed, calling her "Mummy", whimpering and playing the child. She felt disgusted. Why couldn't she have a strong, supportive husband, for God's sake?

She said roughly, "I don't like this 'Mummy' business."

"All right, I'll never call you that again," he retorted, deeply affronted.

Part of his neediness was that they have lots of sex that weekend. A man needs to have sex to feel loved, Annabel told herself, as she responded rather better to this than might have been expected. Her response, though, was nothing to do with lust for him. Still deeply pensive, it had occurred to her that his infidelity freed her from her own vows. She had never so much as looked at another man since she married Ralph. But now…

She found the idea of freedom exciting. She might even act on it. Her thoughts turned to Tom Cormack, who had been sympathetic and kind, and several other fellow-livery male friends. With such fancies in her mind, she was warm in her responses to Ralph. He probably assumed she was excited at the thought of his own manly waywardness.

But Annabel felt a new measure of power in his dependence on her. She told him to amuse himself while she went shopping in Keswick and explored the many antique outlets of the area. He took her out for expensive dinners, and one night when they had a disgraceful amount to drink, confessed to another indiscretion, with a trainee about three years before. Annabel was completely dazed. How like a lawyer, she thought. Asking for other similar sins to be taken into account, to avoid repercussions at a future date. Worse, he confessed his sins with an air of impish glee, as if expecting her to join in the merriment and admire his wickedness. He had never had any girlfriends before her, she remembered. He had been her ugly duckling, and she had thought he would be safe from female predators.

When they returned home, Ralph began to fall into a still deeper depression. He was drinking uncontrollably, she discovered, and she regretted colluding with this excess on the weekend away. He was also sleeping badly, despite taking pills. Sometimes his restlessness disturbed her, and she suggested he should move into one of the guest rooms. But he refused. She did not press the point, afraid that the girls would notice. Under the influence of the two narcotics, his memory deteriorated and his concentration diminished. He became impossibly boring in conversation. Would he ever be the same again?

She was appalled at the collapse of his character and formidable intellect in such a short space of time. Her revulsion for this weak and broken man showed, and he became angry, provoking rows. He had taken some time off work, but was sufficiently senior for no-one to challenge his need for sick leave. Once he accepted he was ill, he showed no great haste to get back to normal, to Annabel's alarm.

The girls were aware of the troubled tension between their parents, but Annabel tried to conceal things from them as much as she could. Poppy seemed to believe that once her mother got another horse, everything in the family would revert to normal.

***

Annabel awoke suddenly as the front door slammed. Dazed, she sat up and looked at the clock, registering it was midday. That must have been Eva leaving, she thought. Guilt added to her general wretchedness, as Eva was expecting to be paid today. Then the doorbell rang.

"Shit," she muttered. "Shit, shit, double-shit." She slithered off the bed, lurched to the door, and ran downstairs barefoot. Grabbing her handbag off the hall table, she wrestled her purse out and opened the front door. It was indeed Eva.

"Sorry," Annabel muttered, shaking hair out of her eyes, fishing out some notes and handing them over. She grimaced rather than smiled, and closed the door abruptly. She hated those eyes taking in her unkempt state, her crumpled sweat pants and top, unwashed hair, red eyes.

In the kitchen she found lukewarm coffee in the pot, and poured out a mugful. Mooching through the hall, heading outside for a seat on the patio, she caught sight of herself in a full-length mirror and stopped in her tracks. Well aware that she had let herself go, she was still shocked by how terrible she looked. Annabel was accustomed to stunning people with her exquisite loveliness – her pale skin and long black hair, her almost perfect model's figure even now in her mid-forties.

The moment had its effect, and she started purpose-fully up the stairs, still clutching her coffee mug, into the en-suite bathroom. She turned on the shower, stripping off her clothes as she went. She had just immersed herself under the hot, comforting water when the phone rang in the bedroom. Grabbing a towel, she ran into the room and lifted the receiver. It was Ralph.

"Hi, it's me. I need your help. Got myself in a bit of a pickle."

"I thought you were seeing your therapist."

"I was. I did. When I came out, the car was gone."

"Stolen?"

"Well, no. It seems I left the handbrake off. The car rolled down the slope and crashed into another parked car. When the owner of the other car came back, he called the police."

"And?"

"They took my car away and impounded it. I rang the police to report my car missing, and they told me I have to pay about thirty quid to get it back. And there'll be damages to repair."

"Can't you sort all that out without my help?"

"Well, no. I'm at the police station. I had to fill in some paperwork. They warned me not to collect the car right now. In fact, they suggested I ring you to collect me."

"You mean…"

"Yes, yes. After my session with the analyst, I went and had a couple."

Annabel looked at his bedside table and the assorted sleeping pills.

"I guess you took some pills to get to sleep last night?"

"Yes. Three at least."

"Right, I'll come and pick you up. I'm just in the shower, so you'll have to wait a bit. Where exactly are you?"

Annabel returned to her shower. "Sod him, he'll have to wait," she thought, soaping herself and applying liberal quantities of shampoo to her hair. Rinsing and drying took time; she wouldn't rush. It felt good to be fresh again.

Going to her wardrobe, she took out clean Armani jeans, a white shirt, a jacket, and snakeskin sneakers. She dressed then applied some moisturizer, powder and lipstick to her face. Swiftly she gathered up the acres of discarded clothing around the room and stuffed them into the laundry bin. She went to Ralph's bedside table and scooped up all the bottles and foil packets – noting three different kinds of pills – then locked them in her own drawer.

She ran downstairs, grabbed her bag and keys, jumped in her car, and set off. Her mind was racing. At some level, she felt as if she'd had a kick-start. Ralph was on a virtual precipice, his whole self disintegrating. How fragile men were! While she had been brooding on her own miseries, he could have done something terminally destructive to all of them. She could not help remembering her mother's words some sixteen years ago, when she and Ralph had announced their engagement. Her mother, planning some aristocratic connection for her desirable daughter, had gone ballistic.

"You'll rue the day, my girl. Mark my words! He's a nobody! He may be very brainy, good at passing exams. But who are his family? He's got no money! How will he keep you?"

Her mother had wanted Annabel to go to finishing school in Switzerland, or at the very least – since she insisted on University – to Oxford, where she would meet people of consequence. But her daughter had insisted on Aberdeen – a "sink of ordinariness", according to her mother. And there, where she could have had almost any man she wanted, she had chosen the brilliant, top man of her year: Ralph – plain, nerdy and bespectacled, a young man who had never before had a girlfriend.

Her mother had not warmed to Ralph, although her father came to appreciate his dry wit, analytical mind, and nimble conversation. Ralph, in spite of his humble origins in a Lanarkshire mining family, was no man-of-the-people but an elitist, a staunch Conservative, and financially most astute.

Two motives sprang to the forefront of Annabel's mind, as she parked outside the police station. The first, not to let her parents get wind of Ralph's disgrace; and second, to restore him to his most important role as chief family breadwinner.

Inside, she was greeted by the officer at the desk. "Had to put him in the cell, he's a bit queasy. Needed to lie down. Seems to have had a skinful."

She found Ralph looking very pale and dazed. Between them, they helped him upstairs and out to the car. Ralph testily shook off the policeman's supporting hand.

"Let's get the hell out of here," he said, slurring his words.

In the car, Annabel questioned him about what had happened at the session; why had he gone for a drink? It seemed the analyst had been brutally blunt and told him that if he went on drinking at his present rate, he'd be dead in two years. He would, even now, find it tough to get back to work, but going to A.A. might help.

"So your response was to drown your sorrows?" she said tartly.

"I guess. I really only had two – doubles."

"You're bloody lucky not to be on a drink-driving charge. Or worse. I think you got confused in the night. I heard you taking pills around five this morning. Probably the combined effects have knocked you for six."

Ralph leaned his head back. "Claire has been given the push from the firm," he mumbled. "With a little persuasion… Tough on her, to lose her job."

Annabel said nothing in reply. It's always the woman that gets the blame, she thought.

***

In sharp contrast to the morning apathy, Annabel busied herself for the rest of the day with multiple tasks. She arranged to collect Ralph's BMW from the pound the next morning, to pay the fine and deliver it to the garage for repairs. She phoned Ralph's psychoanalyst and gave him hell, describing the disastrous effects of his straight-talking. She did the same with their family doctor for prescribing multiple types of sleeping pills to a depressed man with alcohol problems.

The family doctor promptly appeared on the doorstep and gave Ralph a good going-over. He took some blood tests for a check on his liver, and offered some practical advice. When he left, Annabel unfolded the bed-settee in Ralph's dressing room – adjacent to their bedroom – and he crashed out there for the next twenty hours. Then she rang her own law firm, and requested that she be allowed to work full time instead of her usual three days a week.

By the time the girls came in from school and family routine had kicked in, she realized she had not thought of Mimi for a good six hours.

Chapter 3

"Can't say I've ever heard of him."

"Oh, Sue, where have you been? He's on the box all the time and in the papers, too!"

"I never read the papers and hardly ever watch the telly," said Sue sniffily.

Bridget looked disappointed that her high-profile new customer had not caused the reaction she'd expected. As the two women chatted on the doorstep of the bungalow attached to Leatherburn Riding Stable, near Edinburgh, the contrast between them was so great as to be comical. Stable owner Bridget was tiny – not much over five feet – skinny, grey-haired, and carelessly dressed in slacks and a man's shirt. Sue, on the other hand, was a young woman in her prime, with wild blonde hair, a healthy, outdoor complexion, a strong, well-muscled build, and an air of consequence. She wore riding breeches, worn leather boots, a denim shirt and jacket.

"I've got a picture of him somewhere. Come on in," said Bridget, determined to impress Sue.

Inside the house, she scrabbled about among some papers strewn around the kitchen. "Here! In the *Daily Mail* yesterday." She flourished it triumphantly.

Sue looked at the picture of a man's head and shoulders, posed to camera; he was certainly handsome, all Hugh Grant floppy hair and showman's grin, rather full of himself. The feature related to a new television series he was presenting on ethical farming; he looked vaguely familiar.

"Dick Fraser… ethical farming? Well, it rings a faint bell. Is he a horseman?"

Bridget laughed. "No way. But he wants to be one. He's only been for a couple of lessons and hacks. His wife and two kids are coming regularly, but with him, it's the usual – time pressures. That's why I thought of you. He'd be a good one for private lessons. Do you want me to suggest it to him? Drop a hint to his wife, perhaps?"

This time Sue's ears pricked up. "That sounds a great idea," she said, giving the picture another look. "He's a complete beginner, I take it? Yes, by all means drop a hint."

"Right. He's not the keep-fit, sporty type, but seems very keen. Doesn't want the family racing ahead of him, either. He'll be one who likes the excitement of riding more than the finer points."

Sue looked at her watch and turned to go. One of her clients was down at the enormous indoor school doing a work-in on a horse before an hour's intensive – and expensive – teaching session with Sue. The fee was divided between herself and Bridget.

As they walked down to the school together, Bridget had more news to impart.

"I've had another interesting client. Not sure if she'd be one for you, though. Name of Annabel Lindsay. Very posh and well-connected, related to land-owners in Perth and all sorts of high heid-yins. She's coming to the advanced class, and her main motive is to buy a horse. She lost a really good mare after an accident. Needs a quality animal. She's got history. Made it to the junior national eventing team in her youth, and still does affiliated eventing. So if you hear of a suitable horse… money no object whatsoever. She used to keep her mare in livery over at Her Ladyship's." This last word was spoken with a sour expression; Bridget's habitual reaction every time the rival establishment was mentioned.

"But she's loving the class here. I have high hopes that if we find her a horse, she might stay with us. I've got a lot of new horses arriving from Ireland in the next week or so. You might want to look them over, too. Come back up to the house and have a coffee when you're finished."

***

Sue had a lot to digest and think over when she left Bridget's later that evening. She drove her dilapidated Land Rover almost on auto-pilot between Leatherburn and her home forty minutes' drive away in the East Lothian countryside. She was amused that Bridget hoped to win over one of Lady Mandy Morton-Merrydew's livery clients. Why would anyone willingly change the smooth opulence of that establishment for the rough-and-ready, gypsy-fair nature of Leatherburn? This woman Annabel was probably only riding here because Bridget had a huge stock and a rapid turnover.

Sue was well aware of the rumours surrounding the enmity between the two stable-owners. One version said that Bridget's husband, Ned Stark, had been an admirer of Lady Mandy in his youth. But that was so outrageously improbable that Sue had quickly discounted it. Ned was a down-at-heel, foul-mouthed, bad-tempered tramp, while Lady Mandy was aristo-class. The woman had fallen on hard times, admittedly, and was very eccentric.

Of course, Sue had to admit Ned was superbly clever with horses, so there was a possibility of some connection there. A sort of Lady Chatterley thing, maybe?

Sue had known Bridget for a number of years, and had learned a lot from her about how to conduct horse business. Plenty of riding stables run by horse-lovers struggled or sank without trace, because their owners weren't tough enough. Bridget kept her staff to a minimum and drove them ruthlessly. A few of them lived above the public toilets in an unheated flat – accommodation worse than some illegal immigrants had to put up with, Sue suspected. And they had to pay rent! Bridget also relied a lot on a number of regular unpaid volunteers, mostly young girls who would do anything just to be around horses and get a few rides.

Leatherburn's owner's true genius, though, was that her fundamental business was buying and selling horses. She got them cheaply, somehow – possibly through her husband's mysterious networking, and they tended to arrive in lorries late at night. She put them in the school to be ridden by her clients, worked them hard, then sold them on. Sue reckoned the school's clients didn't realise to what extent they were guinea pigs, learning to ride on total unknowns. But Ned Stark certainly had the ability to assess a horse quickly enough, so no grave disaster had so far occurred. And regular riders learned a lot through riding a different horse every week.

Sue thought she could at some stage follow Bridget's example, and perhaps even refine it. She could buy a promising young horse, work it hard in her schooling area, then sell it on at a profit. Perhaps the plan could be tried out on this posh person Annabel. Sue would need some capital to buy another horse, though – and that was a snag. But if she was successful, her finances would take a turn for the better. The possibility of a famous client was a nice idea, but such people were often fly-by-nights, not ready to commit to hard work, so she had better not expect too much from the Dick Fraser plan.

Sue drove along the farm track to the big rambling farmhouse called Brockhollow, where she lived with her husband and young daughter. They occupied the basement flat, thanks to a superb arrangement with Rosemary, the farmer's wife. Sue paid her rent in kind, by taking care of Rosemary's two hunters and keeping them fit for the hunting season. And Rosemary was happy for Sue to keep her own two horses in the stable there. She was beginning to get one or two clients coming with their own horses for training, building up a reputation and a growing business.

After checking the horses, she let herself into the house to find Mike sprawled in a dilapidated armchair watching some mindless TV show, a glass of beer and a bag of crisps at his side. The flat was spacious but down-at-heel, all faded, peeling wallpaper, worn linoleum and threadbare furnishings.

Sue was keen to share her news. "Can I put this off now? Come into the kitchen and chat. Shelley go down all right? Can you get me a beer?"

"Sorry, this is the last," Mike grunted, switching off the television and slouching after her, crumpling the crisp packet as he swallowed the dregs in his glass.

Sue went to put on the kettle.

"Have you heard of a TV personality called Dick Fraser?"

"Sure, of course. He was on tonight. Some new, worthy series, rather boring. I switched channels. Why do you ask?"

"He's a new customer over at Leatherburn. He and his family are regulars."

Mike was more impressed than she had been. "You must get his autograph."

Sue snorted her contempt. "Autograph be damned. He may want private lessons, courtesy of Sue Maxwell!"

She made a dramatic flourish, then swung open the fridge door looking for something to eat. She was famished.

"Christ almighty, Mike, there's nothing here!" She looked at him in horror.

"I get hungry, especially when I'm alone and bored."

"I filled the fridge only two days ago! That was meant to last at least till the weekend."

"I pay for it, why shouldn't I eat it?"

"I left a shepherd's pie that was more than enough for the three of us. Didn't you think of me at all?"

They'd had a similar row last week with Mike saying he paid for everything, while Sue reminded him that she provided their accommodation.

He had become a compulsive eater since their wedding four years ago, and his weight had ballooned. Sue picked up his suit trousers that were hanging over the back of a chair. "What's this?"

"They're split at the back. I wondered if you could mend them for me tonight."

Sue held up the voluminous garment. "They're torn across the seat. I can't mend them. Problem is, Mike, you've got too big for them. I thought you got new suits through your work?"

"Every two years. I'm not due another pair till next year. Look, I need a suit for work. Can you give me some dosh? I can slip into Marks and Spencer's tomorrow between calls."

"Are you mad? I can't give you any money. I've got a delivery of horse feed tomorrow, and I'm going to have to pay by cheque and pray that it doesn't bounce. You just eat up all our money – and it shows." She poked him hard in the belly.

"I thought you were going to ask your doctor about my weight?"

"I did. She said no more cooked breakfasts, no beer, no snacking between meals. And more exercise, preferably every day. What did you expect her to say?"

Mike looked a little pale. "I have to have a good breakfast, what an idiot she is. I don't eat too much."

Sue was weary of arguing with someone so ridiculously in denial. "Well, the new regime starts tomorrow, like it or not, because there's nothing for breakfast. You've scoffed all the bread, I see."

"I thought you'd have something stashed away in the larder. This *is* a farm, for God's sake."

Sue went upstairs to borrow a loaf and some eggs from Rosemary, who showed not a flicker of annoyance. The farmer's wife was highly receptive to her horse news, and very encouraging.

"Look, my dear, how shall I put it? I think you're going places, you're really getting a name in the horse world. And if I can be of more substantial help, don't hesitate to ask. This idea of a young horse to bring on – it's just spot on, just what you should be doing. I could loan you the money. No bother at all. Everyone needs a helping hand at first."

Sue was deeply touched. She was so used to struggling against the odds that such kindness was almost destabilising. She already owed Rosemary a great deal, including her livelihood.

"Oh, while I think about it," Rosemary added, "Jim was out shooting rabbits. Would you like one for the pot?" She hurried off and produced a furry carcass. "Why don't you all come up for a meal the day after tomorrow? Just ourselves. You haven't been up to us for a while."

When Sue went back downstairs, Mike had gone to bed. She felt considerably better as she busied herself making toast and scrambled eggs. With Rosemary's generosity, she could put off any more shopping for two days. She wondered if Rosemary had overheard the exchanges about food and money. While she ate her supper, she scribbled figures on the back of an envelope, and came to the conclusion that she, Shelley, and her own horses could just about live on the money she was making. Mike was a millstone round her neck with his over-indulgence and they were creeping ever more into debt. He was the biggest mistake she had ever made in her life, except of course that he had given her Shelley.

Five years before, Sue had been in a dead-end, low-paid job as head girl in a stable in the Scottish Borders. She did not even have a horse of her own, though she was allowed to borrow a stable hack to go out hunting once in a while. On one hunt, she had met Rosemary, whom she knew vaguely through farming circles. Rosemary had offered her the use of the flat at Brockhollow, with the present arrangement of caring for the hunters. Sue had been desperate to accept, but still needed an income while she built up a client base. She could have got a loan to tide her over. She wished to God she had!

But little Miss Clever had had other ideas. She had started to frequent a pub in her spare time, looking for a wealthy farmer. Mike dropped in now and then on his way home – a smart, urban businessman, with his three-piece suit and his fancy Volvo. The path to matrimony could not have been easier. Sue had been deliriously happy, thinking the days of her hand-to-mouth existence were finally over. She had been bowled over at the impression of affluence, the urgency and demands and importance of his life.

When he took her out, she would thrill to his fast-paced, edgy driving, tail-gating and overtaking, and even once or twice testily passing on the hard shoulder. Such magnificent urgency and impatience! And after he popped the crucial question, he had been willing to come and live in this rural outback, prepared to drive the distance to work each day just so she could live as she wanted. He must love me very much, she'd thought. She'd had visions of them buying land eventually and building their own sanctum, complete with stable and paddock. And surely, with his income, that would happen soon.

It was so obviously a marriage of convenience that her friends had not been surprised. Although, being more worldly, they saw that he was not as wealthy as Sue imagined.

Disillusion came all too rapidly. She soon realised that "businessman" was a euphemism for "sales rep"; the Volvo was a company car – a two-year-old, high-mileage cast-off he'd inherited from his boss; the suit a necessary uniform, payable out of expenses and renewable every two years. And he could not afford a mortgage, so the arrangement at Brockhollow suited him perfectly.

Sue, whose work was very physical, had a healthy country appetite but assumed that Mike would need proportionately more because he was a man and spent the day working. As he left early, she got into the habit of feeding him a farmhouse breakfast of sausage, bacon and eggs. And he always ate massively at the evening meal, invariably wanting extra helpings of pudding before settling down in front of the TV, with brief sojourns during commercial breaks to raid the fridge for something more to scoff – yoghurts, chunks of cheese, cold meat, cakes.

The weekly grocery bill had expanded like Mike's girth, and when she asked for more money he would become stroppy and accuse her of spending too much on her precious animals. There was never enough to squirrel away for that homestead she dreamed of.

Sue needed a plan to control Mike's compulsive eating. Every time she left him alone in the evening – and even when she didn't – her precious hoard of food disappeared down his throat. When she'd had a good week's income, there was no point in buying a treat, like a bottle of whisky, because he just scoffed most of it. He was like a stubborn horse and she would have to manipulate rather than berate him.

She decided to take Rosemary into her confidence. The older woman had all the generous resources and storage places to be expected on a well-to-do farm, so Sue arranged to store the bulk of her food and drink upstairs in Rosemary's fridges and pantry, keeping only essential provisions downstairs. Even if Mike realised what was going on, he could hardly go and raid their landlady's kitchen.

He took up so much of their bed that she had brought in a single divan for herself. Even his interest in sex had diminished to less than once a month, and she usually had to take the initiative. Now and then he had not been able to rise to the occasion, which would make him tetchy and difficult for days. Trouble was, she didn't find him wildly exciting now that she knew what he was really like. But Sue's carnal needs were strong to the point of compelling, and she had begun to realise that she would have to look elsewhere.

***

Next morning, Sue got up later than usual. She threw a housecoat over her shortie nightdress, slipped on some clogs, and went out to see to the horses. Mike was in a sulk, with only boiled eggs and toast for breakfast, which he'd had to prepare himself while Sue got Shelley up.

Later, Sue was having tea alone in the kitchen when there was a knock on the door. It was a plumber, who'd been called to investigate a water leak at the farmhouse. Rosemary had gone out, and the workman needed a signature for his paperwork. Sue greeted him with a beaming smile and an effusive welcome. She invited him in while she looked for a pen. He offered one but she pretended not to notice.

Would he like a cup of tea? Why not? He was rugged, good-looking, easy-mannered, and had a very glad eye. Looking sluttishly dishevelled in her bedroom clothes, she left him in little doubt of her intentions. Before she had finished making his tea, he moved behind her and put his arms round her waist. His sex jabbed her urgently between the buttocks. From there it took next to no time – on the kitchen floor, and with nothing said between them – till it was over.

She remembered too late that Shelley was playing in the room next door. After he had pulled himself together and left – without his tea, but with his piece of paper duly signed – Sue took a peep into the playroom, and found her little girl absorbed and oblivious.

She went back into the kitchen and sat on the saggy old sofa to drink her tea, utterly appalled at herself. Yet she was stimulated rather than satisfied, and urgently needed more. Boy, was she horny!

In the ensuing days, the world didn't come to an end. Nobody dragged her off to the village stocks, or chopped off her hair and condemned her as a trollop, though she dreamed something of the sort. After a few days, she breathed more easily. She had got away with it, but in future – and she knew it would happen again – she must be a little more selective and cover her tracks. One way was to make sure she shagged Mike soon after, just in case. It was belt-and-braces caution as she was on the pill, but you never knew.

Chapter 4

Megan's stomach was churning with nerves and she was unable to concentrate. She'd read the same paragraph three times but still hadn't taken it in.

"This is ridiculous!" she exclaimed aloud. "Just because I've fallen off four times in the last week, it's affecting my work. I'm not focussing. Falls are rites of passage, only wimps get put off by them."

She looked around her rather spartan office in the managerial wing of St Dunstan's District General Hospital, ten miles from Edinburgh. The warm summer morning should have lifted her spirits, but not today. She would normally be actively engaged in several tasks at once – on the computer and making phone calls, reading papers and signing letters. Instead, the papers she was trying to digest before meeting the Chief Executive later that morning were just not sinking in. The reason for her butterflies was the jumping lesson planned that evening at Leatherburn.

She got up from her desk and went along to the cubby hole which served the hospital managers' wing as a kitchen. These were basic NHS conditions, not the palatial offices to be found in the private sector. She put the kettle on. It was early for her coffee – she was usually disciplined about these things – but she needed to pull herself together.

Using her fingers to rinse out yesterday's dregs from her mug – a freebie from some drug company – she wondered why no-one ever remembered to bring in washing-up liquid and a scrubber? The milk in the fridge was just about to expire but didn't smell too awful, so she poured some in.

Back at her desk, sipping thoughtfully, she came to a decision.

"I'll go to the class tonight, but I won't stay on for the jumping lesson," she told herself. Megan explored how that option had affected her stomach; it definitely felt better. She felt a little disappointed with herself at chickening out, but knew her leisure activities could not be allowed to disrupt her work. She loved jumping. She got a tremendous buzz out of it, and looked forward to a time when she could do it with the utmost confidence and no disabling nerves. Unfortunately, they said, you never lose the fear altogether.

Megan glanced at her watch. She had precisely eighteen minutes to complete reading her papers in time for the meeting with the Chief Exec.

"Better get rid of the nerves," she thought suddenly, "or the boss will think I'm scared of him!" She put down her mug and held her hands out, palms down, in front of her. They were steady. She got up and inspected herself in the mirror: smart and tidy in her navy, striped skirt suit and pale lemon blouse with court heels; bouncy curls well-brushed; healthy complexion only needing minimal make-up. The coffee seemed to have done its stuff, but she needed to push all thoughts of the elusive mastery of horsemanship well to the back of her mind.

"I know. Tonight, I'll arrange a couple of private lessons with a reliable horse and teacher, and start again from square one. Rebuild my confidence, bit by bit."

Happy with her executive decision, she switched her focus back to work.

***

Annabel glanced at her watch as she logged out of her computer. It would be almost seven by the time she got home, but she'd extracted a promise from Ralph – still on sick-leave for "stress" – that he would have the evening meal on the table. Her office in the city centre legal firm was furnished with a solid mahogany desk, chairs and filing cabinets, and smart but understated green-patterned soft furnishings. It exuded quiet affluence, for the sake of the company's generally well-to-do clients.

Ralph's duties were neither difficult nor time-consuming; he'd had all day to prepare soup and ham salad. Indeed, all he had needed to do was open a tin, heat the contents, and take stuff out of the fridge. But on arriving home, Annabel found him talking intently on the phone in his study and the girls bickering in their joint sitting room upstairs. The kitchen table was bare.

She registered this with exasperation. She was out all day working to keep the family finances afloat, yet was expected to get the meal on the table, too. She crashed around the kitchen, slamming doors and banging pots together until Ralph shuffled in, looking sheepish.

"You're early, dear. Let me do that. Sit down and have a sherry or something."

"Don't be silly, I'm late. I've got to be away in forty minutes. Get some soup plates out and call the girls. Keep an eye on this saucepan. I'm going to change."

When she came down a few minutes later in her riding gear, the meal had not advanced much. Seeing the brandy bottle on the sideboard, Annabel swiftly snatched it up and spirited it into a cupboard, then went into the hall to call the girls. Eventually they all sat down in the kitchen to a rather untidy and ill-set table.

"Is that all we get?" moaned Lily with a martyred air, surveying the food before her. Too late, Ralph put his fingers to his lips.

Annabel took a deep breath, glared round at them all, then said with an air of restraint, "It's high time you all started helping more. Perhaps then we might enjoy more creative meals."

Her elder daughter sat down with a sullen look on her face and an overdone long-suffering sigh. "I suppose you're going to that *awful* stable." She looked accusingly across the table.

"Is there any reason why I shouldn't?" enquired Annabel coldly.

Poppy quickly interjected. "Of course not. I wish I could go, too."

"You've got your homework," said Annabel, glancing more softly at her younger daughter, taking in the freckled nose, perfect skin, and red-gold, wispy hair.

"I haven't been riding for *ages*," sighed Poppy. "When are you going to get another horse, Mummy? Then we can start going back to the nice stable at Hadley again."

It was Annabel's turn to sigh. "Don't start, dear. When I've got time to go out and look, I might find another decent horse. It's difficult when I'm working full time."

She had already begun the difficult search for a replacement for Mimi, and someone had suggested she should look over Mrs Stark's stock at Leatherburn. Everyone knew how *un-approved* the stable was, by the standards of the British Horse Society, and rumours flew about the number of accidents it had notched up. But the turnover in horse-flesh, and the occasional gem of a hunter or show-jumper that had originated there, meant it was worth a try. To her astonishment, Annabel had found that she was rather enjoying exploring the bottom end of the riding school world. The rides were not the usual bored, trudging cobs, and the lessons were fast, exciting, risky. There was one hour of flat work and half an hour of jumping.

She had not expected to see so much talent among the clientele, either; most were working class, council-house tenants. Of course, she did not join in the joking and ribbing that went on among them. Their accents were so broad she could barely understand them, but she appreciated the degree of bonding which came naturally between good riders.

When she described her experiences to her friends over lunch in town, with her usual sardonic and sometimes cruel wit, she was considered very adventurous. "Do take care," they said, worrying more about her unsuitable human associates than the horsey exploits.

At the supper table, an atmosphere of gloom had descended, prompted by Annabel's martyred air and

Lily's pubescent sulkiness. Ralph tried to jolly things up by small talk.

"When will you be home, Angel?" This was a name he had used when they first fell in love, and she rather resented him using it now.

She replied tetchily, "The same time as always. Around ten forty-five." She glanced at him. This last week or two it seemed as though he might be pulling himself together. Maybe his normal habits of tunnel-visioned ambition and workaholism were re-asserting themselves. Although those traits could be annoying, they were infinitely to be preferred to a man succumbing to mental breakdown. He'd stopped the sleeping pills; if she could just wean him off the brandy…

Looking at her watch, she got up.

"Coffee, Angel?"

"No time, thanks."

"Oh Mum, I need my sports shirt for tomorrow and it's in the wash," Lily complained.

"Well you'd better wash it yourself, hadn't you?" she responded tartly.

Sensing more trouble, Ralph moved quickly to placate mother and daughter. "Don't worry. You go now," he said. "I'll see to the shirt."

"Don't. It's good for her to do her own chores. She can't be slaved over all her life." Annabel strode out.

***

Sue was getting ready to head over to Leatherburn stable. Bridget had phoned to tell her of a rather exciting horse she had recently acquired – a warmblood-cross-thoroughbred called Barney. She had invited Sue to ride him in the advanced class, knowing she was looking for another horse, and thought this one might appeal. He was fit, lively, fast, well-schooled and had a huge jump. One of the advanced class riders had already ridden him really well, bringing out his massive potential.

Knowing Bridget well, Sue was suspicious of the stable owner's generosity and wanted to check on her glowing report. When she rang one of her friends at Leatherburn, she heard a rather different story. Barney had been nothing but trouble ever since he arrived, with few clients being able to cope with him and a few ending up on the deck. That morning he had jumped out of the outdoor school, ditched his rider, and bolted. The rider – a hairdresser – had broken his wrist and was threatening to sue. Mrs Stark was keen to offload him.

Sue wasn't put off; she was game for the challenge, and he might have concealed genius. She had thought hard about Rosemary's offer to loan her money for a horse to bring on and sell. In the end, they'd agreed that Rosemary would actually own the horse, when it was found, take on the insurance – and the risks. Then, when Sue had educated the animal and sold at a profit, she could keep the surplus herself.

Although she admitted this was hugely generous of Rosemary, Sue also thought rather smugly that it was evidence, if she needed any, of what a superbly capable and knowledgeable horsewoman she was.

***

Kitted out in jodphurs and rubber boots, hat and stick – purchased from a mobile saddler at a reasonable cost – Megan waited in the queue to pay and find out which horse she was to ride.

Since their holiday in the New Forest, the family's enthusiasm for riding had not waned. She'd explained to Edie, the teacher, that tonight she would miss out on the jumping. Having witnessed her pupil's rather spectacular falls the week before, Edie was not surprised.

Megan admitted she needed to rebuild her confidence and asked about one or two private jumping lessons on a reliable horse.

"If you wait for half an hour or so, you'll probably catch Sue, who gives private lessons," Edie suggested. "She's a nice girl, a well-qualified teacher; we've been lucky to get her. She is more into flat work, but I'm sure she will be pleased to take a jumping client."

That evening Megan was allocated yet another new horse, one of a pair of carriage horses that Mrs Stark wanted to get some work into. She rode Love – partner-in-harness of Marriage – down to the indoor school, which was a barn of a place that could accommodate twenty horse-rider pairs at a pinch. With the recent warm weather, the soft earth was dry and powdery and the atmosphere dusty, especially when the class of a dozen had been trotting round for a few minutes.

Edie was in good voice, swearing and bellowing as usual, stalking round the centre of the school clutching her ringmaster's whip. Megan struggled to keep Love on the track, finding her board-stiff, lazy and unresponsive. But Edie didn't berate her for once, just telling her to do her best.

When it was Megan's turn to canter, she gave the right signal, heel behind the girth... but nothing happened. Edie cracked her whip. Several horses shied in fright at the pistol shot, and Love shot forward in a lumbering canter, nearly throwing Megan off balance. She hung on in ungainly manner, but in the mayhem someone else had fallen off. There was a brief pause while the rider was restored to the saddle without ceremony. Edie took no prisoners, thought Megan.

The next time she was required to canter, she gave Love a wallop with her stick, producing a buck and a half dozen canter strides. Megan was red-faced and exhausted, not really enjoying herself.

After the flat-work hour, Megan took her horse up to the yard, then returned to the gallery overlooking the school to watch the jumping lesson. The gallery door opened and a tall, slender woman came in – a vision of elegance in expensive, well-fitting jodphurs, polished leather boots, and her hair gathered in a snood. Megan turned round expectantly.

"Are you Sue?" she asked, smiling.

"No, I'm Annabel."

"Ah, sorry." Megan had seen the woman at a distance before. "Oh yes, you ride in the advanced class, don't you?"

"Yes, for the moment. I'm really looking for a horse to buy. There are a couple of new ones in the yard. I'm not sure it's a wise move to buy off Mrs Stark, though. She would always come off best in a bargain."

Megan laughed, feeling a little envious. "Yes, I'm sure. It must be lovely to own your own horse. I'm a green beginner, but I can't help dreaming."

The other woman seemed to withdraw into herself. "Yes. Well. There are ups and downs." As she turned away to watch the class, Megan was aware of some kind of shutter coming down – clunk, like a guillotine – and felt she had been dismissed. Perhaps her admission of novicehood had put her into an inferior order, beneath notice; someone who didn't have the wealth or the pedigree to be immersed in the horse-world from birth.

She looked at the willowy figure with the air of chic, of unmistakable class; rather unusual for Leatherburn. Megan's class vibrissae were alerted. She would test the water.

"You're a horse-owner already, I take it?"

For a moment, Megan wondered if this remote, aloof woman was going to ignore her altogether. But then, as if coming out of deep thought, Annabel turned and looked at Megan in a detached, speculative way.

"No, not at the moment. I had a mare who broke a leg, and had to be destroyed. It's ages ago – well, a few months – and I'm only just getting round to looking for a replacement."

There was a pause. Megan was surprised at how matter-of-factly this information had all come out; no misty eyes or throat-clearing. Maybe the woman could only cope with the topic by keeping it blunt and factual, she thought.

Then Annabel added, as if to herself, "Rather like a broken love affair, it isn't a good idea to get another one on the rebound."

"Did you keep her here?"

"Oh, good heavens, no. I wouldn't do that. Well, would you?" Annabel drew herself up with disdain. "This place is okay for experienced riders and maybe do-it-yourself livery, if that's all you can afford. No, I had her in livery at a place called Hadley. It's a bit south of here, at the foot of the Pentlands." She dropped her voice. "I wouldn't trust Mrs Stark or that gypsy husband of hers further than I could throw them. Leave a valuable horse in their care? No way. They'd hire it out behind your back if they could get away with it. Or even sell it!"

They looked down at the class, where Edie was arguing with someone about the spacing between jumps. "Bollocks! Don't make excuses, you wanker," she expostulated. "Get on with it if you're going."

Annabel gave a fastidious gasp. "God, she's vulgar," she said. Then, after a pause. "This place is not so good for beginners, you know. You are quite plucky to start here. Some people get put off. They have a huge rate of accidents. Not surprising, really, they think more of making money than safety. I could offer my legal services and make a fortune." She gave a little smile which briefly dispelled the aloofness and gave Megan a glimpse of a warmer person underneath.

Annabel described the stable at Hadley with enthusiasm. "It's an old hunting yard, with a little clock tower over the gate, all beautiful grey stone, in lovely rural surroundings. And Mandy keeps it immaculate."

Hadley was, she advised, particularly good for children's lessons; excellent for livery, if a little expensive. As Annabel spoke, Megan's ideas and dreams went into orbit.

"Sounds great. I've two boys who are just starting. It might be better for them. And for me. I've had any number of unsuitable rides here."

Annabel agreed. "I really wouldn't bring kids here. Honestly! No-one gives a toss about safety. But why not go and have a look at Hadley? She doesn't do adult lessons like these, just owner-lessons. But there are kids' lessons and activities galore. The owner is a real character. Hair like a witch, aristocratic to the core, but not at all snooty. A bit like someone Terry Pratchett would invent. She's just great at communicating with kids and horses."

Megan felt Hadley might be the answer to her prayers. The dare-devil attitudes of Leatherburn were rather extreme, and if you didn't go along with them – as she hadn't tonight – you ended up with a disappointing experience. She and Annabel began ferreting in their pockets for a piece of paper and pencil to write down contact details and directions. It was a kind of initiation ritual, the tentative beginnings of a friendship which might or might not flourish in two hectic, modern lives.

"Give me a ring if you decide to go," said Annabel. "I should quite like to re-visit. Haven't been since… I lost Mimi. I could show you the ropes, introduce you to Lady Miranda Morton-Merrydew; we call her Mandy."

The gallery door swung open with a bang, and in swept an athletic-looking blond woman, dressed in leather boots, sturdy breeches, and a waxed coat. She strode to the balustrade, ignoring the two other women, and leaned her muscular thighs on it, spreading her arms out along the rail, seeming to occupy a huge space. Megan and Annabel fell silent, watching her.

From the floor of the school, Edie shrieked raucously, "Oh my God, look what the cat's brought in!"

"Just call me Pussy Galore," rejoined Sue, affecting a smirk and a sinuous body movement. Edie cackled with appreciation and they exchanged a few merry insults. While her minions rearranged the jumps, Edie told Sue about Barney's latest misdemeanours.

"You'll not have any trouble, of course," she said.

"Famous last words," snorted Sue. "Can I bring him down to the school?"

"Sure, just join the next class in… about five minutes."

Waving a hand towards Megan, Edie explained about her enquiry for private lessons. Sue turned with hearty eagerness, introducing herself affably to both women in the gallery. Producing a dirty, handwritten card with her details, she was all-obliging, willing to fit in with any requirements. Almost before she knew it, Megan had a lesson booked for the following afternoon, her half-day. Her solar plexus tingled, but it was excitement rather than fear. She was sure she could trust this wholesome, engaging woman, who radiated confidence and horsey know-how. She caught Annabel's eye and grinned.

"I'll get you over your nerves in a lesson or two," said Sue breezily. "Before you know it, you'll be whizzing round a showjumping course."

"Gosh, my husband will be jealous," said Megan.

Sue's face lit up and she responded with doubled enthusiasm. "Oh, persuade him to come, too. Does he ride?"

"Yes, about as badly as I do. He may well want private lessons, too. He is extremely anxious that I don't get too far ahead of him. You know what men are like, it's about vanity as much as anything with him."

"Boy, do I know," said Sue. "Anyway, you've got my details. Talk him into it."

With a nod she was off, striding away as if she owned the place, and letting the door swing shut with a clatter.

With a swift glance at her watch, Annabel said she'd better go and get mounted up. "You'll give me a ring about Hadley, won't you?" she asked, rather anxiously.

"Sure thing," Megan replied. "I'll look at my diary when I get home. Maybe the weekend?"

Megan felt as though she was performing as much of a service for Annabel as the other way around. But she felt good about that. And it would be useful to have a friend who knew all the pitfalls about horse purchase and owning.

Almost out of the door, Annabel turned back suddenly with an air of furtive conspiracy. "I should warn you, don't talk about Hadley within earshot of Mrs Stark or her staff," she said. "There's terrible rivalry between them. Not ordinary commercial rivalry; it's ferocious, battle-to-the-death stuff. Mrs Stark's been known to turn someone off the premises who was a client of Hadley. So just be aware!"

How mysterious, Megan thought. She would like to have learned more but Annabel had gone. Feeling pleased with the evening's developments, Megan ambled back to the yard where there was a bustle of riders mounting and dismounting. She saw Sue aboard the awesome Barney, sorting out girth and stirrups with consummate ease. While the horse fretted and fidgeted, his rider sat loose and relaxed, continuing the flow of stable-gossip with Mrs Stark, who had come out to chat. Megan would have happily stayed to watch the fun, but decided she was thirsty and tired. It was time to head home.

Chapter 5

Annabel was deep in thought as she guided her skittish chestnut around the school before the lesson started. She could hardly believe she had committed herself to a visit to Hadley; she hadn't been able to face going back since her mare's death. But chumming Megan on a visit felt like a good idea, and the young woman was being blatantly exploited here at Leatherburn, put on all sorts of crazy creatures she couldn't cope with, and then demoted to a complete dud. Megan had related the stories of her recent falls, both in jumping lessons and out on hacks. And tonight the poor woman had been riding a carriage horse, of all things! Anyone else less feisty would have been completely put off by now.

Annabel's horse began to prance and sidle as another rider moved up beside her. A deep, rich, masculine voice said, "Good evening, Annabel."

She looked up in surprise. Although the riders all exchanged banter during their lesson, she had not been on name-and-greeting terms with anyone so far. Beside her was a classmate, in his thirties, rugged, and with the most amazingly blue eyes. She noticed them for the first time now, seeing him at close quarters.

"Good evening… Scott."

"I was looking for you," he said, sternly. "I was going to give you a row!"

Annabel was even more astonished, although she could see from his mock-severe expression that he was joking.

"I was hoping to ride Barney, that great bugger of a horse I had last week. S'cuse my language, hen. They told me that he was already booked for a woman who wanted to buy him. You are the only woman I could think of who could manage the rogue. But forgive me," and he made a half-bow, "I see it isn't you."

Annabel laughed and coloured slightly at the compliment. "No, you'll have to go and quarrel with Sue. Look, here she comes. She's a teacher here. I'd guess she can take Barney on – and you – at the same time."

He roared with laughter and looked at her appreciatively, then twisted round to watch Sue, expertly and confidently astride Barney.

"Guess I'll have to put up and shut up then."

They rode on together for a bit, Annabel happy to keep the chat going. When Edie called them to order, he rode off with a parting grin.

Annabel was amazed at herself. Annabel Lindsay – scion of a tribe of land-owners, judges, sheriffs, diplomats, professors – going pink and flustered because a working class man with nice eyes had flirted with her and called her "hen"! Her lunch companions would certainly not get to hear about this.

As the lesson progressed, he caught her eye from time to time – when the jumps were put up to a challenging height, or when Sue and Barney performed some spectacular exercise – and gave her a wink. She tried not to gaze at him too much, but couldn't help noticing his athletic, muscled body, and his brown, outdoor face and arms.

"Dear me, I must be seriously sex-starved," she thought.

She didn't speak to him again that evening; he and his friends were doing their man-bonding thing, departing in haste at the end of the lesson for a few jars at the local, the Pie 'n' Pint.

***

When Megan arrived home at the family's converted mill on the western side of Edinburgh, she found the house peaceful, the children asleep in bed, and Melanie – their nineteen-year-old nanny – watching TV in her own room. Still in her riding clothes, Megan perched on a stool in the rustic-style kitchen, leaned back against the Welsh dresser and drank beer thirstily from a bottle. She was very tired, and although her riding experience had not been particularly enjoyable tonight, she was pleased with the contacts she had made. Dick was expected home any minute – he was flying into Edinburgh from Heathrow – and she had lots to tell him.

After their slight tiff on the New Forest holiday, Dick had returned from London with lovely presents for them all, generally assuming an air of being chastened, and restored to his position of devoted family man. Megan felt she must work at keeping his feet on the ground and avoid letting all the fame and adulation go to his head. Their riding exploits seemed one good way to do it, as novices had to accept dictatorial instruction, being shouted and sworn at, and made to feel small.

She was just about to take a shower when a taxi drew up outside, and then he was in the hall giving her an enormous hug.

"Just watch it, I'm filthy!" she said. "Covered with sweat and stour."

"I still love you!" he replied, rubbing a finger down her cheek, leaving a groove under the brown dust.

Dick had been travelling in Kenya, researching the issue of flower-growing for luxury Western markets and how it affected food production for that country. The topic was one of mutual interest, as Megan and Dick had originally met in Tanzania a dozen years before. She had been carrying out voluntary work on a gap year, while Dick had been one of a team of British TV researchers exploring the impact of Western volunteers on the country.

They continued chatting as they got ready for bed. Megan was keen to get Dick riding again, and so was he, but he did not seem particularly impressed with the idea of Hadley riding centre.

"It sounds too proper and approved," he said. "I like a bit of risk-taking. But this Amazon Sue person sounds great. If you're taking private lessons, I will, too. I could always come with you tomorrow for this private session."

"Maybe not this time," Megan said quickly. She knew Dick's capacity for taking centre stage, and really wanted to repair her confidence without distraction.

"What's Sue like?" he asked.

"Like a Valkyrie. Oozes equine know-how. Like some-one straight out of *Horse and Hounds*. She'd be the glamour person riding the winner, or the ultimate professional judging the pig-tailed kids on classy ponies."

"Glamour person?" queried Dick, with an expression of wide-eyed innocence.

"Striking-looking rather than pretty. She strode in like a blond Boudicca just down from her chariot. More intelligent than the average horse-mad groupie, I'd say. Very affable and down-to-earth."

***

By the time Annabel arrived home, her domestic scene was far from organised and peaceful. Lights flared from every window, while upstairs she could see the blue light of a television and hear mingled sounds of voices and music. Before investigating, she made a quick phone call before it was unsociably late. Then she looked around for Ralph.

The sitting room was empty, as was the kitchen and his study. She found him in the dining room, out cold, flat on the Persian carpet, slumbering deeply and snoring gently with an empty brandy bottle at his side.

Annabel slumped on a chair and gazed at him, despairing. How old he looked with his sandy-grey, sparse hair, and his prematurely-lined face. There had been talk of him going back to work, but her spirits dropped now as she looked at him.

Roused by a shout from upstairs – "Mum? Is that you?" – she climbed wearily up to sort out the girls, quench the TV and the music, and persuade them to settle down for the night. She then had a hot shower and put on a silk kimono, delaying having to face the consequences of Ralph's relapse, not wanting a row after her pleasant evening. Later, when she looked in the dining room again, he was still there, his position changed slightly, breathing noisily.

"At least he's alive," she thought, as she went to the kitchen to make herself a hot drink.

She wouldn't dream of leaving him; there was the family, and that came first. The girls needed them both. But why, oh why, should she take the brunt of the discomfort, the concealing, the shielding of the girls from his weakness and thoughtlessness? She longed for a time when she only had to think of herself. How nice it would be to have a great evening out with affable people, then come home and watch TV for a bit, have a soak in a hot bath, read quietly, and fall peacefully asleep, dreaming sweet dreams. She thought of her blue-eyed rider friend and his masculine appearance. Inevitably, she compared him with her flawed husband. Wouldn't she like to be inviting Scott upstairs?

She left Ralph alone. If he died of the cold, it was in the lap of the gods. Let him look to himself; she had done all she could. She took her mug upstairs and went to bed, anticipating wicked dreams.

***

Sue drove back to her country home very late. She'd stayed for a gossip with Bridget Stark after mastering the fractious Barney. She'd enjoyed working with the horse but didn't feel his temperament denoted untapped genius, just over-generous feeding. She had no plans to take him off Bridget's hands, but there were no hard feelings between them.

They were both enthusiastic at the thought of the prestigious Dick Fraser as a client; his wife, too, of course.

"Won't Her Ladyship be green with envy?" smirked Bridget.

Privately, Sue planned to maximize any opportunity this new acquaintance would give her. Through him, she might meet more famous names, especially sporty people. Sue's dreams about herself were always exorbitant, and now she imagined herself as mistress of some grand castle, like Blair Atholl, where she would hold international dressage events and horse trials. Quite how knowing a famous man would lead onto such good fortune, she hadn't quite figured out.

***

Lady Miranda Morton-Merrydew chewed her pen and pushed back strands of floaty grey hair. She hated doing the accounts at the best of times, but this month they were especially worrying. She flipped back the pages of a large accounts book, looking for the same month last year. Poring over the figures, she groaned, switching back and forwards to compare then with now.

A gentle tap on the door signaled the arrival of Hamish – Dr Hamish McPherson – her loyal companion of ten years. He placed a cup of tea on the desk, far enough away to avoid being spilled.

"Not good?" he asked, knowing exactly what had detained her so late.

Mandy gave a huge sigh and reached for the cup. "Thanks, Hamish. It's the height of summer and we should be raking it in now. The truth is, that evil woman is trying to do me out of business."

"How so, my dear? Surely she wouldn't."

"She certainly would. The grudge she bears me will go with her to the grave. She – or they – do well enough just trading horses. But she's been stealing my ideas, the things I do with the kids over the holidays: own a pony for a day, gymkhanas, treasure hunt on horseback, all that. Our figures for these are all well down on last year. Just look." She pushed the accounts book over the desk to him.

"And she's doing hunter hire, border raid hire, pub ride-outs. It's as if she's having an all-out drive to put me out of business," she continued wearily. "I'll tell you what hurts most, though. It's Annabel. She's defected to Leatherburn; goes there every week. I've lost a couple of liveries, too, for various reasons. They are the backbone of my business – classy liveries and children's activities."

"Just a moment," said Hamish, perching on the arm of a claret-coloured sofa. "I can actually give you some reassuring news there. Annabel rang a little earlier. She said not to disturb you, but she wants to come over at the weekend and introduce a friend who is interested in bringing her family here for lessons. Annabel hasn't found a new horse yet, but made it clear that when she does, she'll want to come back."

"Oh Hamish, bless you, that's the best news I could have had. Maybe with that, our fortunes will turn."

Hamish fished in his pocket and produced his cheque book, refusing to be deterred by her protestations. He led a delightfully comfortable life in retirement, and it was in his interest, as well as hers, that they remain solvent. But Mandy was uncomfortable.

"I want your wisdom, Hamish, and your ideas. There must be ways of turning this around. Tell me what to do." She turned to him beseechingly, with a loving look that had melted countless hearts over the decades.

"Why not tell me a bit more about this bad blood between you and… Bridget, is it? I don't understand why she has her knife into you so ferociously. You told me it was something to do with that saturnine husband of hers."

"Oh dear, it was all so long ago." Mandy shifted uneasily, and it was clear she felt uncomfortable with the topic.

"Yes, well. When Ned Stark was a stable lad at my ex-husband's estate, he was good with the horses; I mean, more than good. He had that sort of innate know-how that's almost mystical. I suppose I was indiscreet in chatting to him and encouraging him. It was foolish of me, in those days the lady of the house didn't notice underlings, just used them and walked all over them. Can I just say, there was nothing that passed between us! How could there be? He was as uncouth and rough and tongue-tied as a village idiot. He wasn't my John Brown. But after I noticed him, it was as though he worshipped the ground I walked on; everybody noticed it.

"And when my marriage fell apart, it was one of the things that was flung at me. My charming husband tried to destroy me with accusations of infidelity with a stable lad! Poor Ned got the heave, with no reference and much scandal. It dragged him away from Bridget, who worked in the house and who was his intended. Their lives collapsed as a result. And the publicity! It must have been as bad for them as it was for me. You know all about my interesting life since then," she added with a shrug.

Although she had never revealed all the painful details of her eventual escape from the miserable, violent marriage, she had told him of her heartbreak at having to leave behind her two young children, whom she had been forbidden ever to see again. She had left her castle and her Lord, but it certainly had not been with any wraggle-taggle gypsy lad.

Mandy had fled to the continent, living a bohemian life with poets and painters, until eventually she found her place as Mistress-in-Residence to the Ambassador to Morocco; the lively and sociable situation allowed her to shine as hostess and raconteuse, entertaining lavishly and shining in a world of fascinating if ephemeral guests.

But with no official status at the Embassy, the Ambassador's sudden death had left her dispossessed yet again. Before leaving, she had scouted round the Embassy and decided to make her own arrangements for a pension. What would not be missed? Was there an inventory? With a set of dinner plates – hand-painted by Picasso – carefully packed into her luggage, she had scarpered with all possible haste back to the UK; to Scotland, where she bought Hadley riding centre. And over the years she had turned it into a popular and well respected business.

"So she blames you for Ned's fall from favour in the past, even though you suffered more than them?" Hamish looked perturbed. "For heaven's sake, you were cast adrift with less than nothing!"

"I think Bridget, like any other woman, can't take the idea that her husband adored another woman. And that was made hideously public at the time. It's made her the bitter old crone she is now."

"So when were you aware of their appearance at Leatherburn?"

"About five or six years ago. They've been extraordinarily successful, mainly in horse trading. Ned goes round the country, over to Ireland, places like Appleby Fair. Their turnover in horses is phenomenal, and they attract the young folk who want a bit of dare-devilry on horseback."

"So you think she's doing it all out of spite?"

"I think her choice of location was deliberate, certainly. They're only about what, fifteen miles away? You know that nice girl I've got, Julie? She came from there. She told me some horror stories – you know, blatant disregard for safety issues, dreadful treatment of staff, and so on. But apparently Bridget has also badmouthed me to clients as well as staff, and it's clear she holds a massive grudge.

"Things are so bad I think I may even be faced with selling the Picasso dinner plates," Mandy added morosely.

"Oh nonsense, it hasn't come to that," Hamish replied testily. "Don't be bullied by those upstart riff-raff. They get above themselves once they've made a bit of cash. They'll come to grief sooner or later. There'll be a serious accident, a fatality perhaps; one almighty lawsuit and she'll be out of business."

"That won't be any comfort to me if I've already gone out of business myself," Mandy commented.

"Have you ever thought about opening a saddlery shop here on the premises? You know how women love to shop. You all dress your horses better than you do yourselves.

All those different multi-coloured rugs for numerous purposes; those knick-knacks in your grooming boxes; hoof picks, and brushes and things. And riding clothes for humans, come to that. Leather goods, of course. Organic medicaments, equine and human."

Hamish was getting into his stride. "And haven't I plenty of time and capital for the paperwork and stock control? I could really do a masterly job for you. You could even take stuff round to all the events and shows in your horse-box. There's a goldmine waiting to be exploited!"

"Hamish, you are such a gem." Mandy felt her spirits rise for the first time in months. "That's an idea worth working on. I feel quite uplifted. Have you any more ideas up your sleeve?"

"I think we'd better sleep on it. Meanwhile, give me your unpaid bills and I'll deal with them."

Chapter 6

Annabel awoke before the alarm and realised that Ralph was not beside her. She still felt determined to cut him adrift from her duty rota of responsibilities, but she was curious. How would he cope? What would happen next?

He wasn't next door in his dressing room. And downstairs there was no sign of him in the dining room or the kitchen. She went through the usual motions, putting on the kettle, getting out things for breakfast. She observed Lily's aertex shirt was clean and dry, if not ironed. And in the waste bin was the empty brandy bottle.

She fed the cat and went to unlock the back door. It was already unlocked. Opening it, she peered into the garden, scanning over the sweeping lawns to the rhododendron shrubbery, and beyond to a little copse of oak trees. No Ralph.

How odd, she thought. Did he go out and leave the door open all night? She went to shout at the girls to get a move on. When she returned, he was coming in the back door in his T-shirt, shorts, and running shoes.

"Where on earth have you been?"

"I've been out for a jog. I feel great," he said rather defensively.

"You were out cold on the dining room floor last night. I'd have thought you'd feel lousy this morning."

"Not at all. I'm really fine. I'm going to get on my clothes and go into work today. Time I got back."

Annabel restrained herself from asking where he'd slept. She noted how thin and unmanly he was in his sweaty gear, his white legs like matchsticks with a few bulging blue veins at the back of the calves. Thinning hair, damp and dishevelled.

"I'd forgotten how invigorating a morning run is," he said, fishing out the orange juice carton from the fridge and pouring himself a large glass. "I went all around the golf course." He glugged down the juice and poured another, moving away with glass and carton.

"You might leave some juice for the rest of us."

"It's nearly finished," he said, shaking the carton. "I'm determined to get fit. Think I'll go out for a jog every day. I've lost weight, down to ten stone. Think if I keep exercising and miss a few meals, I'll lose more."

"Ralph, you're skin and bone. For God's sake don't lose any more."

Annabel looked at her pale and feeble husband, comparing him in her mind's eye with Scott and those other fit riders last night.

"Yes, I will. I've tried for years to lose weight, now it's easy. You must keep feeding me salads and healthy food. None of your roasts and fries."

"Mine? My bloody roasts and fries? It's my fault that your dietary habits are chaotic? None of your ice-cream and chocolate biscuits, you mean. To say nothing of wine and brandy," Annabel rejoined with spirit. No, she must shut up; she would not start a row first thing in the morning. Besides, he was trying to get his act together, talking of going into work. She'd not stand in his way. He probably still had alcohol circulating in his bloodstream, she could smell his sweet-sour breath as he gave her a perfunctory kiss.

But he'd driven while being very much the worse for wear before, and she would not interfere.

***

Earlier in the month, one of her colleagues had asked her out to lunch. One of the partners, George. She'd initially been rather touched. He had seemed to ask her on impulse, and she wondered if he needed someone to talk to about some personal troubles. She had got the impression he was a bit low. But as she had some urgent stuff to do that day, she'd had to decline. George had looked a bit huffy and did not ask again.

Maybe today she would take the initiative and ask him. Why not? That wasn't being too forward. It was odd how Ralph seemed to have female friends or colleagues whom he would meet for coffee, lunch, or a drink on occasion, but she never had any male friends on an equivalent footing. Maybe she was too reserved. Perhaps she gave out signals that she was a committed, married woman; untouchable and remote. Surely she wasn't too old, over the hump, and just not sexy and attractive any more? Life was supposed to begin at forty, but so far it had just sagged and dragged her down with duties and demands. She felt like a scrap of blue touchpaper waiting to be ignited. But she would wait forever if she did not position herself near some fire-source.

Mid-morning, Annabel popped her head round George's office door. She had hovered in the corridor feeling rather spare until the door opened and his secretary bustled out. George looked up, rather surprised, frowning and annoyed at the interruption. Her heart sank. But he invited her in courteously enough, and she smiled and sat down. Then wished she hadn't. It would have been better to be more casual, a take-it or leave-it invitation from the doorway, as if a thought had just occurred to her in passing. And a quick escape route. Now she had made it heavy and formal, and he was probably busy digesting her needy body language.

"How's things?"

"Fine." He looked at her expectantly, impatiently, poised to get back to some pressing task. Annabel felt rushed and embarrassed, aware she was losing her cool.

"Er. George. You asked me to lunch and I couldn't that day... I wondered if I could ask you today instead?" She was furious to feel a blush mantle her cheeks. Oh God, how stupid! How girlish.

He leaned back, inspecting her with a bland expression, chewing the tip of his pen, then spread his hands and smiled in an avuncular manner.

"Afraid not, my dear. I've got an engagement at the City Chambers. Would love to have, how nice of you to ask. Maybe... some other time, you know. Give me more notice, that sort of thing. Diary so full." He patted his bulging leather personal organiser.

In the midst of her mortification, it struck Annabel how camp he was. The drawl, the floppy forelock, the overdone gestures. He was also thickset, jowly, and well down the spectrum of male desirability. And he was treating her like a gauche schoolgirl with a crush on him.

"Oh, that's okay. I just… wanted to return the compliment, really."

Annabel got up awkwardly, but she was not to escape quite so easily. He jumped up even more impulsively, came round the table with exaggerated, even ham concern, holding his hand out towards her. He laid his hand on her arm, detaining her and looking deep into her eyes. Her cheeks burned.

"You're not in any trouble, my dear, are you? Were you wanting to pour your heart's concerns into my kindly ear?"

"No, no, of course not." Annabel tried to move out of his immediate space. "In fact, I wondered if you were wanting *my* advice that last time. I didn't want you to feel rejected."

Her misery was complete when he let out a bellow of laughter, a guffaw so coarse and loud the whole firm must have heard it, accompanied by a gust of smelly breath.

"Don't you bother your head about *me*," he grinned, and squeezed her arm briefly but painfully. She turned, gritting her teeth and hating him with all her soul, and tried to cover the acre of space between her and the door with nonchalant dignity.

Back in her office, she ground her teeth at her own awkwardness. How hard it was to be sinful. Her main problem was her pride; she hated to crawl and beg. And she was a lousy actress, could never put on an act or even lie convincingly. But would her natural dignity lose the battle with her emotional needs? It seemed quite likely right now, her need was so compelling.

She looked at the pile of files on her desk, and reached reluctantly towards them. Then she picked up the phone instead, and punched in a number without hesitation. A familiar husky voice answered.

"Hello, Mandy. It's Annabel here."

"Annabel! I got your message last night. My dear, how *are* you? I'm so glad to hear from you. We've all missed you *so* much here."

The response was wonderfully over the top, yet so characteristically kind and heart-warming. Annabel pictured the familiar rambling farmhouse and windswept fields, the big indoor school, and the surrounding woodlands. And Mandy herself; her wild grey hair, and her layers of dun wool and waxed clothing.

"I've missed you, too. I have been looking for a horse, though not as systematically as I maybe should."

"There's been nothing in the *Farmer's Weekly*. Not the best time of year of course. I was wondering, though. There's a really lovely fourteen hand two pony, an Arab, that a friend of mine is selling. Genuine reason and all that. I've known the animal from birth, and its history. I must own up, I'd love to have it here. I did think of your girls, but all of you could ride it, and it would be a temporary expedient for you. Not what you wanted, I know, but have a think about it."

As soon as Annabel thought about it, the possibilities gained colour. Hmmm.... she confirmed she'd certainly think about it, then moved on to the subject of Megan and her wish to visit Hadley. Mandy was enthusiastic and eager to discuss times and dates, and Annabel felt much better as she put the phone down. She looked at her files again, glancing at her watch. One at least was urgent. But first she would put in one further call.

Her vet, Tom Cormack, had looked after Mimi and fired the bullet that ended her life. He had been silently sympathetic. Annabel was aware that at moments of emotional crisis she was prone to imprint on some nearby source of support. She so seldom gave way to her feelings that any person who had witnessed her totally distraught seemed to have an emotional claim on her.

Tom had been frequently in her dreams, a shadowy presence, though she could not raise his detailed image in her mind's eye. Compelled by some innate force she could not wholly control or even understand, she rang the surgery number. A bright female receptionist voice answered. Then Tom himself was on the line. Annabel felt a lurch in her stomach.

"Hi, Tom. Look, I wonder if you could give me five minutes. Could I come and see you? I just want to ask one or two things about… Mimi, the mare I lost, you know? I suppose I want to close that episode and move on. Please?"

To her gratification, he continued to sound matter-of-fact. Women grieving over dead horses were part of a vet's daily grind, it seemed. They arranged an appointment for early the following week.

***

Annabel was shown into a small office at the vet's surgery, furnished with a couple of functional wooden chairs and a tiny desk stacked with curling, dusty papers and an old veterinary tome. Talking to relatives of patients was not such a big thing here as in human medicine, she reflected, thinking of the palatial offices of the private doctors she had occasionally visited with her daughters.

She heard a deep voice giving instructions to someone, then heavy footsteps coming along the corridor, followed by Tom himself stomping in wearing his heavy-duty boots and ancient Barbour coat. He greeted her with a nod, avoiding her eyes, and continued his train of discussion almost without a break. He talked on about the farm he'd just visited, the cows he'd dosed. Annabel found herself nodding and smiling politely, saying, "Really?" with feigned interest, aware she had lost the initiative.

He was gabbling, she realised, totally at sea in this heavy emotional situation. He was pleading for clemency. Barely aware of the content of his garrulous blather, she took him in: how he looked too big for this room and the tiny desk behind which he now sat; his short grey hair and weather-beaten face; his hard-working hands; his eyes that always evaded contact; those hobnailed boots clumsily parked under the desk; his wholly masculine ineptitude.

Eventually he ground to a halt and stared fixedly at his desk-top. Annabel – dressed smartly in her elegant city trouser suit, immaculate cream blouse with silk scarf at the neck, and polished high-heeled shoes – felt acutely aware of the contrast between them. She felt as if built on a flimsy, delicate scale compared with this rural, all-weather, craggy farmers' friend. Even her voice seemed tiny. Masculine and feminine took on new disparate dimensions.

"I wanted to be sure – before I think of another horse – that there were no factors that could have been avoided, with Mimi?"

She got no further before he was off again, wordy sentences tumbling over each other, making no sense except to reassure, get her off this fraught topic, and off his back. As he droned on, she was aware of the power of talking; it didn't have to make sense. Just keeping the initiative was the key. She knew she would get no answers, had been aware of this for five months. Immediately after the accident she'd wanted a CID posse to investigate the site of the accident, the events before and after. And knew that was nonsense, of course. No-one to blame, an act of God (in old law-speak), an unavoidable risk with high-spirited animals who nevertheless must be given a good measure of freedom.

How do I get out of this impasse? Annabel thought, looking down at the nervously restless boots. Then she remembered Mandy's pony. Breaking into the monologue quite abruptly, she asked if he knew the Arab Mandy had mentioned. Tom's face cleared as if the sun was breaking through above a cloud-bank. Yes, he knew it. What a great idea. She needed to get back in the saddle as soon as possible. This would be a nice animal, good for the girls, good for the confidence, easy to sell in the future.

Annabel perceived that the interview was over; she'd already taken twenty minutes of his time. What would the receptionist think? She stood up, smiled into his eyes, and shook his hand. He was still chuntering on, go and see it, let me know if you want a pre-sale vetting… happy to help, good to see you, all the best. What a string of platitudes. My God, was he married? she wondered. How did such a man ever woo, wed, and bed a woman?

She left the surgery feeling confused, or maybe challenged. Everything in her mind and behaviour seemed so out of her normal character. On the way home, negotiating the traffic, she thought of her new persona – a modern woman, liberated from her vows of fidelity. She ought to be prepared for what she wanted, even if the moment never came. She ought to carry condoms with her. Even that rebellious act was thrilling to contemplate. But how to swan into a chemist and ask for them? The counter staff were professionals, of course. No raised eyebrows, but the silly minxes would probably have a giggle about it later. *Did you see that middle-aged woman buying a pack? Hope springs eternal! She had a wedding ring on, too. Well I never. I thought people over the age of thirty lost interest in all that.*

She'd go to the supermarket. A pack of condoms could be selected and just mingled with the other things, like cat food, groceries, household stuff. Somehow it was more anonymous. She turned into Sainsbury's, though it would make her late home. But where would she keep them? Where would be safe from prying eyes? The mother/wife in any home seemed to be everybody's property, nothing of her own was sacrosanct. She'd once tried to keep a diary, but somehow Ralph had sniffed it out. She did not want to record her inner thoughts if someone was going to read them, so they were no longer written down. Female creativity and rebellion had struggled and been stifled throughout the ages, subordinated to her service role and intimidated by misogyny, she thought belligerently.

Annabel picked out a pack of five standard condoms, not wanting to draw attention to herself by pausing to select, but not wanting something wantonly adventurous. She gathered a few other items, and was gratified at the checkout girl's total lack of interest. The teenager probably didn't register anything beyond swiping the barcode. Back in the car, Annabel fished out the precious pack and looked at it, then secreted it in her handbag. There would be no point in having them if she hid them at home. They would stay in her bag, in her make-up pouch, and she would risk someone furtling about in there and finding them.

She had not written off Tom yet. His shyness might denote interest; maybe he could be drawn out, led astray? Thoughts of him occupied her to the exclusion of other things. He was something she needed to resolve. At home, she went through the dutiful motions in her quiet way, but no-one remarked on her introspection. It was just Mum in one of her moods.

In the following days, she went about her daily life, her secrets tucked away in the deepest, most private corners of her mind – and handbag – trying hard to feel hopeful and empowered by those secrets and where they might lead.

Chapter 7

A nnabel wrote a note to Tom Cormack, saying there was something else she needed to ask him. *Could he please phone her at 11pm on Thursday evening?* She added her phone number.

The girls were usually in bed by that time, and as Ralph was keeping regular hours, she thought she could guarantee some privacy. She posted the note several days in advance, then got cold feet. Would he think her request bizarre in the extreme? Probably. Well, it was done now. She was behaving very oddly, viewing every man she met in a new light. Ralph's analyst would probably have a name for her deviant behaviour.

When Thursday came, she was nervous throughout the evening. She even dropped a favourite coffee mug, which smashed into smithereens. Ralph had gone back to work full time and was behaving in an exemplary manner, though relations between them remained cool. He had taken to going to bed early and getting up at the crack of dawn to go jogging. His diet had taken on a seriously bizarre aspect, several litres – or so it seemed – of orange juice daily, and nothing solid until evening when he would partake of the usual evening meal, avoiding green salad and vegetables. Then he would have a huge helping of ice cream and chocolate sauce with a drizzle of Drambuie. But at least he was no longer drinking, nor losing any more weight, and only occasionally took sleeping pills.

Annabel watched the clock nervously as ten-thirty approached. The phone rang. She started quite violently, but Ralph did not seem to notice. He picked up the receiver. "It's for you," he said, holding it out to her.

Annabel's mind raced, her hand shook. What was she getting herself into?

"Hello?" she breathed, and thought it sounded horribly come-on and floozyish. Again, Ralph didn't pay attention. He got up and slouched out into the kitchen, just as a female voice spoke. Annabel broke out into a sweat, feeling her stomach drop about three feet.

"Hi, Annabel. It's Jackie, from the stable. I hope you don't mind me ringing?"

She recognised the unrefined accent of a woman she knew slightly from Hadley; not a close friend, just one of the crowd of grass widows whose men never appeared, and who seemed to have transferred all their devotions to their horses.

Jackie went on, "I'll be frank, and you can tell me to go to hell if you want. Listen, we all miss you like crazy. We all feel for you, we know what you've gone through, but we think it's time you came back. I know it's a terrible cheek of me to talk like this, I hardly know you. But someone's got to. Mandy won't, for fear of seeming mercenary. But she wants you for yourself, Annabel, we all do. Honest."

Annabel, in spite of her tension and her concern to speed Ralph up to bed, was deeply touched. Female friends, after all, were the best, the most loyal.

"Thanks, Jackie. I really do appreciate it. I am seriously thinking about this Arab pony Mandy suggested. I don't know if you've heard?"

"Well, I'm really glad to hear it. But I thought I'd make a list of horses for sale or loan, that might suit. "

And she proceeded to reel off a list of horses who might be available on short term loan because their owners were away, or needed to buckle down to their schoolbooks, or were *hors de combat* through injury. She sounded as if she had scoured the countryside for potential horsey candidates. Again, Annabel felt warmed and amazed. The women she met nowadays in the horse world were mostly ordinary working women (and after all, she reminded herself, she had voluntarily joined that world), but they seemed rather more genuine and sincere than many of her social contacts. Well, if people wanted her back so much, she would stir herself and do something about it. Poppy would be pleased, too.

"I've decided to go and see the Arab pony. In fact, the owners know I'm interested and won't sell to anyone else before I've seen it," she told Jackie. "I spoke to Mandy a few days ago. I plan to come over with a friend, probably this weekend, to see her. We've been meaning to for some time."

After she'd put the phone down, Annabel sat thinking about Jackie. The woman had a nice Arab herself, and had asked Annabel to hack out with her once or twice. It was always better to go out into the country in pairs or groups, as the horses liked company even more than the riders. But Annabel had never taken up the offer; she'd not been interested enough, too taken up with her own concerns of competing, jumping and schooling. And, she admitted ruefully to herself, she had looked down on Jackie a bit. Well, now she would be different. The horse world was full of lovely women helping each other in difficulties, and she would be a proper part of all that. She would come down to earth a bit, stop being so aloof. She thought of Megan, and felt glad she was going to be her mentor.

With a start, she looked at the clock just as Ralph put his head round the door.

"I'm off to bed now. Doors are locked. D'you think I could join the porridge-eaters tomorrow?" This was said in an injured tone, as if he had been purposely excluded.

"Sure, you've only to ask. No problem."

When he was gone, Annabel sat watching the clock. She had remembered to disconnect the phone in the bedroom. She picked up a book, read the same paragraph four times, put it down again. She went to the sideboard and took out a pack of cards, shuffled them, and sat down at a coffee table. She put on the television with the remote, turned the volume down, flicked through the channels, put it off again.

"What am I getting so het up about? He'll not ring. For God's sake, what an ass I am," she muttered to herself. "It was madly dictatorial. Ring me at such and such a time, I've got something to ask."

The phone rang. Her heart lurched. She picked up the receiver.

"This is Tom Cormack. You asked me to ring?"

"Oh yes. Thanks for calling," said Annabel, impossibly brightly. She gulped. "Look, I wonder if you and I could meet. Perhaps for a drink?" There's no going back now, she thought.

"What for?" he asked after a pause, sounding puzzled and on his guard.

"Oh… *you* know. Just to chat, get to know each other a bit…"

"Oh, right. Right, yes… thank you. How nice… but not quite at the moment-it's-just-so-busy-with-calls-at-all-hours-day-and-night-I'm-on-call-for-farms-and-out-liers-and-crofts-all-these-small-animals-too-cats-and--dogs-hamsters-rabbits…" He was off, just like the time in his office. She sat and waited for the torrent to cease. "…and-it's-nice-of-you-but-let-me-contact-you."

"Of course." Annabel rang off. The clock said ten past eleven. "Christ, what have I done? I'll never dare speak to him again. Now I'll need to get a new vet."

But the next day, courage and desperation had re-asserted themselves. Maybe I'm just not explicit enough, she thought. Maybe I give up just when I should go in for the kill. Now he knows what I'm after, he'll possibly respond more willingly. Let's try just one more time. Make or break. Go for it, girl!

In the privacy of her office at work, which was much more secure than at home, she phoned his number and got the receptionist with her cheerfully anonymous voice. She asked for Tom Cormack.

"Who's calling?" Annabel enunciated her name, wishing she, too, could remain anonymous. After a pause, the girl returned. "I'm afraid he's not in at the moment. I'm sure he'll get back to you. Bye."

And Annabel knew that he had been there. He'd probably said to the lass, "Oh, not her again. She's a complete bampot, a nuisance, an obsessional time-waster, a stalker. Tell her I'm not in, and don't say I'll phone back."

Annabel put her head in her hands, elbows resting on her desk, and wept hot salty tears. She remembered the days when she'd had more admirers than she knew what to do with; men had even fought over her. How confidently and carelessly she'd taken her sex appeal for granted then. And now, in a few short years, how things had changed. It was not as if she had neglected herself. She was slim, fit, smart, took regular hair and beauty treatments, had excellent dress sense, knew about cosmetics and deportment. I'm innately a good girl, I suppose, born to be faithful, she told herself. Maybe I'm marked by Ralph's family scent which has made me a chemical no-go area for any other man.

Remembering the condoms in her handbag, she longed to have an occasion to use them. She yearned to be wicked, to have some man look at her with lust and desire again, to lead him on and respond. It was twenty-five years since she had made love to anyone other than Ralph, and times had changed so much. Women no longer felt embarrassed about their randiness; they could talk dirty and experiment, do risky things like having sex out-of-doors.

Annabel had picked up a magazine in the staff room recently and flicked it open at a page on "How to keep your man interested" or some such rubbish. To her amazement, the first piece of advice had been "Know your way around a penis". Good grief! If she had bought such a magazine, she would be furtively hiding it, not leaving it around on a coffee table.

She remembered her own mother once talking frankly – or as frankly as she ever got – about her married sex-life, and saying quite matter of factly that she didn't know whether Annabel's father was circumcised. Annabel had not expressed emotion at the time. She'd felt the gulf between such a sex-life as that implied and her own was just too cosmic to be explored, certainly to be explained to her mum. Now her own daughter, Lily, avidly read a magazine each week which Annabel was horrified to discover was explicitly and provocatively sexy.

Yes, sex-etiquette changed with generations, just like fashion. There must be some key to adult-dating that had developed since her day, and to which she was oblivious. Maybe the girls would know. Or maybe her new friend, Megan; she was still young and extremely attractive. Annabel balked at the idea of taking Megan into her confidence on such matters; she was far too reserved for that. But maybe a time would come.

She wouldn't throw away the condoms yet, she decided, though Annabel was beginning to think they were more a thrilling delusion than a safety device. She would take steps to purchase the fourteen-two pony, which appealed enormously. It could be a family pony, which would get round the difficulty of favouring one daughter over the other. And she would talk to Mandy about another vet, implying she had fallen out with Tom. That would raise no eyebrows particularly, for Tom was really more of a cow-man, with a reputation of letting things take their course with horses when illness or injury struck.

There was another man, Annabel knew, who attended at Hadley, and whose knowledge of horses was probably superior to Tom's. Annabel thought bitterly, I'd better not trail my coat for *him* and scare him off. I'm really going to need a vet.

Chapter 8

"I agree she's fun to be with and an excellent teacher, sure, but she really does only have one topic of conversation," Megan told Dick as they travelled to Leatherburn one afternoon for a joint jumping lesson with Sue. Megan was mystified that Dick had proposed a social event with Sue and her husband – a cross-country jumping demonstration, with commentary by one of the outstanding national eventers. It was being held in Glasgow in about a fortnight's time, and he suggested they could stop on the way back for dinner.

"When I ring you at night when you've been riding, you only have one topic of conversation, too!" he teased.

On the whole, Megan was up for the idea and certainly keen to go to the demonstration. They seemed to be becoming friends with Sue rather quickly, but both had reason to be glad of her help, having had several remedial lessons with her.

This afternoon, Sue planned to take them into a field where a few cross-country fences had been erected; very simple and not too big.

"It'll be an introduction to the feel of the sport," she had said. "I think you are both ready for it. Very different from show-jumping in a restricted arena. The horses get keen, go fast, and can jump big."

"Don't chicken!" Sue yelled. "Drive your horse into the middle of the fence, look to the other side. If you look at the front of the fence, that's where you'll stop!"

They both managed fairly well, finishing up by stringing a few fences together on a short course. Megan accomplished this with no run-outs, but Dick had a few problems. As he tensed, his horse became rather gee'd up.

"Relax a bit!" Sue cried. Megan could see this advice was lost on her husband as he grappled with his eager cob, muttering under his breath. Eventually he set off, but was only just in charge. His progress was far from rhythmic as he scrabbled over fences. The turn to the last jump was wrong, and the horse ducked out to the right, tipping Dick out of the saddle to the left.

"I could see that coming," muttered Sue, as she went to retrieve the horse. Megan could see it was not a serious fall, even though Dick was writhing on the ground.

"I don't think there's any damage done," she said, helping him up.

"You two took your time coming to my rescue," he said crossly.

Before he could think about it, he was bundled into the saddle and coming to the last fence again, keeping a correct line this time, and jumping well. Sue praised him lavishly.

Afterwards, as they'd agreed, the three of them went to the Pie 'n' Pint for a half pint of beer. Riding was thirsty work.

"So when do you think we'll be doing an event like Lauder?" Dick asked, not quite seriously.

"You know, if you got yourselves a nice horse, it could all happen quite quickly," Sue responded, knowing that's what he wanted to hear.

Dick turned to Megan and patted her knee. "Didn't I do that last fence superbly?" he asked.

Sue asked about their recent experiences in the classes and Megan explained that she'd introduced the boys to Hadley stable, where they were thoroughly enjoying themselves. She admitted she'd been worried about safety issues at Leatherburn, from observations, her own experiences, and the general gossip.

"I just hope Mrs Stark doesn't hear about it. She won't be pleased," Megan added.

"Oh, she knows," said Sue. "Nothing goes under the radar in the local horse world."

"Oh? What did she say?"

"Not much. But she won't fall over herself to give you good service any more. Still, if you come to me, that'll be a safeguard."

Megan mentioned that Mrs Stark had recently told them they didn't need an escort any more when they went out on hacks. So they had gone out several times, just the two of them.

"There are always adventures," Megan said. "Things you don't foresee. An old mattress discarded in the gutter, and the horses refusing to pass it. Similarly with a bonfire in someone's garden. One of the worst was the sudden introduction of pigs into that top field, the one just by the track. We almost lost control there, and couldn't get the horses to pass."

Sue looked grim. "Horses just hate pigs. Bridget is short-staffed, so it helps if you can look after yourselves. And while I agree it's a bit soon, it is the best sort of learning curve for you."

Dick chimed in with an entertaining account of how they had run straight into a parade, with banners and brass band. They'd seen it coming along the high street, and luckily had managed to escape into a side road just in time.

"It makes for a rather stressful outing at times," Megan said, grimacing.

Sue looked at her with a slightly disdainful expression, and gave a little shrug.

"You only began to ride when you do it day after day, on your own, hacking out in all weathers, over the moors or in heavy traffic, wherever. Schooling a horse, bringing it on by tiny degrees and with patience. Mastering its moods, teaming with it, motivating it. Merging with it like a centaur. Being able to get aboard any animal at all and make something of it."

Dick gazed at her in admiration, but Megan thought it sounded like a speech she'd made before.

They discussed the forthcoming demonstration in Glasgow and made plans to travel in the one car.

"Mike can drive," said Sue. "He won't mind."

"Do you think there will be lots of people from the eventing world there? Ian Stark? Ginny Leng?" Dick asked.

"For sure."

Megan thought, too late, that Dick was already planning a bit of self-introduction and grandstanding, all of which could get tedious.

***

Megan, Jeremy and Sam sat around the oak trestle table in the kitchen, drinking tea and tucking into hot crumpets dripping with melting butter and strawberry jam, laughing and chatting. They had not long arrived back from Hadley stable where, on a freezing cold Saturday afternoon, they had taken part in a Hallowe'en and Guy Fawkes party, complete with pony-club games.

Lady Mandy had ensured that every child went home with a handful of rosettes; much-prized colourful trophies to be hung on bedposts. The Fraser boys had won more than their fair share and both were still on a high, desperate to give their dad a blow-by-blow account.

Megan got up to make more tea. "Do you remember, Sam, not long after we started at Leatherburn, you absolutely refused to come riding with us?" Sam looked blank. "You'd had a bad fall. Your poor bottom had a huge purple mark on it."

"Oh yes," said Sam, remembering. "I went to Granny's instead, and we baked cakes and pies." He licked the golden drops of butter off his fingers.

"You enjoyed yourself so much there I thought you'd never want to come back to riding. But after a few weeks you announced you would. Aren't you glad now that you did?"

Megan was impressed with how these gymkhana games taught the children to leap on and off, tumble and fall about, so that they lost their fears and inhibitions. Flamboyant Jeremy had particularly shone in the sack-race, when his pony charged the length of the school with him clutching on round its neck, while all the other competitors laboriously hopped in their hemp bags along-side trudging ponies. Sam, a little more cautious, showed natural talent in the egg and spoon and in the javelin race, where you inserted sticks into traffic cones while negoti-ating a complete turn.

"You can tell," said Jeremy, "that the ponies loved it as much as we did."

The boys broke into song. "*Please, Daddy, don't get drunk this Christmas. I don't want to see my Mummy cry-y-y-y.*" Giggling, they plotted to tease their dad with this woeful, country-style ditty they'd heard on the car radio on the way home. "I'm going to take my rosettes to school," announced Sam, counting them again proudly. "I don't think Miss Lesley believes I'm a proper rider. She thinks only posh people do it. Fancy. Six! And two are firsts. Any more crumpets, Mum?"

"No more, or you won't want your dinner."

Megan smiled contentedly as the two ran off to play and squabble. She was back in her evening class, with no further shattering mishaps. Dick had been busy with his TV work, but hoped to make up riding time in the holiday season. He loved the ambience at Leatherburn so much that he'd announced he would go along over Christmas and help muck out. Megan wasn't sure how long his enthusiasm would last, but Dick insisted he loved being treated like a worker, getting his hands dirty, doing some tough manual work.

"I get so tired of people kow-towing, as they do in the media world," he had told her. "So bloody pretentious and career-driven. At the stable, no-one gives a damn who I am. They judge you on your merits as a rider or horse-handler."

He had come home from his last private lesson with an invitation from Sue. All of them – boys included – were to go for a festive high-tea, then stay overnight. Megan was again slightly surprised to receive the invitation on such a slight acquaintance, but pleased all the same. It was nice when people invited you as a family. Too many of Dick's colleagues were habitual party animals, with hard drinking and partner-swapping integral to the scene. Dope, too, she suspected.

Jeremy bounced back in. "When will Dad be home, Mum?"

"I don't know, darling. He said he'd be out all day, but was a bit vague about his plans. Must have been something to do with work as otherwise he'd have loved to come and watch you. He should be back for dinner. Don't you think you should change out of those smelly clothes?"

At that moment, the outside door opened and Dick was temporarily overwhelmed by the rugby scrum that was his two sons in a state of excitement. When he emerged, Megan came to kiss him. She noted with considerable surprise that he had his riding clothes on, but the hurly burly did not allow rational conversation until they both went up to wash and change.

"Where on earth have YOU been?" she asked.

"Oh, I've been over to Brockhollow Farm. You know, Sue's place."

"What on earth for?"

"She thought I'd benefit from riding some really good horses. Her own, and the farm owner, Rosemary's, too. It was tremendous. We did some schooling, then went for a super ride. I'm not up to jumping these big chaps yet. But the difference between them and the Leatherburn horses is chalk and cheese, my love. We... er... she's going to take me hunting."

"Hunting!" Megan screamed.

Dick looked startled; his wife was normally the soul of patience and tolerance.

"Yes. Why not? I'm not anti-blood sports, as you know."

Megan had stopped in the middle of piling up clothes for washing. She felt as if she had been struck in the midriff.

"You casually talk about going off hunting with Sue, and it never even occurs to you to include me in your plans!" Megan looked at him aghast, feeling the corners of her mouth quiver and tears come to her eyes.

"My darling," Dick said soothingly. "I'm sorry. If it upsets you, we'll not do it. I thought you would be anti-hunt. And you never usually worry about me going off on my own."

"Dick, you know this is different. I'd give my eye-teeth to go hunting – when I'm good enough, which is maybe not yet. Riding is something we do together, we progress in it together, we share. I've never elbowed *you* out."

"I'm not elbowing you out." Dick was becoming irritable. "Anyway, you often go riding without me."

"You don't expect me to submit to the demands of *your* job, Dick, I'm sure. I have enough constraints of my own. We've been through this before. Besides, there's the look of it. What do I think, what does everybody think, when you go off hunting with another woman?"

"Look, I've said sorry. If it upsets you, we won't do it. End of story. Now stop looking so accusatory."

Dick gave her a hug and a kiss and escaped downstairs. He hated scenes, and they seldom rowed. But Megan was left feeling flat and uneasy. She let the clothes drop on the floor and sat down heavily on the bed, deflated and troubled.

Dick's more logical response ought to have been to include her in the hunting plan. And he couldn't possibly have thought she was anti-hunt, she told herself, remembering how they had once followed the stag-hounds on foot in Somerset when they had taken an early Spring holiday there. They had even been invited to a meet, and drunk sherry with the Master and his Huntsman on the lawn on a fine frosty morning.

Dick was always being invited to classy houses because of his high profile; he was a bit of a snob, loving to be lionised and courted by the gentry and aristocracy. She remembered her husband on the occasion with the Somerset stag-hounds, in his element, chatting man-to-man with the Master, amusing the company with his wit. She pictured him surrounded by the ladies of the manor, elegant in their country clothes, hanging on his every word. He had stood in their midst, a city-dwelling alien but still managing to dominate with his shock of floppy dark hair and his manly frame, charming them all, the centre of attention, the focus of sparkling conversation and bursts of laughter.

Megan had had the two boys with her, drinking orange juice out of crystal glasses. After the first courtesies, she had been left mostly alone; she supposed this class of person did not look after their own children, and perhaps it was deemed eccentric even to have the children in tow. She had enough self-confidence to take it in her stride, but Dick was more thin-skinned. Afterwards, he had asked her anxiously, "How did I do? Did I come over well?"

In spite of her professional life and her own academic achievements, Megan often found herself marginalized in social situations with her husband. It always puzzled her. On her own, she could circulate, introduce herself, talk and discuss, hold the floor, be an integral part of the action. But with him, against her will she would find herself trailing behind, silent and dull like a dowdy female bird. It was why she often excused herself from the invitations that came from his work in the media; she had no desire to be patronised by daringly-dressed and impossibly glamorous young women.

Dick had always been understanding; they did not live in each others' pockets all the time, they had their own lives and interests. Megan usually felt it was an excellent thing that they were so different, that they did not compete against each other, and that they enjoyed their own space.

But this time, alarm bells were ringing over Sue and the hunting suggestion. And the fact that he had backed down so readily did not muffle the strident warning tones.

Why had he not breathed a word in advance of today's trip to Sue's place? He must have intentionally concealed his plans, smuggling his gear into the car, and presumably changing at her house. He had emphasised that his commitments could not be broken for the children's party, as if they were duty rather than pleasure.

A rumpus breaking out downstairs shook her from her thoughts. Sounds of excited laughter, pretended roars of indignation from Dick, strains of "*Ple-e-e-e-ase, Daddy, don't get drunk this Christmas,*" drifted up from the sitting room. Megan folded her thoughts away with the laundry and went down to calm the boisterous high-jinks that could easily end in tears or breakages.

Chapter 9

Annabel was spooning out the porridge into four bowls as Ralph rushed into the kitchen in his overcoat, bringing a miasma of tension into the relaxed weekend atmosphere.

"Here's your porridge, darling," said Annabel, frowning at the coat and briefcase. "You do know it's Saturday, don't you?"

"Yes, but I'm going into work, lots to catch up on." He threw open the fridge door, knocking the carton of orange juice out onto the floor. "Bugger!" he muttered, leaping back and ensuring the juice scattered widely.

Poppy got up from the table to grab the roll of paper towel and mop the tiled floor, while Ralph picked up the now empty carton and looked at it helplessly. "Is there no more?"

Annabel produced a new one from a cupboard. Her husband's need to have everything done for him had disrupted the peaceful scene.

"No time for porridge, sorry," said Ralph. "All right for some to relax at the weekend. I've got to go."

Annabel restrained herself. The porridge wars, as Lily had labelled them, had been fought in this household longer than she could remember. Periodically, Ralph would feel left out of the communal activities, and ask in an aggrieved manner if he could have porridge made for him at breakfast, too. Annabel would say, "Yes, of course." Then one morning some days or weeks later, just as it was ready, he would say, "Sorry, no time, must dash." The next day, the same sequence, the same conversation. So she would stop making it for him. Then he would come and peer over her shoulder and say, "Is any of that for me?"

And so the oscillating irritation would continue. Annabel had repeatedly determined never to be drawn in again, yet somehow it was never possible to extricate herself from his game-playing.

Once he had gone, and peace settled, she brought up the question of the pony which she planned to look at today with a view to buying. Annabel emphasised it was to belong to the whole family, not just one person. But she could see this ploy was not going to work. Lily's habitually pouty face clouded as she worked herself up into a histrionic sulk.

"You say that, of course, so it'll sound fair. But it's not the least bit fair. It will end up being Poppy's. What do I get? I've grown out of ponies, for God's sake. Why should I be bossed around out of school? All that heels down, toes in, sit up, thrust the bust crap. None of my friends go traipsing off to the stable any more. That's for kids. Like, dirty, smelly places. I prefer to be clean, I prefer to be lady-like."

Annabel knew Lily had lost interest in riding when it became clear that she was not as good as Poppy. Unfortunately, her young sister outshone her in many things, and her jealousy was expressed in petty acts of bullying.

"Horses aren't playthings, Lily. People don't grow out of them."

"Well, *you* don't, Mum, that's true."

"Don't be rude."

Lily defiantly tossed her newly-tonged, bouncy ringlets. "Well, I'm the older one and I don't see why Poppy always gets pampered and I get nothing. You always favour her. You're being selfish, just because *you* like to ride. If you get this pony, then I ought to get something costing just as much."

"Like what? What do you seriously want? You've both got as much and more than most girls of your age. You never think about the expense of all the things you take for granted."

"I could have the same amount for spending on clothes, or a holiday abroad with my mates. Then you could get your silly old pony, and I wouldn't object."

Poppy looked from one to the other in an agony of miserable suspense; she longed for a pony. Her hopes had gone into orbits of delight, only to be deflated by Lily's habitual obstructiveness. Her sister's dog-in-the-manger attitude, as well as her cheek, was provoking Mum into a rage. She knew the stages so well. And here came the explosion.

"Oh thanks, big of you, I'm sure. Well, let me tell you this, young lady, you'll get nothing more until you learn…" Lily sat looking both smug and martyred at the rage she had caused.

Annabel's seething rejoinder came to a stop. "Sorry, Poppy, it was a nice idea, but Lily has ruined it as usual. No pony. We'll have to both go without."

Poppy's tears trickled down her cheeks. Lily got up with slow dignity, compressing her lips and walking out of the room with her head erect, as if she had much to bear. Poppy knew that her mother's response to stress was to go into self-denying mode, her "early Christian martyr tendency", as they both called it. No doubt that was what Lily had hoped to achieve.

Annabel tried to protect Poppy, and probably did end up favouring her younger, milder, altogether *nicer* daughter. It was very difficult to be fair, when one was so much easier to love than the other. Often, poor Poppy got punished along with Lily just so that the older girl could not claim discrimination.

She had intended to take both girls to look at the pony, but that plan had now been ditched. She could not possibly just take Poppy along, or that would confirm Lily's accusation of favouritism. But she'd arranged with the pony's owners to visit, so she'd go alone. Bother the lot of them, she thought, though she really meant Lily and Ralph; they were so alike in some ways.

Poppy went to her room and sat, brushing her nose with the end of her wispy, flaxen ponytail, looking gloomily at her prep books and wondering why she always looked forward to weekends, only to have them spoilt by family rows. She glanced longingly at the huge poster on the wall behind her bed, of her heroine Pippa Funnell on Primmore's Pride, winning at Badminton Horse Trials. Her door opened and Lily looked in.

"You're not doing your prep now, are you? We're going into town. We'll meet the gang, get the goss. Come on, you agreed."

Poppy was astonished at how quickly Lily seemed to get over the traumas of rows and quarrels. She never appeared to suffer an aftermath of dull misery and worry.

"I didn't suppose you'd want to, after all that."

"All what?"

"The row downstairs."

"Oh that. Good Lord, you don't get upset by Mum in a tantrum, do you?"

"It was your fault, Lily, you know it was. You provoked the row. If you hadn't, we'd all be going off to look at horses. You've spoilt my Saturday. Why should I go into town 'cos that's what you want to do?"

Poppy observed that Lily had dressed with unusual care. She wore new khaki designer jeans and jacket, with a rather see-through animal print top. She had on orange eye shadow and thickly-applied mascara, coral lipstick and matching nail varnish. Her long brown hair hung in designer curls over her shoulders. Poppy supposed her sister wanted to meet a boy they knew slightly, Adrian, whom she had seen last week in the shopping mall. When Adrian had smiled and said hello in passing, Poppy had noticed her sister's blush at the time, and her self-absorbed, abstracted state afterwards. Lily was a great dreamer, often inhabiting the world of her imagination more fully than the real one, their father would say.

"Come on, Pops. We can't sit here moping. Do your prep later." Lily slid deftly into persuasive mode. "We can go to that cool new trendy café and I'll buy you a Coke. Or maybe a poster of Justin Timberlake. It's time you got into blokes, instead of these butch lady riders." She looked askance at the gymnastic equine feats plastered on the walls. "Do come on. No need to change, you're fine as you are." Lily looked with critical superiority at her sister's blue denims, fleece sweater, and trainers.

"I'd much rather be going to look at horses," Poppy said bitterly. But Lily could see she was yielding, and jollied her along, helping her find her purse and jacket.

"I've loads of stuff to buy. We'll go to the mall. I want to top up my mobile and get the latest Charlotte Church single, *Crazy Chick*. Oh, and we'll go to Boots for some low-carb chocolate." Lily chattered cheerfully, trying, it seemed to her sister, to draw her into her synthetic teenage lifestyle.

"Don't you think Mum is trying to compensate for something with this crazy horse business?" asked Lily, lighting up a cigarette as they waited for the bus. "She's trying not to admit she's, like, getting on a bit."

Poppy looked anxious. "No, of course not. Mum's always liked riding and stuff. She's not changed. She's had a lot to cope with, what with Mimi breaking a leg and Dad being off work. She's had to do everything. You should give her a break."

"She and Dad are circling round each other like a pair of prairie dogs. Why don't they admit they are washed up as an item? I wouldn't stay together just to nark all the time."

"I don't agree. You can't just break up over every passing difficulty. They've got us to think of."

"I reckon Dad's been up to something. I don't believe in this illness he's had. He didn't have to stay in bed, he wasn't off his food or anything. It seems phoney to me. He was supposed to be under stress, or depressed or some such thing. Wish I could stay off school every time I felt fed up."

Poppy shifted uneasily. She liked to stick up for both parents and thought Lily was wickedly irreverent and ungrateful to talk about them like this.

"Dad had something wrong, he was on pills. I saw him taking them. And of course he'd put on a brave face in front of us."

"I know for a fact that one problem was the amount of booze he drinks. Haven't you seen Mum trying to hide the brandy bottle? And trying to put out the empties before we see them? That's not illness, that's self-indulgence." Lily's tone was scathing. "He should snap out of it. How can he lecture me about smoking when he does that? Parents are the pits."

But Lily's upbeat, gossipy mood only lasted as long as it took them to take the bus into town, walk twice up and down the mall, and see no sign of Adrian. She became grumpy with disappointment. "It's your fault for taking so long to get ready. Now I've missed someone I really wanted to see here."

"If you were going to meet someone, why did you drag me here?" asked Poppy reasonably, knowing the answer.

"What a bore. And you are a bore, too. Sulking and creating an atmosphere. We might as well go home."

"You said you'd buy me a Coke at that new place."

"Well I don't feel like it now. All very well for you, you're not upset by these rows at home, because you're never the target like I am."

Poppy knew her sister was being unreasonable after her disappointment over Adrian. Normally she would deal with the situation by not answering; she hated rows and bickering, so had developed a technique of just mentally removing herself, floating off into another world. Sometimes Lily would get angry, saying they should have a good old dingdong barney and clear the air. But Poppy knew the air never was cleared that way, it just grew progressively more and more murky.

This time, however, her tolerance had been sorely tested, and something went "ping" inside her head.

She turned to face her sister, screwed her face up with rage, and screeched at her, "Oh, go back and look for your bloody boyfriend. That's the only reason you're picking a quarrel now. You were all sweetness and light when you wanted me to come out with you." Poppy tossed her ponytail, turned on her heel, and marched off in the direction of the bus stop.

Behind her there came a strangled sound, a sort of roar of rage. "You bloody little prig, I hate you–"

Poppy felt a violent thump between her shoulder blades. The impulsion sent her flying forwards, over the edge of the pavement onto a side road, and into the path of a car. Her arms stretched forwards to regain balance, but she slid headfirst over the bonnet, collided with the windscreen, and was projected into the air. She was conscious of all this in slow motion, accompanied by a sickening, squealing noise. This is like a bad fall from a horse, she thought. Then she crumpled in a heap on the road with no more coherent thoughts, just a terrible panic and pain as all the air left her chest, and she battled agonisingly to get her breath.

When Poppy came to, she was surrounded by people, all bombarding her with instructions or questions. "Lie still, dear." "No, she should be moved off the road, can you move your toes? Where do you hurt?" "Don't sit up, keep quite still." Someone else was gabbling, "She just appeared from nowhere, I stood on the brakes. I tried to stop, the lights were green…"

She became aware of a terrible noise, a screaming undulating wail, an animal noise of infinite distress. At first she wondered if it was coming from herself. It roused her more effectively than anything to a sense of anxiety. Someone seemed to take charge, a man in a tweed jacket who smelled of tobacco.

"What's that horrid noise?" Poppy choked out, thinking that perhaps a dog or a cat had been hit by the car as well.

"It's all right, my love," he said soothingly, as people do when it isn't all right. And then she realised it was her sister screaming hysterically, "She's dead! She's dead! Omigod, omigod, what will I tell Mum? Noooooooo,noooooooooooooooo! Please say she's not dead."

Poppy managed to sit up with assistance, and saw Lily being taken into a nearby pub by a little knot of people. She looked like a rag doll, floppy and falling about, hair and clothes awry, mascara running, lipstick smudged, like... like a ham tragedy queen, Poppy thought. How typical of her to grab all the attention.

"It's all right, dear, she's just upset about you. But she'll be better inside, a tot of something will calm her down. You've got a scrape on your face, and you're a bit mucky, but is there anywhere else you hurt or can't move?"

An ambulance came. Poppy was lifted in, then Lily was brought out of the pub and helped in, too. She looked a complete wreck, so different from the girl that had set out this morning.

Poppy asked, "Are you okay, Lil?" But her sister, still rolling her eyes and making harsh sobbing noises, was unable to answer. One of the ladies climbed in and announced she had better stay with Lily.

***

Ralph came home to an empty house. As he looked from room to room, he noticed the light flashing on the answering machine. The brief message informed him to ring St Dunstan's District Hospital on the following number as soon as possible.

His first thought was Annabel and a horse-related mishap. Then he was hearing, but hardly taking in, that his two daughters had been involved in a road accident; neither seriously hurt, and one was ready to be taken home. Would he please come and collect her? The other was badly shaken and would be kept in overnight. Perhaps he could bring in her toothbrush, washing things, and a nightdress.

***

Almost an hour later, Annabel breezed in. Ralph met her in the hall, and she knew immediately something dreadful had happened. He stood, white as a sheet, his face fazed and grim.

"Come and sit down, my love," he said carefully.

"Ralph, don't be a bloody ass. Tell me what's happened, tell me. Where are the girls?"

"There's been an accident. You must keep calm." Ralph doled out the information in small rations, as if to a child; as though she would be unable to deal with too much at once and must be led cautiously up to the shock-horror bit.

"Where are they? What's happened? For Christ's sake, tell me!" Annabel felt the rising hysteria and fury at his cruel ineptitude.

"Lily's in hospital. She's been kept in. Just for observation overnight."

"Ralph, what happened, for Christ's sake? Where's Poppy?" She was screaming now.

"Poppy's upstairs, she's asleep. She's had a shock and mustn't be disturbed." As Annabel immediately made for the stairs, Ralph stood in her way. "No, you can't see her, you're too overwrought. The doctor said–" He grasped her in both arms, but he was no match for her. Annabel flung his restraining arms away and when he tried again, she gave him a thump with her fist in the stomach, not too far above the groin. With a gasp he was on his knees, while she stepped over him and bounded up the stairs.

Poppy was awake, lying in bed. Annabel knelt down and pulled her into her arms. Poppy started to cry on her shoulder. "My darling, my darling. Don't cry. It's all right, just as long as you're safe. Oh my God, your father made me so worried."

After the first embrace and tears were over, Annabel wiped Poppy's face tenderly with her hanky, stroking the silky hair, and asked gently what had happened. Poppy looked embarrassed. "It was all my silly fault, Mum." Annabel held her closer. "I just stepped off the pavement in front of a car. It wasn't going fast. I got knocked down. It didn't hurt much, though I couldn't get my breath for a bit."

"And was Lily knocked down, too?" Annabel sat back on her heels, both puzzled and alarmed for her other daughter.

"No."

"Why did they keep her in hospital then? What happened to her?"

"She was terribly shocked, I suppose, seeing me getting knocked down. She thought I had been killed. She was screaming and carrying on; out of her mind for a bit."

"I see," said Annabel, with an inkling then of what might have happened. "How did you come to step in front of the car, Poppy? Had the two of you been quarrelling?"

"Honestly, I was just careless, Mum." Poppy did not meet her eyes, and the tears began to flow again. Annabel cuddled her and coaxed her to lie down. Tenderly smoothing her daughter's brow, she realised now was not the time to press for details.

"I'll bring you some tea, sweetheart, in just a moment."

She went down to Ralph, who was sitting on a chair in the hall, doubled over, looking grey. "That was pretty bloody brutal."

"I'm very sorry, darling, I really am." She tried a tentative smile. "Come through and I'll make some tea. You should have told me straight out, though – like, the girls have had an accident, no-one's killed or seriously injured. I was left in suspense, thinking they were both in the morgue or something." Her eyes narrowed as she looked at him. "Never, ever come between me and my child, especially when she's in trouble."

"She's my child, too."

"Well then, tell me just what's going on. Poppy gets knocked down by a car, and she comes home from hospital while Lily's kept in! Which hospital? St Dunstan's!" Annabel wrinkled her nose. "That's an NHS hospital. Hope she doesn't catch anything nasty, like MRSA! Did they say anything about Poppy? Injuries? Advice? Any tablets?"

Ralph produced some paracetamol. "Just these. She's not had any yet. They said she was bruised and scraped. She got an X-ray and anti-tetanus. Bed, rest, keep her quiet for a day or two."

Annabel busied herself making tea, and handed a mug to Ralph, who was swallowing a couple of the paracetamol himself. "Tell me about Lily. Did you see her?"

"Yes. She was sedated and a bit dopey. They said she'd had hysterics, screaming and crying and flinging herself about. She thought Poppy might have been killed. But when she was told Poppy was fine, it didn't stop. She'd wound herself up in the way we know so well. They gave her diazepam, then didn't feel they could send her home all doped up. Probably she'll get out tomorrow."

Annabel leaned against the sink, clutching her mug and sipping her tea. "You know there was a row this morning? When I brought up the question of this pony, Lily made a scene, and I blew up. Then the next thing, to my surprise, they were off into town as if nothing had happened. I wonder if they started quarrelling when they were out?"

"Who can say? Lily's such a drama queen, she uses any situation to take centre stage." Ralph sipped his hot tea.

"I think that's a bit unfair. It must have been a real shock seeing Poppy flattened on the road, especially if it happened after they'd been arguing."

Annabel went upstairs with tea and tablets for Poppy, then set off for the hospital to check on Lily. But the girl was sedated and asleep.

She was allowed home the next day, with a supply of sedative tablets to be taken in tapering doses. Lily was still very fragile and weepy, and any mention of the incident threatened to bring on hysterics again, so they all kept off the subject. She stayed in her room and was waited on for a couple of days, but didn't speak a word to Poppy, behaving as if her sister was beneath her notice.

***

Life gradually got back to normal. Poppy insisted on going back to school after a day or two, but Lily stayed off for a week. When she returned to school just before the Christmas holidays, Poppy heard through the school grapevine that Lily had been given the celebrity treatment for being so highly strung and caring so much about her little sister.

Some days later, Poppy was working at her prep when Lily walked in, sat down, and fixed her with a sinister stare.

Poppy shuddered. She looks positively demonic, she thought.

Lily glared, trying to pierce her sister with her fiercest look. "If you tell anyone about what happened in town that day, I'll kill you."

Poppy, to her own amazement, burst out laughing. Something had happened to her since the accident. She was beginning to realise that, of the two of them, she might be the stronger after all. She said, not unkindly, "Don't be silly, Lil. If I told anyone, you'd be accused of attempted manslaughter, or worse. You'd be sent away to a borstal. You wouldn't be in a position to kill anyone then."

"Have you told anyone?"

"No. And I won't… on one condition. You must do something in return."

"What?"

"At supper tonight, you tell Mum and Dad you don't mind if we get this pony Mum was talking about. And you won't make any more fuss about it."

"Do you swear you won't tell, if I do?"

"I'm not going to swear to anything. That's my offer. Take it or leave it. And I might tell you that Mum suspects we were rowing, so if you're nasty to me ever again, just remember, I could change my mind. Now go away. I've got lots of work to do."

When Lily left the room without another word, Poppy hugged herself delightedly; she had never felt so pleased with herself, or so content. Today she had become a woman, on two counts. Her first period had started that morning – possibly brought on by the stress of her accident, her mother said – and she had bested her sister for the first time ever. She was free.

***

Over supper, Lily came up trumps and said her piece about the pony; quite convincingly. Ralph and Annabel both thanked her and praised her maturity and generosity. Poppy smiled in Mona Lisa fashion at everyone, and said not a word. Ralph looked as if he might start asking probing questions until he saw Annabel's warning frown and slight shake of the head. Later, when the girls had gone to bed, they discussed things more frankly than they had for years.

"I didn't want you asking what had caused the change of heart," explained Annabel. "There's no need to go into that. It's clear they've come to an agreement; a bribe if you like. I wonder what did happen. Also, I didn't want you blurting out that I'd already bought the pony. Let Lily think she's done a generous thing. I think Poppy is growing up and won't be under her sister's thumb so much in future. Lord be praised for that."

Chapter 10

"Oh let me see him, the poppet," enthused Jackie. "Isn't he just gooourge-ous? Hello, fella, welcome to Hadley. He's a friendly, lovely boy." She wrapped her arms round his neck, vibrant with adoration, her eyes closed with an expression of bliss. "Oooooh!"

No-one else could get near the new Arab pony. Annabel caught Mandy's eye and briefly glanced heavenwards. Mandy, who'd learned a thing or two in her time as a diplomat's courtesan, moved in and firmly disengaged Jackie.

"If you do that, no-one can see his finer points," she said kindly. But Jackie was not so easily deterred.

"I can't help it, I'm so excited!" she gushed, beaming round and surging forward again.

Poppy was outraged. What right had this person to take the worshipful high-ground over *her* pony, and using such excruciatingly uncool baby-talk?

Mandy took charge. Glancing round at the two stable girls who had also come into the spacious loose box to view the new arrival, she said sternly, "So many people around him are going to make him nervous. Julie, Anna, you go back to your work now, and Jackie, I'm sure Piper is waiting for you."

The new pony had been delivered by his previous owners that morning. There had been the usual formalities, papers and money exchanged in the house over chat and coffee. Then Annabel and her daughter had come into the stable box to admire him, along with – it seemed to Poppy – half the world. She fervently wished that all these people would go away so she could quietly bond with her new soul-mate.

Mandy smiled at Poppy. "She's well-meaning, but a bit intrusive," she said. "Now you can get near him."

He didn't look the least bit nervous, rather he seemed to like being the centre of attention. He was an elegant dark bay gelding, pure Arab, with a small indentation at the side of his neck. Mandy assured them all this was a "thumb-print of Allah", carried by all the best Arabs and which guaranteed long-life, success, and many other good things.

Poppy stood drinking in his beautifully proportioned limbs, his generous eyes, his gleaming coat, and feathery luxuriance of mane and tail, while her mother and Mandy stood back a little, discussing practical details like shoeing, worming, feeding and vaccination. Poppy knew she had to take an active interest in all these rather boring things if she was to be a proper horse owner.

"He's got a very posh name," said Mandy, "but you can change it if you want, of course. Don't believe all this nonsense about it being bad luck to change a horse's name. Or you can just use it for competitions and give him a stable name. It's Shah Suleiman. I think his previous owner wanted something which sounded oriental. I rather like it. It's got a good ring to it, rolls off the tongue. I can hear the announcement: 'Miss Poppy Lindsay riding Shah Suleiman', as you enter the arena looking so proud and confident."

"I like it, too. Shah Suleiman." Poppy beamed and glowed with delight. "We can call him Solly for short. What do you think, Mum?"

At last, when everyone else had gone and only she and Annabel were left in the box, Poppy complained, "Gosh, doesn't that Jackie woman gush! You'd think she owned Solly. I could hardly get near him."

"Oh, Jackie's a bit like that, but she means well. Not everyone has your advantages, Poppy. I'm afraid you have to put up with everyone's interest," said Annabel, trying to be fair. "It's like a new baby in the family. Everyone has a claim. When you were born, grandparents, aunts, uncles, cousins, all wanted to stake out their own little bit of you. I had to rescue you once or twice."

A face suddenly appeared in the doorway. Poppy groaned quietly; yet another admirer.

Megan had come to collect the boys from their lesson, but Annabel noticed she had a man in tow. An extremely good-looking, tall and broad-shouldered man. He had flaxen-blond hair like a Scandinavian, and a matching moustache. She was conscious of staring open-mouthed, until Megan said hurriedly, "Oh sorry, this is Alex, a surgical colleague of mine. We collided – almost literally – at the gate. I didn't realize that his daughter, Fiona, was one of the girls who helps out here on Saturdays."

Acknowledging Solly, Alex supposed ruefully he would come under more pressure from Fiona, his daughter, to buy her a horse. "I'm holding out as long as possible," he told the two women. "I sometimes think that if the world were populated with horses, men would become obsolete."

Annabel looked enviously at Megan and thought, *lucky thing. She's got a fabulously attractive husband, and now seems to have this Adonis of an admirer, too.*

After Solly's fine points had been rehearsed all over again, Annabel invited Megan and her boys to come along and have lunch at a nearby garden centre, the Shrub and Grub. She and Poppy would have to return to see the mobile saddler later in the afternoon.

Looking around to check that Mandy was not in earshot, Megan lowered her voice to a conspiratorial whisper and declined, explaining that she was riding out with Dick that afternoon at the rival establishment at Leatherburn. Dick had started his Christmas holiday sessions of voluntary stable work there, and seemed to be amazingly enthusiastic at mucking out and carting manure. He had even been allowed to take out a hack.

Clearly surprised, Annabel suggested Mrs Stark shouldn't be allowing him such responsibility so soon, it was almost courting disaster. Megan agreed but said Dick was so proud of himself and would brook no dissuasion.

"A garden centre, did you say?" asked Alex, looking at Annabel. "Sounds a good idea. I'm under orders to look for a Christmas tree. Mind if Fiona and I join you?"

Annabel tried to sound cool and not too eager. "No, not at all. You're most welcome. Shall we go?"

***

Later that afternoon, when a great deal of money had been spent on Solly's wardrobe and grooming requirements, Poppy finally got to ride her new best friend. Mandy and Annabel took the chance to chat in peace, while keeping half an eye on the youngster as she put him through his paces in the outdoor schooling arena.

"One reason I was really annoyed with Jackie this morning, was that I'd promised her to ask you if – once you get to know Solly a bit – you would hack out with her and Pied Piper. She's nervous on her own. But, of course, she was hardly commending herself, being so irritatingly OTT and gushy."

Annabel smiled reassuringly. "It's fine. I had already made up my mind I would do that, Mandy. She's asked me before."

Mandy looked relieved, and patted Annabel's arm. "That's very kind, dear. I know she's not really the sort of person you'd normally expect to be friends with."

Annabel cringed inwardly as she thought of the damson-dyed hair with the mousy roots, and remembered the vulgarities and commonplace expressions which often littered Jackie's speech. Her lunch friends would raise their eyebrows if they knew, and tease her mercilessly about consorting with the great unwashed.

"I think one of the reasons I feel kindly disposed towards her is that in many ways her background is like mine," said Mandy. Annabel couldn't hide her look of astonishment.

"You'll get the whole story on your first trip out with her. She likes to let it all hang out. Her first marriage was a disaster – an alcoholic, violent husband, just like mine.

She clung on for twenty years; imagine that! Then he put her out and installed a dolly-bird receptionist from his work. Jackie called her a 'brainless minx with her skirts up to her backside'.

"Anyway, she found an older man through a dating agency," Mandy went on. "Apparently, he's got a chain of video shops and lots of money. Jackie gets to spend what she likes and do what she likes, more or less, as long as she housekeeps for him. In some ways, she's done better than me! I still have to work!"

Annabel smiled. Only Mandy would draw a parallel between herself being ejected from a Borders castle and estate, and a shop girl thrown out of a council house.

"The most important similarity is that we've both pulled ourselves up out of the mire by the bootstraps. Though I would much rather be independent than rely on a man."

Annabel reminded her, "You do have Hamish!"

"Indeed, and he is a gem among men. But after all that I've been through, I prefer to be at least a little independent. Jackie is a bit insensitive, and not good at knowing *comme il faut*. She used to come bursting into the house without so much as a knock. I had to get one of the livery ladies to mention to her that it wasn't acceptable. But she is learning! And she loves gossip. Well, who doesn't? But she'll be nosy and ask you all sorts of personal questions. Just be blunt if you have to.

"As a rider, though, she's a lot better than she thinks. You'll have fun."

***

Driving home later, Poppy sitting beside her, both were silent, engrossed with their own thoughts. Poppy was delighted, although the day had been fraught with adult-generated irritations; her mum was not usually so unpredictable and irrational. But at least she seemed cheerful again, more like she had been before Mimi's catastrophe.

Glancing sideways, she noted a little smile playing around Annabel's mouth. She was probably thinking about how smart Solly looked when they had kitted him out with his bridle and new lightweight saddle, suitable for dressage. And those lovely new rugs – wool-lined canvas New Zealand for outdoors in winter, quilted stable rug for indoor wear, and a very smart navy travel rug with red piping. Matching travel boots, too. Poppy had spent some of her own money on a new set of brushes and grooming kit. Solly deserved the best of everything.

They had dithered about so much over lunch at the garden centre that Poppy had got quite impatient and restless. Her mum had been so difficult. Poppy was too excited to eat much, though it was quite nice to chat to Fiona about horses while Mum and Alex were talking of something else entirely; but she was impatient to get back, and worried that they might be late for the saddlery van. The adults had lingered over coffee, and then they had followed Alex and Fiona to look at Christmas trees! She'd had to remind her mum for the fourth time about how near it was to three o'clock, and even then they were a bit late. If they hadn't got any tack, she wouldn't have been able to ride at all!

Solly was pure heaven to ride, though. She was going to have lots of fun, and they were going back tomorrow to try him over one or two small jumps.

After all the stress and excitement, Poppy suddenly felt quite tired. She wriggled down in her seat. "What do you suppose he thinks of us?" she asked.

"Who?" her mother glanced over at her, sounding surprised.

"Why, Solly, of course. I hope he loves us as much as we love him."

Chapter 11

M egan brought her car to an abrupt halt and leapt out, grabbing her hat, stick and gloves. She'd just dropped the boys off at their grandmother's, and had tried to escape quickly but her mother-in-law had no concept of urgency. Megan had almost had to be rude to get away. It was so difficult near Christmas. There were thousands of things to be done, and the little established rituals that the boys loved all had to be religiously observed.

She could have done without this afternoon's ride, but Dick wanted it so much. Now that he was, as it were, a member of stable staff, he wanted to show off a bit and lord it about as her escort.

It was mid-afternoon on a crisp December day, with twilight only an hour away. Dick was waiting with two horses tacked up, looking anxiously for her.

"You're late," he said. "We'd best get going, before it starts getting dark." As they climbed aboard, helped by one of the girls, Megan recognised her horse as one of the more sophisticated rides – a somewhat temperamental mare called Lucinda, prone to bolt if she was not tactfully ridden.

"Who's that you're on?" she asked.

"Barney."

"Barney! I thought he was terribly difficult! Are you sure you shouldn't take something a bit quieter?"

But Dick pooh-poohed the very idea. "I've ridden him in a lesson with Sue this week. No problem. He's a reformed character."

Megan knew she was beaten before she opened her mouth. Underneath his suave confidence, Megan knew he was extremely concerned about looking cool and in charge. She thought of asking for a smaller, more sedate horse for herself, but Dick was already heading out of the yard. Aware of a little knot of foreboding in the pit of her stomach, she knew she would be better in the lead to try and keep things calm and not too hell-for-leather. But with Dick in this look-at-me mood, there was no chance of that.

They rode out along the pathway leading to a rocky stream, and the horses stumbled across placing their feet carefully. At the other side, the pathway meandered a little before opening out to a muddy track beside the stream. Usually they trotted a bit here, going into canter when the horses settled. Dick glanced back.

"Ready?"

"Yes, trot a bit first till I get used–"

But Dick had gone off at a brisk trot; too fast, Megan thought. Barney was tossing his head and looked very skittish. To her dismay, she saw Dick's heel go back behind the girth, the canter-signal. Barney shot forward like a train, and so of course did Lucinda. Megan tried to remember all she had been taught. *Sit up, sit back, still and deep in the saddle, don't hold on too tight.*

Both horses were plunging and excited now. Barney was bouncing on the spot, then suddenly his heels shot up – almost in Lucinda's face – and Dick sailed over his head, landing in a heap on the grassy bank. With great good fortune, he held onto the reins.

Megan settled Lucinda as much as she could. "Are you okay?"

Dick nodded, pulling himself up slowly and painfully, looking furious.

"Dick, I'm sorry but I do think this is crazy. We've two horses here that are the most difficult rides in the stable. And they're both in a tiz and already worked up to high doh. Can't we just go back and get two calmer and more sensible ones?"

"No," he answered gruffly, managing to remount awkwardly from a nearby rock.

"Well then, do you mind if I go in front?" Megan said rather than asked, and manoeuvred herself ahead. There was no fun in this at all, she thought. Dick was out to prove his mettle, and she must attempt to limit the risk even if he got irritable and called her wimpish.

"OK. If you must."

Megan walked Lucinda ahead as calmly as she could, but Dick was still having problems settling Barney. She knew that once a rider got anxious, the horse tuned in to the tension and things just spiralled from bad to suicidal. She concentrated on keeping calm herself.

"I think," Dick bellowed in a strangled voice, "that if you got a move on, he'd settle better."

Megan picked up to trot and then as gently as she could into canter. There was an explosion from behind, a roar of anguish as Barney pranced, half reared, then did a monumental buck. Dick had no chance at all, and he soared into the air, landing seconds later with a sickening thump on the muddy path. Before Megan could do anything other than swivel to witness the fall, Lucinda's fuse lit up and she was off like a rocket, galloping away down the path. Megan sat up, wrapped her legs round, pulled on the reins, heaved, rattled the bit. Still they flew like the wind; and worse, she realised that Barney was hot on her heels.

Every time there seemed a chance that Lucinda might answer her brakes, Barney fizzed up behind and set them off again. Megan knew she must try to get control before meeting the road in about half a mile. But by then they were still thundering along. She could see at a glance that there was no traffic about. Astoundingly, she was now thinking lucidly of what she should do. She must find a way of slowing Lucinda and at the same time stopping Barney. And there was help just over the lane, where a narrow tree-lined track, locally called the Tunnel, ran steeply uphill between high banks.

Lucinda galloped onto the road, hooves clanging with a metallic echo on the tarmac. Megan still could not stop her but she could steer her into the Tunnel, where she let the mare have her head a little. Lucinda actually slowed perceptibly on the slope and rough going. A few hundred yards on, the slope was at its steepest where the alley narrowed. Saving her strength until this point, Megan pulled with all her might and yanked the mare's head round to the right so that she came to an abrupt halt, blocking the path. And – praise be! – Barney stopped, too.

Megan sat for a moment, gathering her breath. The horses snorted and their hot breath condensed in the chill air. It seemed an eternity since they had charged off, and she wondered what state Dick was in. Then, as both horses stood quietly, she gathered up Barney's reins and headed Lucinda at a walk down the Tunnel. But Barney was not finished yet. Still full of bounce, he resisted her attempts to lead him and lashed out with his hind leg, just catching Lucinda's hock. With a wild shake of his head, he snatched the reins out of Megan's hand and galloped off downhill, flourishing his tail in triumph. Luckily, Lucinda seemed to have spent her bit of temperament, and was happy to walk on without fuss.

"Sod him," Megan muttered to herself. "I'll just have to leave him and get someone else to come and find him. Hope he doesn't cause an accident. Better go and see to Dick."

She retraced her steps without mishap. As she crossed the road, there was no sign of Barney. Along the path by the river, she at last came upon Dick, slumped by the path, his helmet on the ground a few yards away, head in hands. At least he's alive, she thought. Distracted by hoof beats as loud as a whole cavalcade, she turned to see Barney thundering along towards them.

"Whoa, whoa, steady boy, easy now." Megan was amazed at her own authority. But it worked. Barney slowed abruptly and stopped beside them, panting and lathered in sweat.

She got down from the mare and leaned over Dick, who looked very white and sickly. A cut above his left eye was bleeding, and he was mopping his nose which was also dripping blood.

"I began to wonder if I'd ever see you again," he said, with the ghost of a smile.

"It was hell. Didn't think I'd stop before Jedburgh. How are we going to get you back? Can you get up?"

"I'm a bit dizzy. Don't think I've broken anything."

Dick painfully pulled himself to his feet, then winced.

"Could you walk back?"

"Don't think so. And there's the river. Have to get aboard somehow."

"Let's get you on Lucinda, and I'll see if I can handle Barney. If he's difficult, I'll just leave him. Looks as if he's burned his rage out, though."

With the determination of desperation, they got Dick's foot in the stirrup and heaved him up. Then Megan, wishing there was someone she could pray to, mounted Barney. Thinking hard of how she had seen Sue sitting lightly on him, loose and relaxed yet authoritative, she took the lead towards the river. And to her utter amazement, he was docile as a lamb.

Their little procession did not go unnoticed when they reached the yard. Megan felt the shame of coming back with one horse lathered in sweat and the other with an injury, but she was also angry that there had been no-one sufficiently in charge to say a firm NO to such crazy risk-taking. She or Dick could have been badly injured.

Joanne hurried forward, looking concerned. "What happened?" She could see Dick's bloody face and slumped posture, and Barney's sweaty state.

Megan explained as succinctly as she could. They checked Lucinda's hock, but there seemed no significant injury. A large, swarthy, shabby figure loomed from the tack room; Mr Stark. Usually bad-tempered and foul-mouthed, he was not one to cross.

"Oh aye," he sneered. "Ye think ye're so bloody good, and then ye find out ye're no'. Ye're brought down to size wi' a bang." He stood, hands on hips, his mouth twisted in an evil grin.

Megan and Joanne helped Dick to dismount, which he did with muffled groans. Joanne and a helper led the horses away to their boxes, where Ned peered critically at each one, rubbing his hands down their legs, and barked orders with many a venomous look at the pair in the yard.

Dick stood precariously, leaning on Megan with his legs and back bent, unable to move. She propped him against the wall, brought a chair out from the office and eased him down onto it, then rushed off to get her car, which she drove into the yard. They gingerly edged him into the passenger's seat.

Dick looked so seedy that Megan decided to take him straight home, leaving his own car behind. She settled him in a chair by the fire with a large tumbler of whisky and a couple of aspirins, then left to collect the boys. She did not tell the grandparents about the accident – no need to worry them unnecessarily – but the boys got the full story on the way home.

"Gosh, poor Dad. I'm glad he's not seriously hurt though, just before Christmas," said Jeremy. "You were terribly brave, Mum, to ride Barney after all that."

"Yes, believe me, I thought so, too."

At home, Dick was sufficiently revived to consider going upstairs for a bath, then crawling into bed. But moving was excruciatingly painful, mainly in his lower back. He gave Sam his glass of whisky. "Go and put it at the top of the stairs, son," he said. "It will be an incentive. Jeremy, you shout encouragement."

By now, a spirit of hilarity had taken over. Megan was pleased that, as always, Dick had taken his mishap on the chin and was enjoying the ludicrous side. She didn't think for one moment that he would learn from the experience, of course; he was incorrigible. Right now, he was crawling on his hands and knees up the stairs, while Sam flourished the glass at the top and Jeremy produced a camera to record the moment. "What a sight you are, Dad. All bloody and scraped."

Dick thought as he heaved himself, groaning, into bed, that he had as usual left his shopping till the last minute. He had two days before Christmas Eve to recover, then he'd have to face the shops.

Chapter 12

A smouldering Ned Stark stomped into the house to find his wife sitting on a high stool in the kitchen. In front of her on the counter were piles of banknotes and cheques held down with brass paperweights, heaps of coins, papers, and her account book. She bent over them like a bony old witch over her ghastly ingredients, her pen busy as if stirring trouble. Dressed in baggy woollen clothing of an indeterminate colour and shape, her hair lank, straight and unwashed, she was a striking contrast to her ultra-modern kitchen; all smart shining pine, Dutch tiles, and gleaming steel. She looked more like the kitchen maid she had once been than the owner.

"Ay," Ned growled, announcing himself. Bridget looked up, surprised and alarmed. He didn't usually appear till later when his meal was on the table. She put her pen down, knowing something was up.

In his surliest manner, he relayed the bare bones of the incident with Dick and Megan. Horrified, Bridget slid from her stool to rush out, more concerned about the horses than the humans. But Ned caught her firmly by the arm and pushed her roughly back to her stool.

"Best get on wi' counting yer cash, woman," he said. "The horses are aw right. Have I no' seen to them?"

Bridget returned uneasily to her task. She did not dare cross her husband in this mood, and was aware of more trouble brewing. It might take half an hour or more for him to bring it to the surface. Meanwhile, he lounged against the door with his arms folded, a dark, ominous presence, watching her. She bent her head, feeling prickles of fear at the back of her neck.

"I dinnae like yon fellow," he announced eventually.

"Maybe not. He's a good customer, though."

"He's no' a horseman, ye ken that as well as I dae. What the hell wis he doing riding that bugger Barney? Are ye out of yer mind?"

Bridget kept her head down and tried to keep her voice mild.

"I didn't know the girls had let him out on Barney. I'll bawl them out for that. But remember, the Frasers could easily get snapped up by *her*." Bridget's leathery, lined face contracted into a study of concentrated malevolence. "Her Ladyship over yonder," she jerked her head approximately west. "So we want to keep them sweet."

Ned had silently moved to her side, in the peculiar cat-like way he had of sliding like a shadow. He towered over her in a threatening stance. "You'll no' keep them sweet if you break their bloody necks. Pit them on beasts they can handle, woman, no' the two finest horses in the place. Aye, keep them sweet, and keep them here. But dinnae let me catch him treating my horses like that again. Or ye ken whit tae expect. They're lathered in sweat, it'll be a wonder if neither's lame."

Bridget cringed, nodding submissively. He sat down beside her at the corner of the counter, breathing foully in her face, jabbing a dirty finger on her books.

"Have ye no' managed to pit Her Ladyship out o' business yet then?" He leered hideously.

"Give me time," Bridget answered, beginning to shake. "We are raking it in, Ned. And I hear she's struggling. But there's Mrs Lindsay, whose got another horse – not from us – and she's gone back over there."

Bridget was gabbling out of terror, and realised as soon as the words were out of her mouth that she'd said the wrong thing. He was still boiling up and the explosion was yet to come.

"Then ye've missed out again. Ye were going tae sell her a horse and offer her full livery here," he said, his mocking tone more frightening than plain anger.

"Well it didn't happen. Anyway, I can't do full livery without the staff. I'm down two already, and Joanne was furious she had to come in today. Should be her day off, but I needed her."

"Mebbe if you were out there yersel' more, instead of aeways in here counting yer cash, there wouldna be so many problems," he said on a rising pitch of fury that warned of imminent explosion.

Suddenly he stood up, sending his stool crashing to the floor. Bridget let out a yelp and tried to scramble out of his way. But he didn't hit her. Instead, with a wild sweeping gesture, he sent all her neat piles of cash, paperweights, boxes, and books flying, crashing, clanging and spinning around the kitchen. While the spilt brasses and coins were still vibrating on the floor, he bent down to where she was cowering between her stool and the counter.

"Whit a mess, eh? Get on and tidy it up. You lazy, useless besum."

As he aimed a kick at her, she scrabbled out of his way, scuttling to a far corner to start picking up the coins and cash, trying to get as far away as possible so that her bent form would not be a target for his boot. She saw him sweep up a bunch of notes from the floor and put them in his pocket, then heard the metallic clang as he kicked at a brass paperweight. He strode towards the door, pausing only to swipe with the back of his hand at a vase of flowers brought in by some horse-mad child. The water cascaded over the banknotes and soaked the accounts book on the floor. Then he slammed out of the door and away.

Dizzy and almost sick with fear, she sat on the floor, whimpering and waiting for her pulse to settle. The clock told her she should be getting on with food preparation, but instinctively she knew he had probably gone on one of his wandering trips. The trouble was, she never knew how long they would last. Struggling to her feet, she found some kitchen roll and tried to rescue the sodden accounts book, drying the wet bank notes and spreading them out on the worktop.

With another glance at the clock, she grabbed a jacket hanging on the back of the door and rushed out to the yard, not wanting Joanne to come and witness the havoc in the kitchen. If she met Ned, she would say she needed to speak to Joanne, which was true. She had to know that no-one had been seriously hurt in the afternoon's escapade.

***

Before Ned had burst in on her that afternoon, Bridget had been enjoying two of her favourite occupations: counting the day's takings, and stoking her bitter resentment towards Milady Morton-Merridew. In Bridget's mind, all the misfortunes that had befallen Ned and herself over the years could be laid at Her Ladyship's door. If she could have known that Lady Mandy viewed Bridget's enmity as being all about romantic jealousy, she would have shrieked with bitter mirth. There was no room for the softer emotions in her relationship with Ned; it was all fear and submission on her part, threatened violence on his.

Decades earlier, when Ned and Bridget had been servants at the Morton-Merrydew estate, My Lord and Lady had been objects of everyone's admiration, awe, and almost-worship, so Ned's idolisation had hardly been out of the ordinary. When Her Ladyship had been sent away, it was received wisdom that she had done inconceivably wicked things to have been so disgraced and demoted. Milord was certainly not to be criticised. The rumours that Milady had been too free with her favours to a stable lad, of which much scurrilous publicity had been concocted at the time, painted her as a Jezebel and an amoral minx, and Bridget had wholeheartedly bought into that version. If Milady had kept the proper distance, had duly observed the class distinctions, Ned would never have been accused and disgraced in her wake.

Bridget knew a little of Ned's life after his fall from favour. He had taken to roaming widely through Scotland and Ireland, doing seasonal farming and labouring work, joining other travelling folk, living rough. With no references, it had been impossible for him to get another stable job. He had also lived by poaching and petty thieving – sometimes not so petty – and he did time in jail. Joining others for some raids, he had discovered his associates had no loyalty and would betray anyone to save their own necks. There had been major fall-outs. Relating this episode, Ned always glossed over the details. Someone had come to grief, it seemed; probably at his hand. He had then moved to the south of England and found rich pickings from saddles and leather goods left hanging in tack rooms, sometimes without even a lock on the door. He had no difficulty handing them on, and had even extended his activities to horse theft.

In time, having amassed a tidy sum of money, he had appeared in Bridget's life again. They bought a cottage, from where he continued his roaming life, often disappearing for days at a time. She was put to work in a stable. He bought a field adjacent to the cottage, pieced together some wooden buildings, and brought her some ponies with which they opened their first riding school. By then, Ned had discovered his common law wife's capable nose for business. He would provide the raw goods, she would sell them. They made a successful team.

Life had been hard, all the same. Bridget had had to be very creative in her dealings with the Inland Revenue, explaining where their astonishingly cumulative wealth had come from. Yet even this she managed without significant forfeit. But instead of congratulating herself on her success, Bridget had become more bitter with the passing years. Her husband was not an easy man to live with; his surliness and his demands. He exploited her mercilessly, yet blamed her when things went wrong. No-one knew what torment – mental and physical – she suffered at his hands. She never complained to anyone. All her resentment was directed against another person – Miranda, Her Ladyship. Illogically, Bridget was convinced that this woman's influence on their fortunes had blighted them for life.

It was Ned, with his invisible information networks, who had informed Bridget that Miranda had returned to Scotland in considerably reduced circumstances, and taken up the same line of business. And a few years later, when they were able to buy up the stables at Leatherburn, they found themselves only a few miles distant, and on the same business and social level as the woman who had previously been so dizzyingly far above them.

Bridget's business acumen had gone into overdrive. She hardly knew what gripped her. It was not difficult to keep tabs on what went on at Hadley through the bush-telegraph. Yet Bridget's passion drove her to foolish lengths; once she furiously turned someone out of a class because they had also patronised the rival establishment. Ned looked on passively at this emotion. He was becoming lazy, contributing less and less to their income. He hardly needed to. She was a money-making machine, as long as her anger worked positively and didn't backfire.

But Bridget was acutely aware that, although her business was booming, the social gulf was as impassable as ever. Miranda's title and her upper class accent attracted the grand and the well-to-do. Blue blood, connections, and string-pulling, Bridget fumed to herself. Her own main income from horse-trading was generally seen as a rather sleazy occupation, a bit like betting.

She tried to build up other activities so that public perception might be of a respectable riding school, and she put up new notices renaming the stable the "Leatherburn Equestrian Centre". But she did not qualify for the British Horse Society's stamp of approval, which Hadley had won with ease. She did some hunter hire and loaning of horses for the local traditions of "common riding", but these lucrative activities were also high risk, with horses often injured, which meant vets' bills and a horse off work for weeks. In the past Ned would have worked his own magic on sick and injured horses, but nowadays, even if he was around the place, he was too idle.

Class lessons were now well established, but very few of her staff had qualifications. Sometimes a girl would be pitch-forked into teaching when she had only been employed for a matter of weeks. Yet Her Ladyship, who had no qualifications either, was an affiliated dressage judge and regularly invited to judge at the major Scottish international horse trials, like Blair Atholl and Thirlestane.

There were plenty of working class kids, whose parents had no hope of buying ponies, who loved to spend a day at Leatherburn. They often came just to hang loose about the stable, especially the girls. So Bridget engaged them to do chores in exchange for a little free riding. She had known days when, without this source of help, she would have had to shut down altogether. Recently, she had begun to hold competitions – mainly show jumping – for non horse-owners, and these were proving to be extremely popular. Miranda's competitions, by contrast – dressage and show jumping, as well as gymkhanas and mixed shows – were all for horse-owners; a more polished clientele.

Bridget realised that ordinary working people were her stock customers, her bread and cheese. Teenage boys and young men had a tremendous lust for excitement and adventure, so she set up a special class for them. Ned had provided her with a teacher, a young man called Danny with dark curly hair and olive skin, who seemed to be a relative. "Don't pay him," Ned had said. "I'll see to that."

Bridget divined that Danny was beholden in some way, possibly hiding from the law, so he was paid in kind. Sometimes he stayed for a meal and slept in the barn, and he was allowed to escort the day rides. He was certainly a superb horseman in an untutored sort of way and immensely popular with the boys-only class, where they got up to various wild capers like riding backwards, jumping in pairs, and tricks more appropriate to a circus ring. Bridget knew it was risky, but she now had ten regulars who came twice a week.

She would grind her teeth with fury when she saw Her Ladyship's picture in *Horse and Hound,* or when she read an article penned by her in one of the horse magazines. For all her capability with figures, Bridget's spelling and grammar were rudimentary, and no-one was likely to ask her to write words of wisdom or to be photographed for such journals. Yet Bridget considered she and her husband between them were infinitely more conversant with horse-lore than a woman who had been brought up with servants to do all the hard and dirty work for her.

Having an eye to profits meant that Bridget sailed dangerously near the wind over safety issues. She knew she would have to stop sending out clients on their own;

there had been some nasty accidents, and now this fiasco with the Frasers.

Recently Bridget had been exultant, thinking her rival was on her uppers. She had blatantly copied Miranda's practice of "Own a pony for the day" during the school summer holidays, but while Her Ladyship only took two or three children at once, Bridget took ten times as many. If she ran out of ponies, she would simply allocate two children to one pony, and still charge them the same. Most parents were unaware of how unsupervised their precious children were for most of the time, and the kids themselves did not complain.

By the end of the summer, many of Miranda's young clients had defected. Children preferred un-supervised thrills to boring old safety. Bridget had allowed herself to dream of a time when Her Ladyship would be so impoverished that she would come begging her, Bridget, for a job. And she mentally tossed up whether it would be more delicious to send her packing with vitriolic scorn, or give her the most arduous jobs of scrubbing the loos and clearing out the deep litters.

Now, though, these trends in her favour seemed to be going into reverse. She'd had staff problems. Mrs Lindsay had proved fickle. Bridget hadn't seen the Fraser boys for a few weeks, and their mother no longer came to evening lessons. And a whisper had reached her that Miranda was going into retail, selling small items of horse-gear.

Bridget was troubled, not wanting to lose the initiative. How could she finish off her rival before she had time to recover from those competitive setbacks?

Chapter 13

Christmas at the Fraser household had been a riot of genuine family fun, with both sets of grandparents staying for a few days. The culmination had been the gift opening on Christmas morning, in their huge circular sitting room that used to be the mill where horses plodded, dragging round the mill-stones. The magnificent tree, which reached to the ceiling, spread its aromatic branches over the sea of presents spilling out from underneath, all shapes, colours and sizes.

It took an hour for the three generations to unwrap them all; with everyone on a high, the laughter and chat seemed to ebb and flow like a tide. At the end, the floor was awash with paper and everyone sated with pleasure. Then it was discovered that Dick had been surreptitiously recording all the sounds of glee and delight, so they listened to the present opening all over again, the recorded sounds of their own merriment prompting a different sort of laughter.

"I hope you didn't expect to find Lucinda in that big bumpy parcel," Dick said to Megan, his arm round her shoulders and nuzzling her cheek.

By the following weekend, all the relatives had gone back home and Dick, his health restored, anticipated a few more days as a stable hand. Megan was thankfully getting some time to just sit and relax with one of her new books, while Jeremy and Sam had plenty to keep them happy and absorbed. On the Saturday, they were going to Sue's for a festive high tea and sleepover.

"It will be nice to get out of the hot-house atmosphere of home for a bit," said Dick. "Sue said not to worry about dressing up. Just wear what's comfortable."

"I don't suppose there will be any horsey activities?" asked Megan.

"Don't think so. I must have a lesson soon, though. You know how important it is to get confidence back after a disaster."

"Have you told Sue what happened?"

"Yes, I spoke to her on the phone. She said I was a fool for riding Barney outside. Apparently he's been pretty volatile since then. She thinks he's a real lunatic – you know, changes with the moon's phases. Guess I must have caught him in a waxing phase. I must say she's very good as a mentor; she's so intelligent, got some interesting theories. She doesn't laugh at the idea I might do a cross-country course some day. How about that? Get yourself a nice horse first, she says."

"What sort of theories?"

"Oh, just ideas really. She thinks that a man who's a good horseman is usually a good lover, too."

"Does she indeed! I wonder how much research has gone into that! And don't you get drawn into any controlled experiments."

"She thinks one of her horses is interested in her in a physical way. When she has her period, he'll come over to her and follow her round the field."

"Not a very bright horse then. Males are only supposed to take an interest when a woman is fertile. But, Dick, I don't think you should be talking about such intimate matters. Her periods? It's scarcely proper. I'm not sure I approve."

"Oh don't be silly. You know how physical the whole horsey world is. Nobody's squeamish about talking of bums and fannies."

"Ah well, you haven't heard Mandy. She calls your fanny your 'fork'. You mustn't sit on it, you must keep the weight on your 'seat'. Very decorous."

"She sounds boringly proper," Dick drawled.

"Oh no, she's a marvellous character. I just love her. She co-habits with an eighty-year-old doctor, you know."

"Isn't there a Lord Morton-Merrydew?"

"Mandy's ex went the way of all flesh a long time ago, so her son has the title now. Annabel told me that as a young divorcee Mandy was the paramour of the British ambassador in somewhere exotic in North Africa. She acted as hostess and consort for years, keeping the Embassy running smoothly for him, the staff in order, the social wheels well-oiled, all that. Then he died suddenly. So ungrateful! And, of course, she got nothing for her pains; no golden handshake, nothing left to her in his will. So before she could be turned out ignominiously, she did a bunk and took some valuable plates and stuff with her. Including – wait for it – a dinner-service hand-painted by Picasso! It must be incredibly valuable. If you are invited to dinner, you get to eat the Walls ice cream off it. Annabel said she was terrified of dropping the dish."

"Maybe you'll be invited now."

"Who knows? If I am, will you come, too? I can't imagine she's a very good cook if she's been accustomed to having a large staff most of her life. She doesn't even have a cleaning lady now. Must be difficult coping with everything, but the animals always take the lion's share of her attention. Annabel said that when a horse is sick, she'll do anything for it, sit up all night, even walk a horse with colic round the yard at three in the morning. You must come over and meet her, Dick. It's a shame we've split the family riding activities."

"Mmmm. I like Leatherburn, even though it's a bit down-market and Heath-Robinson, and fabulously risky. I do like to feel some electricity between my thighs, some primeval wildness under me."

Megan laughed. "I'd have thought Barney's exploits would have put you off primeval wildness for a bit. There's a bit more finesse to riding than sheer speed, danger, and deer-leaps, Dick, honestly. I was watching some dressage practice the other day, including someone on a side saddle. It's amazing. The cerebral end of riding. Dressage to music, too, which is incredibly skilled."

Later, they all tumbled into the car and drove off to Sue's place. Jeremy and Sam sat in the back engrossed in a serious conversation, quite incomprehensible to the adults, about a series of adventure game books they were both into. Megan relaxed and enjoyed sitting doing nothing, watching the December countryside speed past. On Monday she would go back to work, and everything would crank into high-speed gear again. She reflected ruefully that during the festive season she had the shortest holiday of all the family but the most to do.

"Think I'll spend the day at Leatherburn on Monday." Dick's voice cut into her thoughts.

Megan looked at him sharply. "You can't, Dick. You're on domestic duty. I start back at work, remember? The boys aren't back at school till Wednesday, and Mel is off till then."

"Oh bugger. Why didn't you tell me? Sod it all."

"We discussed this in great depth before Christmas. You said you'd love to spend those days playing with them."

"Well, they could come to the stable, too, or maybe Granny…"

Instantly, there was a chorus from the back. "NO, Dad, no. We've only got two more days. We want to play at home. We've done enough visits and things. Don't make us."

Dick pouted his lower lip and looked pissed off. Megan knew things hung in the balance. "You know you promised, dear," she said quietly.

"Oh, all right." There were sighs of relief from the back, and a hearty, "Thanks, Dad!"

"I guess I can go on Wednesday then. And maybe get a lesson from Sue, too. I should have brought my gear today, after all."

"If she's having us all for tea, she wouldn't want to be bothered with a lesson too."

When they finally drew up at Brockhollow Farm, Dick fished out his comb and tidied his hair, looking into the mirror. He caught Megan looking at him rather sardonically, and laughed self-consciously.

"You're very understanding, darling," he said.

Am I? thought Megan. *Is this really just vanity?*

He led the way to a little wicket gate that led to the garden. "This way," he said. "Then we don't need to traipse through the farmhouse." Winding round the rambling house, they came to the kitchen door of the basement flat.

Sue greeted them and was introduced to Jeremy and Sam. Inside, they met Shelley, after which the three children stood staring at each other with the incomprehension of age gap and gender difference. The shabbiness of the kitchen was camouflaged by festoons of paper streamers, balloons, real holly and mistletoe; the delicious smell of warming mince pies added to the festive feeling.

"I'll make tea, shall I?" said Dick, as he strode unbidden through the kitchen into the scullery, and began filling the kettle and organising a teapot and mugs. Speechless, Megan stared at him with undisguised horror. Not only was he completely at home and melded into the domesticity here, but he had the insensitivity to show this off quite blatantly to her and the boys. She swiftly looked at them to see their reaction. The two were normally quick to pick up on behavioural nuances, reactions, and atmospheres, but they were engrossed with Shelley, who was coquetting at them with some cuddly toys.

Sitting at the plastic-topped kitchen table clutching her mug, Megan let the family noise swirl around her. If she was gobsmacked and withdrawn, no-one noticed. Mike appeared, and then two other families, and there was no more time for pondering. Sue was a cheery, capable hostess, obviously greatly at ease in the pandemonium. Later, when they had progressed to wine, she engaged Megan in friendly chat, quite open and unselfconscious in her manner. Surely she wouldn't behave like that if there was anything going on, Megan thought. Would she?

"You've heard all about our disastrous ride, I gather?" Megan asked, trying to look into Sue's eyes and read her soul.

The other woman looked seriously disapproving. "Indeed I have. Mrs Stark was furious, didn't Dick tell you? He was utterly mad to try to ride out on Barney. Riding in the school, with me there, is one thing. Taking you out hacking on him was crazy, suicidal. And you were on Lucinda?" she asked, frowning and staring at Megan accusingly.

"Yes. I had no choice in the matter. As it happened I was late arriving, and was bounced onto Lucinda without knowing who I was getting on, then wheeled out the gate. I thought it had been approved from on high. Why did no-one on the staff try to stop us?"

"Well, you know, with Dick being famous and all that, and a favourite with Mrs Stark, I think no-one felt bold enough to tell him not to be so stupid. You could both have been killed."

"I know. After the first fall, I tried to get him to go back and change horses, but he's so bloody stubborn. It's all about macho pride and vanity with him, you know. And if I had gone back, he would simply have gone on alone."

"God, I didn't realise he had fallen twice!"

"Oh yes. And did he tell you about Lucinda bolting and then both horses running away with me?"

Sue looked even more appalled as Megan related the details, but commended her for keeping cool and handling the situation.

"Sue, he admires you, so he might listen to you a bit," Megan suggested. "Try and talk some sense into him, please. He's got ideas that are light years beyond his capabilities and he won't listen to me. Fact is, I won't willingly ride out with him again without an experienced escort. I like to do exciting things, but I've got the kids to think of."

Megan found she was rather wallowing in this all-girls conversation, which was critical of her husband on both sides. Normally she was one hundred per cent loyal to him but she felt as if she was testing the water. If Sue was his lover, she would not have been so disapproving, surely?

They had both been knocking back the wine freely, and Megan began to feel giggly and uninhibited. "He said you thought prowess in riding equated with prowess in bed," she said, astonished at herself. "Dick must be the exception to the rule."

Sue laughed rather too heartily and for once seemed lost for words. "Well, I'm not sure I have much influence except when I'm teaching him," she demurred eventually.

"Mmmm. You do rather encourage his grandiose ideas, Sue. He sees himself out hunting, playing polo, doing a cross-country competition."

"He can't really do any competing unless he's got his own horse. And I take it, with his lifestyle, there's not much immediate prospect of that. Oddly, if he did take on the responsibility of ownership, it might do him the world of good. For a man, it's much the same as getting his own car." A look of ineffable scorn flitted across Sue's face, which did much to reassure Megan. "You should think of getting a horse, though. You're much better than Dick, and you've got the right attitude. It's a woman's thing, riding and horses."

At that point Dick came over, looking flushed and merry. "What are you two gossiping about so earnestly?"

"It's an all-woman discussion, my sweet. You wouldn't want to hear it, I assure you."

Feeling much better for the conversation, Megan let herself go a bit and began to enjoy the party. As a result, she drank rather more than usual.

When the other two families had left later that night, the Fraser family all bedded down in one immense room, in two double beds whose coverlets smelled of mothballs. Megan woke in the wee small hours with a dry mouth and pounding pulse, and stumbled through the sleeping house, avoiding dogs and abandoned toys, to the kitchen to get some water. She was dying for some aspirin, but did not want to wake everyone by fishing round in her overnight bag. After rehydration, she soon fell asleep again.

Next morning, they left after a hearty breakfast, climbing the garden steps to the wicket gate. Megan wondered if she had been effusive enough with her thanks. She turned back to wave and caught a typically vigorous gesture and jovial, beaming smile from Sue, so responded with equal energy and jollity. Then, turning forward, she caught the last of Dick's sly grin and goodbye salute, and knew instantly that the send-off had been a secret farewell passing between the two of them. She had intercepted a message that was not for her. She felt both foolish and slighted. How little one knew the man one was so intimate with. Their paths crossed briefly at tangents, and most of their lives they spent apart, doing things the other was unaware of, pursuing thoughts, and tasting experiences.

Life was as erratic as the boys' adventure game books, she thought. She had never kept close tabs on Dick, and had just assumed he was trustworthy. She had taken it as read that, as he had done so much sewing of wild oats before marriage, he would be properly tamed and faithful ever after. Maybe she had been a bit naïve.

When they were home and the boys out of earshot, she asked in measured tones, "Is there anything going on between you and Sue?"

"No," he said emphatically. "Mind you, I'm aware there could be if I wanted to. She's very friendly."

"Well, you seem to me to meet her halfway. Shouldn't you be a bit more reserved?"

"No, I don't think so. I've always believed you can admire a menu even if you're not eating."

This observation hardly reassured her.

***

Bridget Stark waited anxiously for Dick to reappear in the stable after Christmas. It had been such a feather in her cap that this famous TV presenter was not only a client, but had opted to spend his festive holidays working in her yard. After the disastrous ride, when Dick had been given a humiliating tongue-lashing from Ned, he had not returned nor had he phoned. He might have suffered an injury, of course. That was a worry, but since he had not had permission to ride Barney, Bridget would contest negligence if he decided to sue. She and Ned were becoming very alert and sensitive to possible legal suits, and were desperate to protect their hard-earned wealth.

Bridget did not usually trouble herself much about individual clients. But this one was different, and she perceived many ways in which he could be used to her advantage. She looked him up in the phone book, but no joy; he must be ex-directory. She thought of Sue, who would probably have his number. Bridget was aware of something going on there, but it didn't bother her. If Sue kept Dick coming to Leatherburn, they could do as they pleased. Maybe it was better if Dick's family did not keep tabs on him and he came along footloose and fancy-free.

She rang Sue, and was reassured to hear that Dick had indeed recovered, and planned to return to his mucking-out duties in a couple of days. She noted mentally that Dick would be returning on the very day that Sue would be there for lessons. She also took the opportunity to pump Sue about the rest of the Fraser family, knowing they had been ensnared by that insatiable black widow spider, Miranda.

When Dick eventually appeared, to his surprise he was waylaid by Mrs Stark waving from her front door, fluting, "Mr Fraser! Mr Fraser!" He knew she could put on a refined voice for her quality customers.

To the open-mouthed amazement of one of the stable girls who happened to be passing by, she cordially invited him in. Even more gobsmacking, the lass later reported to the rest of the staff, was that he greeted her as "Bridget"! No-one, but no-one, ever called her that, and only special teachers like Sue and Danny ever made it through her doorway.

All smiles and concern, Bridget asked if he'd been badly bruised, and apologised for her husband's brusqueness. If Dick was relieved at this cordial welcome, he did not show it. He lapped it up as his due, responding with his usual charm and even flirtatiousness, and she seemed to like it. *Poor drab thing*, he thought, even as he laid it on with a trowel. *Let me bring some sparkle into your dreary workaday life.*

She made him a mug of instant coffee, a brew of such awfulness that he could hardly suppress a grimace, then asked brightly after Megan and the boys. "We haven't seen them much lately," she said, a hint of a question mark in her voice. Dick was only remotely aware of the inter-stable rivalry and did not appreciate its intensity or know its cause, yet he was as much of a gossip as all the women put together. He admitted they were going to Hadley because Megan had this thing about safety.

Dick assumed Bridget knew little of Lady Mandy, and proceeded to repeat Megan's description of her. He loved to hold the floor, and she was hanging on his every word. He repeated with embellishments the gossip about Hadley's owner living as a courtesan in Paris and other favoured cities of the *beau monde*, then becoming the kept-woman of an ambassador, stealing the Embassy's valuable riches and absconding with them when he died. By the time he was finished, Bridget was open-mouthed.

Elated with his success, yet feeling slightly uneasy, Dick ploughed on. Oh yes, and she lives with a sugar daddy now. A retired doctor. He's very discreet and keeps out of sight.

"Well!" expostulated Bridget, sounding like a prim Morningside lady. "How some people live!"

Dick put down his mug. "She's certainly led a colourful life. No-one quite knows how she could afford to buy that place of hers. Best not to enquire, I guess." He moved towards the door, leaving his coffee only half drunk.

Bridget stood gazing after him as he left. What a piece of good fortune! Through the Fraser family's split riding loyalties, she seemed to have established a hotline to the very centre of Miranda's dark secrets.

Chapter 14

The winter was proving to be particularly harsh. Annabel drove to Hadley early three mornings each week to see to Solly and exercise him, while Poppy rode one night a week and twice at the weekends. It was all working out well. But the early mornings were harsh, with car windows to scrape inside and out, ungritted country roads to negotiate with delicate care, and thick ice to smash on the horses' water buckets. Annabel's woollen gloves stuck to the bolts and even the brick walls when she touched them.

When she took Solly down to exercise him in the school at seven in the morning, with not another soul about, they picked their way carefully over the icy ground and she struggled to open the frozen doors. All these extra little things took time. Sometimes she had to get up at half past five to leave enough time to do everything, then rush home for a shower and get into work for nine-thirty.

She was, however, delighted with Solly, and even more with the way Poppy was handling him. There was a club dressage competition coming up and Poppy was working hard to take part. She had discovered a way of getting to

Hadley from home on her bike, using off-road cycle paths, which meant she could take herself at the weekends. She often stayed there all day, helping round the yard and even doing escort duty with the larger hacks, either on Solly or on a school pony.

This left Annabel free and she had continued to meet Alex, the blond, hunky surgeon, for Saturday lunch – just the two of them – after his morning golf session, and before he collected his daughter, Fiona. They chatted endlessly about themselves, as lovers do. But they were not lovers; *not yet,* she thought. But it could only be a matter of time – and opportunity. There was no doubt he liked being with her and enjoyed her company. She hoped and believed he found her attractive.

It was all very public at the Shrub and Grub, of course, with its potted plants giving minimal screening between the tables. They gave each other little affectionate pecks on the cheek when they met and when they parted; nothing more. It was a beautiful friendship, and it was Annabel's secret, which she hugged close to her bosom like a precious newborn babe. Thinking about it sustained her through many a difficult time, when Ralph was obstructive, or Lily stirring trouble. Or when George at work was in a supercilious mood, as one day recently when she'd asked him how he was coping with the weather.

"The *weather*?" he had queried, screwing up his face in mock-incomprehension. "There's problems galore with conveyancing, wills, and litigation, all demanding my closest attention, and you ask about the weather!"

She did not bother to respond. George had never forgiven her for turning him down, and probably never would. Afterwards, she wished she'd retorted, "If you got up at five-thirty to exercise a spirited horse as I do, you'd be more in tune with the bloody weather." She was glad she had not tangled with him; he would probably be a selfish and sadistic lover, not one you would treasure with joy and satisfaction in the inner recesses of your mind. Her female devotions were pearls to be offered up to a worthy recipient, a man of charm and culture like Alex; not cast before a sneering, sardonic creature like George. Alex came from a long dynasty of medical leaders, which in modern times almost translated into aristocracy.

Now that the high spot of her week was Saturday lunchtime, everything seemed directed towards that magical interlude. The other members of her family were taken up with their own immediate concerns – even Poppy – and no-one queried where she vanished to. She never communicated with Alex between their lunches; she didn't even know his phone number. They just said on parting, "Same time next week?" And smiled and nodded.

Annabel was acutely conscious of the packet of condoms in her handbag. What would he say if he knew? She was almost tempted to let it fall out by accident. Let him know that this impeccably-mannered woman had a touch of the witch about her. Sometimes over their lunch, with him so close, it was agony to restrain herself from touching his hand, his face, his neck. Her eyes strayed frequently to certain parts of him; his chest, hidden by the casual buttoned shirt. Was it covered by delicious blond hairs like his moustache? She imagined undoing the buttons one by one. Was he well-muscled? Her eyes would fall to his crotch. She pulled her gaze rapidly away from that area, afraid she might do something impulsive. But her eyes would drift back, especially when the coffee came and he drew his chair away from the table and lounged comfortably. Men's clothing was so all-concealing, but sometimes there was a visible bulge.

Mostly as they talked, they held each others' gaze. She tried to project across messages – *I love you* – so powerful that he must receive them. She fantasized about being in bed with him. She could imagine the warmth of his flesh, his breath on her neck. Winding limbs around limbs, pulse racing, taking his weight on hers, belly on belly, and then aaaahhh... But letting her mind run riot was only possible later, when they were apart. Thinking of Alex when she was alone in the bathroom or anywhere secure, she hardly needed to touch her erogenous zones before being overwhelmed by a sustained climax. When had she last been as receptive as this? It must mean something.

For a few weeks she had been satisfied with simply having that brief but concentrated claim on him. They talked of their families, especially their daughters, and it was clear that Alex was inordinately proud of Fiona. She had heard the girl's life history almost from conception onwards, but he seldom mentioned his wife, Rachel; only when absolutely necessary, and in neutral tones. Annabel had tried to enlist his sympathy by telling him of her mare's accident, but his response had been so bland and perfunctory that she had known not to raise the topic again. A surgeon must have too many claims on his sympathy, she thought, excusing him.

She had thought about telling him of Ralph's infidelity, but decided against it. Maybe later, when they were closer. He had acted as an expert witness in a few court cases, which provided some common ground between them. And he was a good talker, regaling her with amusing and hair-raising anecdotes of surgical life, and of their running battles with the managers. Megan was a good egg, though, he'd said hurriedly.

Each week the physical yearning grew. Annabel pondered the accepted precept that the man should take the lead in affairs of the heart. Alex, however, seemed quite content with the relationship as it stood. Although she was dying for progress, she was also terrified of destroying the delicate bliss by demanding too much too soon. She told herself to be patient, but each time of parting it got more difficult. Maybe next time she should ask something very small, like, if she could have his phone number? That was a good idea. Surely that wouldn't be construed as being too forward?

She was well aware that her secret had wrought changes in her appearance. With the new lease of life, she was taking more interest in herself, though she had never been neglectful. She had gone out several times recently on extravagant shopping sprees for new clothes. But there was more than that; there was a hormonal glow, an aura, which was almost palpable when she looked in her mirror. Her hair shone and arranged itself naturally in pretty little wisps around her face. Her complexion was perfect, peachy-amber and flawless. Her figure was slender, having shed the surplus pounds through regular riding. In spite of her busy life and early start to the day, she looked wide awake and full of sexual energy. And happy.

Each week she reviewed their conversation, wondering if there were hidden meanings in anything he had said.

She knew of no precedent for the sort of friendship she had with him. Young folk had their own etiquette. In her day it was a kiss on the cheek at the first date; maybe a mouth kiss on the second; full French kiss maybe the next time. Heavy petting, as it was called, was reserved till you were deemed to be going steady. She wondered if there was some signal she should be making, without which his middle-class courtesy and the rules – whatever they were – prevented him from taking the next step. What would he do if she just said one day, "Alex, take me to bed? Love me. Fuck me stupid." But always there was the fear that the spell would be destroyed like a beautiful fable on the stroke of midnight.

The next Saturday, Annabel drew up and parked in front of the garden centre. She was usually first – so anxious to see him – but he was never more than a minute or two after the time. She had put on a new bra that hoisted up her bosom, and a flattering, embroidered, black silk V-neck jersey. She watched from their favourite table, facing the window, looking eagerly for that familiar, sleek and shiny Jaguar, such a contrast to her mud-plastered Honda. These delicious, anxious moments were resolved as ever with a lurch of the heart when his car turned in at the gate and he emerged like a Norse film star, with his ruffled blond hair, his leather and tweed jacket.

They greeted each other with joyful exclamations and the momentary magic of the kiss. For the first time he progressed to a brief mouth-to-mouth kiss, which sent vibrations throughout her body. She continued to savour the soft, warm feel of his mouth on hers. Was it possible, she wondered, to have an orgasm from a kiss?

"You're looking very good today!" he said teasingly, glancing at the hint of cleavage. "There must be a new horse in your life." Her passion for equines was a standing joke between them.

"Why don't you come out riding with me sometime?" she asked, suddenly inspired. Fancy not thinking of this before.

"Oh no. It would be unfair to the horse. I'd flatten it."

"You're tall, but not that hefty. Plenty of big men ride – some are even overweight – and find horses to carry them. You are at least fit and athletic in build."

"Well, thank you for that. But no, it's not my scene. I'd disgrace myself by falling off or something. I prefer to keep my feet on solid earth."

End of subject. What a pity. He hadn't returned the compliment and asked her to play golf either. But setting up a meeting elsewhere, somewhere private, seemed the next imperative. She would work on it. She knew that he liked concerts, theatre, cinema. Going to one of those together would be no different from lunch in the morality scale, the things forbidden to a man and a woman whose first loyalties lay elsewhere. She pondered this as they ordered their food and a glass of wine, while chatting easily as always.

Annabel seldom ate much, the talking and eye-gazing was so much more important. When her dessert came, it had icing sugar scattered over it, and somehow a speck landed on her nose. Not wanting to appear ridiculous, she hurriedly reached down for her handkerchief in her handbag. But he said, "Hang on, Annabel, you've got sugar on your nose." Then he wiped it off with his own hanky. She got the briefest scent of masculinity from it, and watched it vanish into his trouser pocket. Just think how close it's been to him, she thought, her eyes dwelling on his groin – and was almost overwhelmed. Glancing up, she caught his eye and they both laughed. Surely, surely there's more. This was their most intimate moment to date, she thought.

"Alex." She said his name with an air of ceremony, a change of gear.

"Annabel." He responded, flirtatiously mimicking her tone.

"I wondered if you could give me your phone number? Just so that, if I was going to be held up or couldn't make it some Saturday, I could let you know."

Alex was still for a moment, looking down. Oh God, she thought. But then he began fishing in his pockets, and finally produced a rather crumpled card and gave it to her.

"Alexander Temple, F.R.C.S., Consultant Surgeon" it said, with his hospital phone number and his private office details. She noticed his home phone number was not on it. As if reading her thoughts, he said, "My home number's in the directory. But you probably wouldn't be ringing me there."

"No," she said quickly, taking in that she had been given a gentle hint. Fair enough. "Oh, you'd better have mine. We're ex-directory, being lawyers." She gave him a card, which he secreted in a capacious wallet.

There was the merest hint of awkwardness between them, which they covered up by suddenly discovering they needed to be somewhere else fairly soon. After parting, Alex rushed away waving rather cursorily from his car. Normally they went their ways reluctantly, after sauntering around the garden plants and implements before he gallantly saw her into her car. For the first time, Annabel felt uneasy and apprehensive.

***

True to her resolution, Annabel had offered to go hacking with Jackie on her Arab, Pied Piper. It suited them both: Jackie was not confident riding out on her own, though Piper was very safe; Annabel was very experienced, but Solly was not. He needed the company of the older horse to assure him that those heavy lorries with noisy brakes were no threat.

To her surprise, Annabel found that she rather enjoyed the trivial chat and gossip, and her initial tendency to patronise dissolved into something like real interest. She reflected that one-to-one female friendships had not been part of her lifestyle since her pre-marital days. Her social circle was just that – a *melange* of idle ladies with gossip, ample means, and leisure as their defining features. Her work colleagues were predominantly male and, apart from family, she had no close bosom-chum. At Hadley, she tended to know the clientele mostly as so-and-so's owner. But horses were amazing mediators, creating unlikely friendships.

As Mandy had predicted, Annabel heard the story of Jackie's life in unsparing detail. It read like one of those reports Annabel received regularly from the Social Work Department on domestic abuse cases. For twenty years the woman had clung onto her alcoholic husband, on whom she was financially dependent, having given up work when her baby arrived. Indeed, she would probably be with him still if he hadn't taken up with the tarty receptionist, and put her out on the street. Jackie had gone home to her mother, found a job, and started over again; rather like a game of snakes and ladders, she said.

Her mother had pushed her into joining a dating agency, and lent her the fee. Everyone was doing it, according to her mum. "Oh well, I thought," said Jackie, "nothing will come of it. What sort of guys sign up to dating agencies?" But it had filled up the odd evening. Then she found herself being pursued by a client, a man fifteen years her senior. He would not take no for an answer, so she met him in a pub. He was kind and ordinary; not disgustingly ancient, crippled or overweight, as she'd feared.

After a couple of dates he had – in an efficient, businesslike sort of way – got her into bed, and then laid his cards squarely on the table: An arranged marriage, with some mutual obligations and maximum freedom (Annabel compared this swift but unromantic progression with her own quasi-affair with Alex). Jackie would stop work and housekeep for him; he would keep her in the style to which she was certainly not accustomed. That included riding lessons, which she'd longed for since childhood, and even a horse of her own.

After some deliberation, Jackie had agreed. That had been five years ago, and she claimed to be contented with her lot. Her husband needed to be "managed" and "understood", and she left it to Annabel's imagination to divine what that meant. But he continued to be gentle, and she never stopped being thankful for that. She had feared that she was one of those women who subconsciously pick out violent men.

Annabel was amazed at the lack of shame Jackie displayed in talking of her dating agency venture, and suppressed the memory of having toyed with the idea herself when Ralph had been unfaithful. She knew very thoroughly from her legal work how the other half lived, but she was half-ashamed to find herself socialising with someone from that milieu. Ignorant of the rates of exchange in girly friendships, she did not appreciate that confidences were given in the expectation that they would be reciprocated. She did, though, observe that Jackie asked many personal questions and that Annabel's answers did not deflect further questioning, as she had hoped.

They did not talk all the time. Comfortable silences would descend as they wended their way along old railway tracks-turned-bridle paths. Annabel loved being out in the countryside in all seasons, loved to watch the progressive changes, buds appearing in the early Spring, birds chirruping, all that. And she was pleased that Jackie engaged with her in appreciating these things.

It was a perfect bright early February morning as they rode through woodlands with nodding clumps of snowdrops and enthused over the clouds of tiny, pink flower-heads adorning the stark, nut-brown branches of early-flowering plum-trees. Sometimes there would be a fallen log across the path after a storm, and they would ride at it and leap over. She loved the crunch of dried leaves under the horses' hooves and the smell of earth and of conifers.

"Do you like cross-country courses?" Jackie asked.

"Yes, I love cross-country jumping," replied Annabel.

"I can't wait to do another trial. I missed out the whole season last year, of course. This chap's going to be terrific, but I'll have to share him with Poppy."

"I'm hoping to do the one at Duncanshill in the Spring," said Jackie. "It will be my first. I've always dreamed of doing cross-country, but never thought I would. This one's supposed to be very easy, fences not too high, well-designed, idiot-proof and that. Mandy's been great, really encouraging. The only problem is… I don't have anyone to go with me. I don't think I could manage, or even have the bottle to go, without someone to chum me along. I wondered… if you might come with me?"

Annabel was taken aback. The request struck her as rather presumptuous. Jackie's company was tolerable for an hour maybe, but a whole day? What if she met some society friend while in Jackie's company? Stalling for time, she replied, "Er… what day of the week is it? Do you have dates yet?"

"It's a Saturday in April. Near the end."

"Mmmm. Saturdays aren't usually possible, not for a whole day. I've various family things on and," Annabel focussed on the major reason why a Saturday could not be given up, "I always meet a friend for lunch." She innocently implied the "friend" was female, but realised too late that she was putting herself at the mercy of Jackie's bottomless interrogation.

"Oh… right. Would that be the gorgeous Mr Temple you meet at the garden centre?"

Annabel was so dumbfounded she nearly fell off her horse. "How in God's name did you know that?" She had assumed they were incognito, somehow invisible.

"Oh, someone saw you. Sorry if I wasn't supposed to know. It's like, all round the stable. This week's gossipy story. Maybe I shouldn't have mentioned it."

"Who told you?"

"Honestly can't remember."

Annabel understood that the more fuss she made, the deeper she dug herself in. But her mind was whirling. Did Fiona – Alex's daughter – know? Did Poppy know? How squirmingly embarrassing. How awful. Somehow her lovely friendship seemed besmirched. But she must try to stay cool, though her face was on fire. Could she protest that it was a purely platonic friendship? That sounded like the very stamp of deceit, yet it was true.

"Are you having an affair with him?" The question was put teasingly, while Jackie's eyes investigated the give-away hue of Annabel's complexion.

"Well, against all appearances, I'm not. Much as I would like to." Annabel said it lightly and with humour; it was the plain truth, yet she knew it would not be believed. Saved by an inspiration as to how to wrestle down and change the subject, she added, "I've got a great idea who you should ask to go with you to Duncanshill. Megan."

Jackie wasn't taken with the idea of Megan. "With her famous husband and all, it would be a bit of a cheek to even ask," she said. "She's got a young family, a high-powered job, and isn't even a horse-owner."

But Annabel was not easily put off. She pointed out that Megan was wildly keen to learn and might be delighted to get the flavour and atmosphere of a cross-country day. She offered to broach the subject with Megan herself. Feeling that this resolved the obligation question, Annabel fell into musing the implications of being the innocent subject of stable gossip.

Chapter 15

It was late on Sunday evening when Megan made a final review of her preparations for the following morning. She had an eight o'clock meeting as usual, so wanted to get to bed early. With Mel safely returned from her weekend, all the domestic machinery in Megan's complex life was running smoothly, free of hitches, just as she liked it. School kits and the breakfast table were all ready, her own briefcase was packed; clothes laid out upstairs. She pulled her feet up on the sofa, wrapping the chocolate tweed throw around them, and flicked through the channels for something relaxing to watch on the box for half an hour.

The phone rang, and she knew it would be Dick, who was on one of his periodic visits to London in connection with his television work. When away, he rang every evening at the same time. Sometimes the conversations were difficult, particularly if he was still in working mode and on a high, shooting questions at her like Jeremy Paxman, while she had slowed her tempo to a pre-sleep drowsy pace. She was definitely a morning person. If she was very sleepy, he would spark her into life by asking about the boys or about her riding exploits. She tried to save up little anecdotes to amuse him; conscious that he wasn't much interested in hospital politics and even less about disease and death, she had to be selective.

"I've been asked by one of the girls at Hadley to go to a cross-country event with her in April," she told him. "I'm ever so pleased. It will be fun to watch, and hopefully I can pick up lots of hints. I'd really love to do it myself some day. I've looked at the diary and you're away on that date, but I'm not sure if I'll take the boys. Maybe better not the first time, as it will be a long day. I'll need to make myself useful, tacking up, grooming, loading up, and all that. I'll be the dogsbody, but it should be a great time."

"Is it an affiliated course?"

"Oh, Lord no, nothing at all advanced. It's Jackie's first time. Highest jump is two foot six, I think. It's organised by the Pony Club."

"Well, who knows? This time next year, maybe it'll be you."

"Well, I'd love to do it. But it'll have to wait a few years till the boys are older, or I can afford to work part-time."

"What's Jackie like?"

"She's good company. Quite tough, bit of a rough diamond. She had an abusive husband who left her high and dry, but then she went and found herself another man – through a dating agency, would you believe? It's like an arranged marriage. She's amazingly frank about all this. I'm fascinated. He never appears at the stable. Actually, most spouses don't. You included."

"Well, I'm too busy for the social side of stable life. I like to dash in, get my tuition from the best available horse and teacher, and dash out again. No time for inane chat and idle gossip."

"Oh yes, speaking of gossip, there's a rumour going round the network that Sue is pregnant."

"Good Lord."

"I haven't seen her myself to talk to, but they say she's pissed off because it doesn't fit in with her work-life balance right now. Though knowing Sue, she will go on riding till the last minute."

"Mmmm. Well, I hope I'll still get my lessons. Look, I'd better go. We won't be finished here for another hour or so. Bye, my love. Speak to you tomorrow."

As soon as Megan put the phone down, it rang again. She looked at it in annoyance. Her precious relaxation time and early bedtime were slipping away. Who would be so inconsiderate as to ring at this time on a Sunday night? She lifted the receiver and announced herself rather briskly.

"Hi, Megan, it's Annabel. Sorry for ringing so late." The voice sounded strange, rather muffled.

"No problem, Annabel. Anything up?"

There was a brief pause, with some curious background noises, which weren't immediately identifiable. To her horror, Megan realised that Annabel was crying.

"Annabel. Are you okay?" Stupid question. The sobs were more audible now. Somehow it was doubly traumatic coming from someone who was usually

so regal and self-possessed. Great shuddering sighs and gasps came down the line.

"Take it easy, my dear. Easy, hush, hush, it's okay. I'm here, I'm listening."

"I'm… sorry, so…rry… be all right… in minute…"

Megan murmured softly, soothingly, till Annabel got possession of herself. She had an idea what lay underneath all this.

"I'm so sorry, sorry. Look, I shouldn't have phoned at this time, I know. But I'm at my wits' end. I think I'll go mad if I don't talk to someone. You're always so kind and… and dependable, I hope you don't mind…"

At work Megan was often perceived as an agony aunt figure, a shoulder to cry on. This cry for help sounded rather serious, probably not one to be put off to a more suitable time.

"Annabel, I'd offer to come round, but I can't leave the boys. Oh wait, Mel's back. I can come, if you'd like that?" Her heart sank at the thought.

"Oh Megan, you are an angel. I'd come over to you but I don't think I'd be safe to drive, the way I am just now. You know where to come? I'll look out for you. My husband's in bed, so are the girls. Don't ring the bell, will you? I'll hear the car."

***

Megan returned home about one in the morning. She felt like a Catholic priest, loaded down with the shameful secrets of someone's inner life which had suddenly proved too much to bear alone. Poor Annabel. Having her husband cheat on her, she was obsessed with getting her own back, against all her better judgement and normal standards of behaviour. His wandering misdeeds had wounded her pride more deeply than she realised. But her repeated attempts to be unfaithful had been thwarted.

Even though she was a little older than Megan – well into her forties, probably – Annabel was still an attractive, even striking, woman. A little stand-offish perhaps, and unfashionably class-conscious. Megan had been told all the details; Annabel had spared herself no humiliation. The George episode, the Tom saga. Even the condoms in the handbag. But the last disappointment was the one which had precipitated the crisis. It seemed Annabel had fallen for Alex with a sacrificial intensity that must have bewildered and finally terrified the poor man.

Megan had already overheard gossip at the stable about the Saturday meetings at the Shrub and Grub, with much added innuendo about Annabel's body language, which had been easily read by the clientele there. Some had watched the saga unfold with spiky amusement. Megan had wondered if Poppy would hear it – or worse, if Fiona had already done so. It seemed hardly possible that the two would be left in ignorance.

According to Annabel, she had gone to the rendez-vous as usual the previous day. And waited. And waited. He had never been late before. This part was told with a storm of such sobs and tears that Megan had feared the entire household would hear. The Shrub and Grub was not the sort of place where Annabel felt at all comfortable on her own. With Alex, of course, it had been charming in a rustic sort of way. She had waited for an hour, then been obliged to go and pay for her wine, steeped in misery and suddenly conscious of the many interested stares and whispers behind hands. To make things worse, the lady at the till had asked, "Has he no' turned up the day, hen?"

Annabel had got into her car and driven like a madwoman up the hill to the moors, half wanting to crash, not caring either way. But just her luck, nothing happened. She then drove home – not so late as to raise eyebrows, or draw questions – and held herself together in front of the family. She'd phoned the numbers she had for Alex, but as it was the weekend, no-one had answered. By Sunday night, her burden of sorrows had become intolerable.

Megan understood that listening and sympathising uncritically was the best therapy she could offer. Annabel had swallowed a couple of brandies to release her inhibitions enough to ring her. When she arrived, Megan had made them a pot of strong black coffee and promised on her honour not to repeat any of these bitter confidences, not even to Dick – especially not to Dick, she'd added hastily. Finally, she'd encouraged Annabel not to regret in the morning – as one often does – the impulse to spill the beans. And not to tell anyone else, but to allow herself a cooling-off period.

Annabel would ring Alex the next day. She clearly still had hopes the relationship would continue; indeed, that declarations might now be made. Megan had grave doubts. Standing her up in such a cruel way was a sufficient statement of intent, or lack of it. She tried to suggest he should be given up, without in any way sounding moral or priggish. But Annabel had no thoughts at all for his family. Her attitude seemed to be that they could take care of themselves. Knowing the madness and the power of love, Megan made no further comment.

Taking Annabel's hands in hers, Megan had said, "Look, I must go home or I shall be a zombie tomorrow. How about meeting tomorrow evening, and we can talk some more? I think you need to get away for a bit. I'll think of something. Come round to my place for supper. We'll just have it together, you and I. Dick's away, and Mel can have her tea with the boys."

***

It was almost midnight and Sue was tidying up in the kitchen, grumbling at Mike as he hovered in his dressing gown and slippers, hoovering up scraps of food from the fridge and larder. When the phone rang, she moved swiftly to answer it.

"Oh, hi… Yes, sort of… No, not right now…That's right, how did you hear?" Sue cleared her throat and paused. "The mare fell… oh, December, I think it was; just after Christmas… I can't say. She was got at by someone. Just no way of knowing for sure. Yes, I'll be over there this week as usual, Wednesday. Sure, we can discuss it then. See you. Take care. Cheers."

Mike looked up from his plate of cold bacon and potatoes. "Who was that?"

"Oh, just a client, wanting some advice about an injured horse."

***

The following day, Annabel rang Alex's number from her office. His secretary answered, but he picked up the phone promptly. She was trembling, but tried to keep her voice under control, desperate not to let him know the agonies she had been through.

"I'm really sorry about Saturday, Annabel. I should have phoned you, I know, but I'd lost your phone number." She could hardly believe that. He sounded cold, distant.

He told her that when he'd picked Fiona up after their lunch date the previous Saturday, she had laid into him like a fury, accusing him of betraying the family and so on. She wouldn't believe that nothing sinful had happened between them. She retorted that he had not let anyone know he was meeting "that snooty woman", certainly not herself or her mum, which was unarguably true. He was most upset that the word had gone round Hadley that they were having an affair, but realised that appearances were against them.

"It's awful to be the subject of scurrilous gossip, when nothing could be further from the truth," he said jokingly.

Annabel was cut to the quick. "So what now?" she asked.

"In what way?" he replied evenly, giving nothing away.

Annabel felt everything drain from her. She realised that she'd stupidly had high hopes of a declaration of love or an instant elopement, but he was an empty, emotionally constipated, uncommitted male, just like all the rest. For a moment she was torn. Should she take his light tone, and try to continue a friendship as before? Or should she tell him she worshipped the very hairs on his neck, that she was dead without him, would go to the ends of the world for him?

"No more lunches then?" she gulped.

"No, I'm afraid not," he said firmly.

"I've enjoyed them so much."

"And I have, too." She felt him edging towards the end of the conversation.

"Alex, am I not to see you again?" Her voice wobbled.

"Well, I'll probably see you at Hadley, won't I? Look, I really must go now, Annabel. Patients waiting. All the best. Goodbye." And the phone was put down before she could even respond.

***

Megan knocked on Alex's office door later that afternoon, when she knew he would be dictating operation reports. She must not give away Annabel's passion if – as was probable – she found it was totally unrequited.

He looked up, smiled a welcome, then immediately looked guilty and self-conscious.

"I can guess why you've come," he sighed, putting down his handset. He looked her in the eyes with an air of taking his punishment like a man.

"Annabel," she said, reproachfully.

"Yes, Annabel. She's spoken to you, obviously."

"I've seen her and heard all about it, Alex. I know nothing happened between you. But all the same, I think you've been playing with her affections, and now you've hurt her."

His face closed in as he played with the handset.

"I'm no more to blame than she is. We're grown-up people, for goodness sake. She's married, so am I. Surely it's possible to have a pleasant lunch or two with some-one, without making statements or creating obligations, for God's sake."

"Well. That's a bit naïve. You know how people talk for a start."

"Indeed, my daughter made that clear to me. Load of dirty-minded busybodies. Look, Megan, I know I've been a bit of a shit. I've hurt Fiona. She's been a brick and hasn't told my wife, but there may be other folk who will. I've not behaved well, I know that. And if I've hurt Annabel, I'm deeply sorry. To be honest, I was keen to get out of the arrangement. It was getting embarrassing; she was obviously determined to get me into bed. She's an attractive woman, and who knows? I might have been drawn into it. I'm grateful to my daughter for pulling me up short."

He paused. "Is she very badly hurt?"

Megan was not prepared to play to his vanity. "She was very annoyed at being stood up. You can imagine how humiliating that feels."

"That was particularly shitty of me. I'm sorry. Cowardly, in fact. I was afraid that a show-down would lead to the very sort of situation I was anxious to avoid."

Megan was determined he should have his nose rubbed in it a bit more. She said, "The worst of it was, she felt everyone at the garden centre knew she'd been let down. Even the lady at the till crassly commented on it, apparently." Alex groaned. "So, yes. She is sore. Women take these things differently, you know. They invest more. And she was only just getting over the loss of her horse and… other things. She's a bit mixed up, and lots more vulnerable than you."

"What can I do to make amends?"

"Nothing. Stay out of her life. Leave it to her female friends to piece her together again."

"Should I send flowers or something?"

"Alex, don't be a prize ass. If you do any such thing, it will be misinterpreted. You've got a guilty conscience, and you'll just have to thole it."

***

Annabel needed a break from work, from family, from her suffocating insular friends, thought Megan. She was so proud and reserved, she'd struggle to keep up her defences among them all.

"Perhaps if I could get her away, even if only for a weekend, she could bend my ear if she wanted to, cry her eyes out, or go for solitary walks, breathe freely in a little space," Megan muttered to herself, turning ideas over in her head.

Her holidays from work were precious; sacrosanct as opportunities to spend time with her boys. But she could probably spare a long weekend to take Annabel to a health farm or something. A country retreat. She'd mention it to Annabel then they could go on the internet and explore options.

Megan changed out of her working clothes, then put some nice white wine in the fridge, prepared a pleasant little meal of ham with hot peaches and salad, and warned everyone to steer clear of the dining room. She'd suggested the previous evening that Annabel should get a taxi over, so that they could enjoy a relaxing drink or two with their supper.

They would need to get some baggage out the way first. One way or another, Megan knew she would need to squash any hopes Annabel may harbour that Alex might still be available. Megan had to admire the way fifteen-year-old Fiona had handled things. Men were always the weak link, the blowable fuse, drifting into infidelity against their moral judgement, as Alex had almost done.

Megan would try to explore Annabel's feelings for Ralph. Maybe the marriage was on the rocks, held together by the dreadful thought of fission and the effect on the girls. She glanced at the clock. It was twenty minutes after the agreed time, and she began to feel anxious. Oh dear,

Megan could really have done without this complication in her life. But the hand was on the plough now, no turning back.

Tired from the previous late night, she sat down on the sofa, leaned her head back, and dozed. Twenty minutes later the phone rang. Startled and momentarily disorientated, she looked around, saw the clock and grabbed the phone.

It was Annabel, sounding a bit harassed, but nevertheless in command of herself.

"Sorry for this, Megan, but I can't come. Disasters multiplied. Can't give the details, but Fiona – determined to nip our 'affair' in the bud – told Lily at school. She told her dad. Little bitch. Poppy knew, too, but kept schtum. Bless her. Ralph has gone all mortally wounded and reproachful, and walked out. Lily took an overdose. No, she's all right. They pumped her stomach. But RALPH! What a bloody hypocrite. Seems to think his infidelity was excusable, but mine was an unforgivable attack on his pride. I've been painted like a slapper in this household – ME, who seems to have some malign guardian angel stopping me from getting up to anything and having any fun."

Megan could hardly get a sympathetic word in, but realised afterwards that having to cope with family problems might be the best immediate therapy for getting Annabel functioning again. Although there would no doubt be an aftermath.

Wearily she ate a quick supper and went off to join the boys and Mel playing board games before bed.

Chapter 16

On Sunday afternoons, Hadley was a big draw for members of the local horse world, who arrived in horse boxes or trailers for an afternoon of jumping. During the winter, this took place in the indoor school and offered experience of the world of competitive show-jumping at a reasonably non-challenging level.

Mandy had offered to talk Megan, Jeremy and Sam around the course – set at its lowest level – on reliable school ponies, and they arrived early, nervous and excited but all kitted out and looking smart. Mandy immediately swooped on them like a benign dragon, her grey hair floating in the breeze like trails of smoke and her layers of clothing flapping like mythical, multi-layered wings. Her eccentric appearance never worried children in the least. She was like a character straight out of their story books.

"Now, boys, you're looking very well turned out. Let's go down to the school and look at the jumping course." She shepherded them along, with Megan following, smiling at how well Mandy related to them. Down in the school, various stable girls were putting the finishing touches to the course and Mandy briefly surveyed their handiwork.

"Right, boys, before you jump any course, you MUST walk it at least once. Never forget that, it's SO important. I'm going to show you how to walk a course. You see where the first jump is?"

As Megan tagged along behind the trio walking around the curving, looping course, she admired Mandy's tact, giving the boys instructions while making sure that their mother could hear as well.

Without giving them time to get anxious, the boys were going to go now before the crowds began to arrive. Jeremy was hoisted up on Puck, looking so confident that Megan felt a lump in her throat. He trotted round the school then had a short canter.

"Okay, Jeremy, let's be off. Bring him round on the right rein, just as you walked it. Keep to trot if you want."

But Puck had other ideas coming round the curve. The pony seemed to intuit that his jockey was something of a daredevil. Into canter they went, and over the first jump, on to the second. Mandy shouted encouragement. "Good, look at your fence, look round, steady on this corner. Sit now, let him do it." Jeremy wobbled a bit on the changes of direction but kept his head, hopping fluidly over each jump. And then he was coming to the last, and they were over.

His face was one round rosy glow of delight as he and Puck were patted and congratulated. Jeremy was offered a rosette, choosing scarlet and white. Another one to add to his collection.

Then Jeremy dismounted and Sam was helped aboard. Megan was more worried for Sam, who was an accident-prone child whose adventurous spirit was expressed in strange experiments; once he had taken his feet out of the stirrups when trotting – "to see what would happen" – and found himself sprawled on the ground.

Megan murmured to Mandy, "I hope Puck hasn't been lit up too much for Sam."

But Mandy reassured her with a pat on the arm. "He understands all about riders, you'll see. He'll be quite different with Sam. And he knows his way round the course now so that will give Sam one less difficulty."

And amazingly, Puck did seem to know who was on his back. Megan could hardly believe it was the same pony. After his work-in, Puck came nimbly trotting round the corner, perfectly steady, and over the first in fine style, then sedately trotted between the jumps allowing Sam to mentally keep up, neatly and economically leaping over each fence. He had adjusted his pace perfectly to Sam's more dawdly nature. Sam was quite serene about his clear round, and chose a pale green rosette.

"I went round faster than you, Sam," said Jeremy.

Sam snorted. "Lady Mandy says you've got an electric bum."

Then Mandy brought Peaseblossom forward, a lovely shaggy Welsh mare. "Okay, Megan?" she said, rather than asked.

"Come on, Mum," encouraged Jeremy. "It's lovely."

Sam prodded her gently in the ribs. "You can do it if we can, Mum."

As she mounted, Megan prayed that she would not let the side down; falling off was so undignified. The nerves settled a little as she guided the biddable mare through her paces. Then, throwing caution to the winds, she cantered on the approach and found herself sailing fluently through the eight jumps, hugely enjoying the sensation.

"That was marvellous," she breathed, selecting a bright orange rosette. "It's so different, though, when you actually have to string the jumps together."

Mandy smiled to herself. She could recognise an equine-addict and prospective horse-owner when she saw one.

The Frasers decided to stay and watch the fun, which became more thrilling and highly competitive as the jumps got higher, and people with clear rounds in the classes did a shortened, more tortuous round against the clock. The lorry park was already half-full of vehicles, riders and horses, and their attendants.

Sam spotted a snack bar selling hot dogs with fried onions, and Megan tried not to notice the grimy hands and black fingernails of the chef. Food tasted so delicious outside in the cold. The weather was threatening snow, and very raw, so they fetched warm jackets from the car, blankets, and flasks of hot tea to keep them cosy on the hay bales in the school.

***

Later in the afternoon, during the Novice class, Megan was surprised to see Poppy come in with Solly but there was no sign of Annabel. She had heard nothing more from Annabel since the phone conversation on the night she was supposed to come for supper. Megan had phoned several times, but only reached an answering machine. What should she say to Poppy?

They watched the young girl and her mount complete a competent clear around the Novice course, and qualify for the jump-off. Then she went clear in the jump-off with the third fastest time. When Poppy lined up for the rosettes and trophy-giving, Megan caught her eye and smiled. Poppy nodded briefly and looked away. She seemed composed, if a little solemn.

The jumps were put up a bit more for the Intermediate course. First in was Poppy with Solly. At the door, stable girl Gail helped her slide Solly's rug off his hind-quarters as Mandy asked, "Does your mum know you're doing this, Poppy?" The girl adopted a blandly innocent expression and nodded. Off she went, and managed another clear round.

Megan was fascinated with the human interactions as much as the equine endeavours. There were mothers and fathers who hovered over their youngsters, giving them last minute instructions, and watching anxiously. Some of the kids seemed to be grossly over-horsed, sacrificed to parental ambitions; one poor child on a newly-acquired, flashy-looking pony, was barely in charge. The pony was nervy and erratic, and everyone had their hearts in their mouths. It seemed inevitable when the child came to grief at the double fence.

Jeremy and Sam watched with silent attention as the sobbing child was hoisted up again, with terse injunctions from the father to try again and to use the stick. The pony's eyes stood out on stalks when the stick was flourished, and it took the double with enormous leaps which unbalanced the rider, then sped frantically twice round the school with the child hanging on like grim death.

When the duo finally came to rest, the family all slunk out looking hangdog, with damaged pride and unfinished business to transact. Megan felt sorry for both child and pony. "Crazy parents," observed Jeremy loudly.

They were joined by Jackie, and made room on the bales for her. She explained that she usually entered the fray on the Sundays when the horses competed. There was a league, with trophies awarded for the highest accumulated scores, and there was hot rivalry. Jackie had only attempted the first two classes up to now, but was psyching herself up to do the Open the following week.

"I get so nervous that I can hardly eat for twenty-four hours beforehand, but I guess it's one way to keep the weight down. By the time I've done the open a few times," she joked, "I'll be the new Naomi Campbell."

Taking in the action on the course, Jackie went on, "That kid that won the Novice, look she's coming in now." Mandy announced her as Mary-Jane Peutherer on Magic Mushroom. "She's the one to beat. Usually skims round like a flying saucer. Comes from one of the few landed families hereabouts."

"Landed gentry?" queried Megan. "*Are* there any locally?"

"Not gentry. Just landed. Made money in brewing, I think."

Mary-Jane performed as expected. In the end, only she and Poppy had clear rounds, and Poppy was first to jump off. There were six jumps only, with the possibility of one or two brave shortcuts, which were rather risky as the horse needed to be balanced, alert and willing. Poppy did a good clear, but not especially fast.

"Wise girl," Jackie murmured. "Won't win, though, against Magic. He could take the cream off of the milk, he cuts it so fine."

But Magic was having an unusual off-day, and screeched to a halt in front of the wall. Mary-Jane took him in again, and he leapt over it, but she had blown her chances. The young girl came out looking on the verge of tears, clearly unused to Magic being less than perfect.

Poppy won the Intermediate, and glowed as she received her rosette and little trophy, then rode her lap of honour.While the course was being changed and raised for the Open, Mandy came over and scrambled up towards Megan and Jackie, looking troubled.

"Do you know anything about Annabel?" she whispered, conspiratorially. "I'm worried about Poppy doing this on her own. She's fine, of course, but I suspect her mum doesn't know. The Open is quite a challenge for her, though I've no doubt Solly is up to it."

"I haven't heard from her since last Monday," said Megan carefully. "I think there have been some family upheavals." All three grimaced at each other, a wealth of female sympathy short-circuiting between them.

"Hmm. It's a bit delicate," said Mandy. "If Annabel really doesn't know Poppy is doing these classes, I could get my head in my hands."

Megan had planned to leave before the Open, but the boys were so riveted that she decided to stay. There were only six entrants, the champion Magic Mushroom having been withdrawn with suspected injury.

Jackie nudged Megan as Poppy came trotting in with a businesslike air, shed her rug, and set off. She completed a competent round and left everything up; everyone applauded vigorously. While the next contestant was entering, a paper message was delivered to Mandy. She announced the names of the horse and rider, then looked at the paper. The group on the hay bales observed this by-play, and saw Mandy pause, then pocket the note.

In the end, only three qualified for the jump-off. Mandy announced the course on the loud-hailer. No-one was allowed to walk the jump-off course, and they had only moments to work out how best to tackle it. The first one went clear, in reasonable time; the second shaved off a second. Last came Poppy.

Jackie whispered, "Always an advantage to be last, in terms of tactics. Wonder if she'll play safe or go for it."

Poppy paused and looked around. Then with queenly composure, she set off at a strong canter for the first. In mid-air she was turning towards the second with an impossible short stride into it, but Solly's ears were pricked and he jumped it gamely. She was brilliantly up on the clock. Jackie and Megan clutched each other in amazed excitement. Poppy sat up and held him together, round the corner and met the wall – a formidably solid obstacle – just right. Through the finish, and she'd shaved off fully three seconds.

"She's been studying how Magic does it," chuckled Jackie. "Clever girl, clever Solly."

Her excellent performance saw Poppy collect yet another trophy – the coveted Open. When the competition ended, there was a general exodus, with some noble volunteers helping to dismantle the jumps while others found urgent reasons for a prompt departure. Megan found Poppy still on Solly outside, and went to congratulate her but the young girl's main concern was to beg a lift home; it was dark, and she only had her bike.

"I've got to see to Solly, untack, and rug him up. Won't be long, promise. Thanks ever so much, Mrs Fraser. Don't suppose you can manage my bike as well?"

***

Driving her home, Megan fished for information, but didn't need to delve too deep. Poppy told her frankly that her mother hadn't known she would stay for the competitions. She'd only had permission to do the first round, then was supposed to come home on her bike before it got dark.

"I think Lady Mandy got a message from Mum just before the Open jump-off," she said. "She made out she hadn't had time to read it before, otherwise she'd have had to stop me. She's a real trump. Mum is being a bit over-protective, though, just 'cos she couldn't be there herself."

"Is your mum all right?"

"Well… not really. We've had problems at home. My dad's left."

It was said far too matter-of-factly. Poor kid, Megan thought. Everyone in her family is behaving badly in one way or another, and she's the only sane one amongst them.

"I had heard," Megan said softly. "Is your sister recovered?"

"Oh yes. She loves scenes and atmospheres. With a capital S and a capital A. There's some talk that she'll go with Dad, and Mum and I will stay together."

Megan divined that this was a much-to-be-desired option.

"Where is your dad just now?"

"He's with his own mother, our granny. Dad needs a lot of looking after."

"Will you be in a lot of trouble when you get home?"

"Probably. But bringing home two firsts might help. It might also help if you came in with me? Please?"

When they arrived at the house, Megan and her sons went in to hold Poppy's hand and act as mediator. Inside, Annabel looked hollow-eyed and unhappy, her hair a mess, her face free of make-up. She seemed too apathetic for anger. Megan was horrified at the change in her. Even when the three Frasers enthusiastically described Poppy's brilliant riding and triumph, she reacted with indifference.

Conscious of her own hunger, Megan could detect no signs that a meal was ready for Poppy. "Well," she said, hands on knees, her body language preparing for departure. "We'd better get home for dinner. These two will be hungry as hunters. I expect you are, too, Poppy."

Annabel raised her head. "I haven't put anything on Poppy, sorry. Can you manage to get yourself a pizza?"

Poppy saw them to the door and Megan ushered the boys out first, then turned back to the girl.

"Poppy, dear, your mum looks very depressed to me."

"Yes. I recognise it. She was like this after her horse Mimi died, and my dad went through the same a few months back. What should I do?"

"Mmm. I'm no expert, but it seems to me with depression that you need to get at the cause. How would you feel if I took her away for a long weekend? And if I did, what would you do yourself?"

Poppy's face lit up. "Cool. That might just work. It would do her so much good. Dad has been terribly unkind to her..."

"I know, dear. And don't believe rumours about her. I happen to know for absolute certainty that they are untrue, and you may trust me on that. But if we went away, what would you do?"

"Not a problem. I'd go to my grandma's with my dad and sister. You're very good, Mrs Fraser." Poppy gave her a little hug and a kiss on the cheek.

"It's a pity we can't go for longer than that," Megan mused, wondering if there was any way... But no. She had so many duties – to her sons, her husband, home, work. It would be difficult enough to rejig her timetable at St Dunstan's at the last minute and sweet-talk her colleagues into swapping meetings and responsibilities. She always had to work like a trooper in the days before and after all her holidays, almost as if she had to earn them twice over. And although the boys liked going to their granny's well enough, they liked being at home best.

On the drive home, Megan had a brainwave. She and Annabel could go to the New Forest for a long weekend. They could fly to Southampton and hire a car, stay at one of the many old coaching inns, have some rides and rambles, greasy breakfasts and delicious bar-meals. She knew the power of the place to soothe away cares. She'd enthused about it to Annabel before.

Later that evening, when the boys were in bed, Megan phoned and put the proposal to Annabel. She was accepting but not enthusiastic, almost as though she was hardly able to concentrate on the details. Megan offered to do the bookings and arrangements, and Poppy would sort out her own temporary move with Lily to her grandmother's.

***

When Lily heard of the plan, she was not amused. "Bloody hell," she said to Poppy. "Grandma's an old battle-axe. She treats me like a five-year-old. How did you let us in for this? All that decorum and duty crap. She'll expect us to go to church! Christ! No wonder Dad's neurotic."

She tried – and failed – to persuade everyone that she could be trusted to stay at home. "Grandma and I come from different planets," she spluttered. "How can we live under the same roof for even twenty-four hours? She'll think my iPod's a bloody hearing aid."

Chapter 17

Sue sat at her kitchen table, her tattered diary open in front of her, chewing on a half-eaten pencil. The flat was draughty and she wore a thick fleece, body-warmer, and riding breeches. Shelley lounged on a rug in the corridor, well covered in a long woolly pullover and tights, playing quietly, chattering *sotto voce* to her dolls. Sue looked at her in the doorway, thinking she'd been lucky in having a child who was so good at amusing herself and making relatively few demands. She knew from various acquaintances that it was the luck of the draw. Some perfectly sane people seemed to have the most monstrously demanding infants. She wondered uneasily just how her new one would turn out. Could she be so lucky a second time?

Back to the diary. She was charting her last two periods as far as she could remember them. This was her work diary, full of idiosyncratic shorthand and squiggles, totally incomprehensible to anyone but herself. She didn't want Mike to be able to read the contents; no way. Sue's life and work tangled inextricably so needed to be recorded together.

In November a mark had been made in green, which she remembered meant that she had stopped taking the contraceptive pill then. The green light. Seemed a logical connection. Hadn't told Mike, of course. He was the drone, and she would prescribe his role in her life. The half-formed wish had been to sneakily get pregnant by Dick. She'd expected her system to take a month or two to get up and running after stopping the pill, but she had been astounded when she was late and the home pregnancy test had come up positive.

Her first reaction had been to punch the air with triumph and hiss, "Yesss!" But mature reflection and checking the dates convinced her that this was improbable. Her times with Dick had been few and far between, heavily dependent on opportunity. It had been difficult to engage him in impassioned encounters at her most fertile times. Though, by God, they'd taken some phenomenal risks! When he'd been there with his wife and family at Christmas, they'd slipped into the bathroom when everyone else was playing a riotous game of forfeits. It was the only room with a lock on the door. Standing up against the shower cabinet, trying not to shake and rattle it, then a quick wash and many snorts and giggles at how rashly they were behaving. At one point, a child had come banging on the door demanding entrance, and had looked surprised when two people emerged. Thankfully the little horror hadn't commented publicly.

That was the last time with Dick, and her period had arrived on time the next day. So that meant it had to be either Mike or her farmyard cockerel – she didn't know his name – who was often ready to oblige, and keep silent.

This particular man was a huge, coarse farmhand with whom she'd provoked two or three wordless, carnal encounters out in the tractor shed when she had been feeling particularly lustful. She'd supposed he had the wit at least not to betray the golden goose, but, she thought wryly, she didn't want to lay his particular eggs. "I do not want my child to be a gormless thicko," she muttered to her diary.

The thought occurred to her that she could have an abortion, but it would be difficult to do it without anyone knowing. Anyway, the word was out now; she'd told Bridget Stark, and instantly everyone knew.

But all was not lost. She wondered how clued-up Dick was on female matters. Could she convince him that the child was his? That would give her a claim on him, might destabilise his marriage and – even if not immediately – edge him towards her. He was bound to prefer her to that insipid wife of his, always fussing over her kids, too smiley and irrepressibly nice. He'd even hinted as much: Megan was so wearyingly busy; she tired herself out what with that hospital job and her boys, her books and crafts (knitting, presumably!) and her puny riding efforts. What a silly woman, to be married to such a man and yet she never seemed to have a clue what he was up to. If he was mine, I'd keep the closest tabs on him, Sue thought grimly. Megan employed a full-time nanny and must have a fabulous income, yet did not have the first idea of how to make the most of it. It would be her own fault if someone snatched it all from her.

Sue thought briefly of the surprise phone call she'd received from Dick. He had heard about her pregnancy from his wife, who didn't seem to have any suspicions. Sue had not been able to discuss it on the phone without using coded speak, of course, as Mike was around. Dick hadn't sound either alarmed or delighted, but men were unpredictable in their reactions at such times. Sue decided to let the possibility sink in that the child might be his. Men needed time to get used to these ideas.

A few days later, she drove to Leatherburn for Dick's previously arranged lesson. She'd left plenty of time to have a chat before the lesson, if that was what he wanted. She would feign her belief that the child was his, and watch his reaction. If things looked unpromising, she could always discover later that she had made a mistake with her dates.

She pulled up with a scrunch on the cindery ground and went to call on Bridget, only to be told that Dick had phoned about half an hour before to say that he was unavoidably detained and couldn't come. Very sorry. Most disappointed. He'd tried her home number but she'd already left.

Sue flushed with rage and anti-climax. Unavoidably detained indeed! Never one to dissemble, she had an enormous struggle to conceal the surge of her anger. *Take a huge breath and count to ten, twenty, a hundred,* her inner voice warned. Bridget, who was nobody's fool, watched with detached interest as Sue battled to control herself.

"Oh bugger, fuck, sod and damn it all!" Sue expostulated, thinking it would be better to express the rage rather than swallow it or she would erupt and just evaporate. She flashed her furious gaze towards Bridget, who stood with raised eyebrows and a wry expression.

"It's just such a waste of time. Bloody men. Bloody fucking men. Why could he not have told me sooner? And I need the money, for God's sake. I hope he's not getting saddle-fright and going soft. He's been one of my best clients."

"He said he would make another appointment in a couple of weeks' time," Bridget soothed. "He'll probably ring you. It's too bad. Both of us lose out. I think another time he should be told that cancelled lessons at such short notice should be paid for. You'd think a rich fellow like that would offer, wouldn't you?"

Sue nodded, biting her lips. If indeed she ever saw him again – which she doubted – she would insist on payment. Grinding her teeth and unable to simmer down for small talk, she flounced out and drove recklessly away. Bridget saved up every turn of phrase and expression to relate to her husband later.

***

"He stood her up! Didn't turn up the day for his lesson, only rang in half an hour before. Neatly timed, eh? Should have seen her when I told her he wasn't coming. She went beetroot, I didna ken if she would break down in tears or explode with rage. It's his baby, I'm sure of that. Watch this space, Ned, I tell ye. We'll have the *News of the World* reporters snooping around before long. I don't suppose it'll do us any harm if they do. But I hope he's not going to desert us."

"He's too fancy for ma taste. Strutting around here like he owns the place. I've a good mind to sell the story masel.

Think we'd get ten grand for it?" Ned's eyes glittered with greed.

"Aye, and lose my best customer and teacher. Probably get sued, too. I feel sorry for the wife. D'ye think she knows?"

"Maybe no', and don't any of you gossiping busybodies go and tell her. She's a nice lassie, aeways smiling and polite. Deserves better than yon fancy-pants of a peacock."

Bridget back-tracked a little, trying to sound sympathetic. "Two families with two lots o' kids likely to be broken up, just on account of a bit of how's-your-father."

But Ned was brooding. "What d'ye think, hen? Is the story worth selling?"

She liked the idea of a few grand in her hand for merely telling a tale. But she was cautious, too. "They're shagging each other. No doubt about that. Joanne caught them necking in the stalls, they can't keep their hands off each other, everyone's seen them. Bloody shameless they are. But he'll deny the baby is his. And who's to ken for sure?"

Ned rubbed his fingers together, as if appreciating the feel of pound notes between them. "There's a pile in it, hen, and I want us to grab it. Leave it wi' me."

***

Sue's wickedly foul temper, which lasted for several days, was put down to female problems; pregnancy by those who knew, PMT by those who didn't. Mike kept out of her way as much as he could, and Shelley, too. It did not occur to Sue to phone Dick; in any case, it wasn't always easy to locate him. He was a past master at making himself scarce when he wanted.

Bitterly accepting defeat, Sue finally told Mike of her pregnancy. She had held back while she was planning her campaign, but too many of her horsey friends knew. He was ebullient, over-the-moon, so pleased that he'd have turned cartwheels if he'd been able. He rushed around looking for Shelley, picked her up, and shared the news with her. Sue could not help being touched, and quite enjoyed their renewed family togetherness.

Mike became more tender and caring, the way he had been in their courting days. He talked of her giving up on some of her riding activities and private lessons. But not wanting to get into confrontations, she merely said they could face those decisions as her time advanced.

As Sue had suspected, she heard nothing from Dick for some weeks. "Bloody coward," she thought. "He might at least have done the decent thing and met me to talk about it." She had grudgingly admired the tactic of pulling out at the last minute so that he did not have to make excuses to her. Remembering the effect of her last pregnancy, which had made her horny as a hippo in heat, she wondered how she would cope.

To her surprise, a month after the missed lesson, Dick called on her home phone.He was, of course, instantly forgiven; simply by being there, back in her life. She could not conceal the joy in her voice.

"I've just been so hellishly busy," he sighed. "It's unforgivable that I've not been in touch."

"You're always busy, always busier than anyone else," she observed, trying not to sound too accusing. "Oh, but it's been worse than ever. You've no idea."

You always say that, too, she thought to herself. There must be some plateau where this arms-race of a frenetic lifestyle can level out. But she didn't say it. It was only wives who nagged. Dick had a day or two free, and they arranged to meet for lunch at a favourite pub near Leatherburn.

Sue's spirits soared as she put the phone down. "Gotcha!" she said, laughing as she headed off to sort out some smart sporty clothes to wear, and find someone to babysit Shelley.

***

Sue arrived a few minutes late at The Wear and Tear, a country pub not patronised by anyone they knew. She was still there ahead of Dick, who was notoriously bad at time-keeping because he jammed so many things into his schedule, never allowing for turn-around time.

She was sitting in a corner seat in the snug, watching a desultory darts game, sipping a half-pint of lager, when he breezed in, greeted her effusively, and went to order himself a pint of McEwans. He glanced back with open admiration as he waited. Sue smiled beguilingly, knowing pregnancy gave her a glow. He came and sat down, facing her over the small table, placing his pint mug carefully on the drip mat.

"So. A bun in the oven." He spoke softly, checking no-one was near enough to overhear. The joshing from the darts players provided suitable cover.

"You know it's yours, don't you?"

"You sure about that?" Dick asked after a pause. He deliberately made direct eye-contact over the rim of his pint glass, his normally engaging expression suddenly transformed into something challenging, unnerving. His pale grey eyes seemed to protrude like pebbles. Sue was well-practised in deceit, but quailed momentarily, and it was enough to lose her the game.

He smiled at her hesitation, like the sun breaking through, and patted her knee patronisingly under the table. He produced his diary and a pen from his pocket with a businesslike air.

"Now then, here's the date we last had high-jinks. Your December party. No sign of the curse since then?"

"No. That means I'm getting on for three months gone. More actually."

"But you told me at the time that it was safe."

"I thought, having stopped the pill only... less than a month before... I'd still be infertile."

"Why did you stop the pill?"

"Well, I had intended... I mean, you really shouldn't be on it too long. I was putting on weight."

"You're the slimmest, most athletic woman I know. You're not the least bit worried about your weight." Dick laughed sardonically, eyeing her with an impish, challenging air.

"Why am I getting this interrogation?" Sue was flustered and annoyed. It was like being questioned by a bloody supercilious doctor.

Dick became instantly serious. "Well, Sue, you've presented me with a very serious challenge. Here am I – a public figure, a married man with two children – and you're saying that I'm the father of your child. Before I take any steps towards acknowledging that, I'm entitled to a measure of proof." Again she was treated to the penetrating, almost hostile, intimidating stare. "And honesty."

"Do you think I'm lying?"

"Could Mike be the father?"

"Yes, it's possible."

"Anyone else?"

"Dick, NO, of course not. And I don't like being given a grilling like this. You'll be producing the thumb screws next." She became slightly tearful.

"I'll put my cards on the table, Sue. Sorry to be a bit cruel, but I've a lot to lose. I don't think you are pregnant by me for three reasons. One. You've not heard from me for nearly a month. If you knew it was mine, I think you'd have been chasing me in indignation by now." Sue pulled herself up and turned away from him. He was maddeningly right, but how coldly manipulative. Where did he get his insight from?

"Two. You may have forgotten, but the day after the last bonk, you and I were up before everyone else and I tried to take you again. But you said the curse had come in the night and it was heavy and messy."

Sue blushed furiously. She hadn't forgotten that episode, but had hoped he had. She did not in the least mind fucking during her period, but Dick was as fastidious as they came. He would be put off by a bit of gore.

"And, finally. It's not foolproof, but I've had a vasectomy."

Sue looked at him in horror. Good God, why had she not worked that out? He always was devil-may-care, the question of condoms had never arisen, and he had never asked her about the pill.

She said huffily, "Okay, you've proved your point."

Dick went to the bar to get her another half pint and give her time to come to terms with his efficient dismantling of her ruse.

He eased himself down close to her and took her hand. "I had a vasectomy after a previous paternity accusation. Some silly chit at work. Flung herself at me and I took her in the broom cupboard. Only once. But you wouldn't believe it, some of these girls are so eager to catch a man that they time their seductions according to their fertile times."

"Incredible," muttered Sue, closely inspecting the contents of her glass, and letting her blond hair hang over her burning cheeks.

"I was in a pickle. She was pregnant and insisting I should leave my wife and marry her. I didn't want it getting out, and above all I didn't want my wife to know. I saw my lawyer. We could have paid her to keep mum... sorry... but there's always the risk of blackmail and endless demands. So I hired a private detective to look her over. She was living with a man, but she was also quite a nympho, picking up men in pubs for one-night stands. She had a sex-drive that would scare the pants off you."

Sue sipped her cold lager, her face expressionless.

"So my lawyer presented her with this evidence, told her that she didn't have a leg to stand on if that was her lifestyle. And if she made an issue of it, all this would come out and she would be in the tabloid press, lambasted as a tart."

"Surely everyone at your studios would know."

"Yes, of course. But that's the culture there. No-one thinks anything of who's into whose pants. Still, people like me do not want the scandal of press interest and adverse publicity. So I decided that my family was complete and I would avoid such a challenge in the future."

"You're a bit of a Lothario then?"

"Believe me, it's expected in my world. Straight or gay, doesn't matter, but part of your credentials are doing the rounds. Since I met you, I've not been interested in bimbos at work. Your raw, animal passion is what turns me on, big time. But don't ever expect me to leave my family. Plenty people would tell you 'my wife doesn't understand me', all that, and pretend that some day they would make an honest woman of you. But my career comes first, and I can't have a scandal or desert my family."

He paused briefly to sip his drink before continuing. "Megan is ideal, trusts me, lets me get on with things. She's got her own life, her own income, and never wants to know about mine. We don't even share a bank account. She's a great manager, never pesters me to pay bills. She's a super mother to my boys, who are the apples of my eye. So as long as all that is clear, we'll go on as before, shall we? I'd hate to lose you, you've given my life one huge sparkle. Fireworks. The dangers of riding and copulating running in tandem."

Sue was mortified. Clever bastard. She was dumb-founded at his own libidinous lifestyle. How stupid she had been to think he had one wife and one mistress.

"Do you really think your wife doesn't know you carry on?" Sue could not bring herself to utter Megan's name.

"Incredible though it may sound, I don't know for sure. Women's minds are beyond me, and Megan is constantly showing some unexpected and surprising facet of her nature. She is so good at turning a blind eye that I wonder if she does it on purpose. But maybe she assumes men like me prefer intelligent women and find bimbos a turn-off as soon as they open their mouths. Very naïve of her. She's certainly been worried about you, she actually asked me if there was anything going on between us."

"You haven't gone out of your way to hide it, have you?"

"No more have you." Dick looked at her speculatively. "But sometimes I almost feel I want to test the water. To find out just how much I can get away with. Men like me can't make do with loyalty to one woman. I need a harem, with some stable and some fleeting members. All of them scratching the others' eyes out."

"A woman's jealousy can sometimes fuel a man's wanderlust. Maybe she's being very canny by keeping cool," Sue said, feeling both bitter and resentful.

"Maybe. Anyway, I've some news. Megan has got involved in some missionary stunt with a woman whose man has walked out on her. There's some involved tale which I won't bore you with. But the treatment involves the two of them going off somewhere together. At least, that's the plan. Megan thinks she can only take a long weekend off; Thursday to Sunday it is. She doesn't want to be away from the boys too long. It's this coming weekend, and I'm free as air." He treated her to his beaming, television star smile. "Can you fit me in? To your timetable, I mean?"

Chapter 18

Megan spent some of her precious spare time on the internet on Monday evening, searching for cheap flights, an inn that answered their requirements, and a hire-car company at Southampton Airport. They'd have four days including travel; scarcely enough really. She paid for everything by credit card. Once it was halved between herself and Annabel, it wouldn't look so costly.

Melanie would be at their home till Friday evening, but the grandparents would come and stay for extra security, then they would take the boys home with them for the weekend. Dick had announced some last minute demand for his presence on a programme – a chance not to be missed – but he would be free on the Sunday and could meet their home-coming plane.

"Ring me from Southampton," he'd said, "and I'll be sure to be at Edinburgh Airport to sweep you away in your carriage."

Megan was exhausted with all the extra arrangements to make, but provided Annabel's mood perked up a bit, it would be a worthwhile break.

She rang Annabel to give details of the weekend, but for a whole day could not get an answer. She began to worry. Annabel couldn't be suicidal, could she? Eventually, in the evening, Lily answered.

"No," she said, "Mum isn't in. She's at Hadley."

Megan was amazed. Only a few days ago, Annabel had seemed too depressed to bestir herself. Megan explained to Lily the arrangements she'd made for the mini-break and asked her to pass them on to her mother.

"Oh, Mum isn't going now," the girl announced pertly. "Sorry, didn't she tell you? She's decided she needs a complete break from all of us. I expect that means you too, Mrs Fraser," she added with a malicious giggle. "She's got some really wild plans, going off to the Amazon or something. I don't think she's going till next week, but obviously she can't go away with you this weekend. Sorry and all that. I'll tell her you called. Must go. Bye."

Megan had never been so astonished or offended in her life. How odd. But thinking back, Annabel had not really been quite on the same wavelength when the mini-break had been mentioned. She had been rather vague, agreeing but not seeming to care much. It seemed Megan had been too precipitate, and now she had paid all that money out!

She was furious, steaming with rage. She phoned Dick. He was sweet and commiserative, but told her she was too kind and people always took advantage of her. He questioned whether Lily had got it right, and suggested she check with Annabel in person.

Too agitated and angry to do anything else, Megan phoned Hadley and managed to reach Annabel.

"Oh Megan, I'm so sorry! I didn't realise you were going to go right off and get the tickets and things. Gosh, I'm sorry. I didn't know I'd even agreed, actually. Will you be able to get someone else to go with you? I'm sure you will. You must go, though. I'm sure you deserve some time off, you work so hard."

Megan could hardly trust herself to speak.

Annabel continued, "I'm afraid I just decided... the hell with the lot of them. I need some time and space. I never did the backpacking or gap year things like you did, you know. I was too cosseted. I envied you that... Yes, I've signed up for a week, sailing down the Amazon in a dug-out, on a wildlife-watching trip. It's all about camping in the wild; quite primitive by all accounts, but well organised for all that. The son of a friend of mine did it last year, and absolutely raved about it. I thought, why the hell shouldn't I do something like that? Yes, one of my friends is coming, the mother of the chap who went, actually. He thinks we're both mad and will get eaten by a jaguar or something."

As Annabel chatted on, Megan was barely listening. You never stop being amazed by people, she thought. And there was I, worrying that she was going to top herself.

Annabel had the shallowness of all the upper class, Megan thought, with sweeping, lefty prejudice. She was mildly mollified, but not much.

After the call, she rang Dick again. Her first reaction was to cancel and see if she could get refunds. "You won't on the flight tickets," he told her. "Why don't you just go? Take someone else. Why don't you ask your sister to go?"

It was actually a good idea. Her younger sister, Lynn, worked for a design company in London. She wouldn't be able to use the plane ticket, but might well enjoy the break if she could get away. They were close, despite living so far apart.

"Dick, you're a genius!" Megan said, her spirits rising. "At least Lynn hasn't got monster hang-ups about sex and will be easier company."

She rang her sister, who was delighted with the plan, and they spent an hour gassing on the phone. Lynn offered to meet Megan at Southampton in her own car.

"Thank goodness for someone rational who's prepared to meet me halfway," muttered Megan, ending the call with a sigh of relief.

***

Lily and Poppy went to stay with their grandmother as arranged; the first with mulish resentment, the second with patient resignation. Her house was in the centre of town, and their father had already taken up residence there. The girls would be able to reach their school easily enough, but the stable was going to be a few miles extra on busy roads for Poppy. She had taken her bike but, fearing that the combined authority of the older generations might restrict her horse-riding activities, simply did not raise the subject.

She and Lily were sharing a bedroom for the first time in years, which was not a pleasant prospect. Lily was going through one of her dignified-older-sister phases, in which Poppy was ignored as far as possible. On the whole, that suited Poppy. At bedtime they undressed in silence, and she was amused at how prudish her sister was, turning her back as she undid her bra, and removing her knickers from under her skirt. Poppy rather liked her own naked, undeveloped body, and happily stripped everything off knowing Lily would be offended, then pulled on her nightie.

"You've no modesty, have you, Pops?" her sister muttered contemptuously, clambering into bed.

"I remember a time when you weren't so prudish," replied Poppy, amazing herself. She had found that since her periods began and the power gradient between them had shifted, ripostes came readily to counter her sister's barbs, and she was no longer afraid of the consequences. It seemed that Lily was nonplussed, too; effectively silenced.

Poppy's gibe was a reference to an episode the previous summer, when they had stayed at their cousins' farm in Perthshire. There were three cousins – two girls of similar ages to themselves, and an older boy. There were also three ponies which they had been allowed to ride. One searingly hot afternoon, tired of riding and generally gambolling around, the four girls had lolled in the sweet-smelling hay in the shade in one of the barns. Too hot for comfort, someone had the idea of taking their clothes off. They had all thought this would be a laugh, a great way to chill-out, and no-one protested. It was gloomy and dusty, they could not see each other properly.

"In case anyone's listening," Lily had said, "don't anyone talk about undressing. Say, I'm moulting, or something like that."

Poppy had been curious to see Lily's adolescent body. She was aware of her sister's growing bosom and that she had just started to wear a bra. Poppy thought breasts were nice things, and was envious. Once everyone had undressed, they wanted to do something more. It was all curiously exciting.

The younger cousin ordered the two older girls to sit on a beam, so that she and Poppy could look properly at their breasts. After a bit, she asked, "Can we touch them?" That was allowed. Then, "Can we suck them?" That was allowed, too. Poppy was amazed. It was as if she was dreaming in black and white. She was very aware that the two older, pubescent girls enjoyed having their breasts handled. The uninhibited younger cousin then wanted to look at bottoms, but the others fought shy of that, it was a step too far. When they came to dressing, the younger cousin could not find her pink knickers. They hunted everywhere, getting more and more anxious, but no pants came to light.

"Will anyone notice?" asked Lily. "Just pull on your jeans. You won't go and clipe on us all, will you?"

They decided the garment must have slipped down between the stack of hay-bales and the wall. When they thought of the farm hands using up the last of the hay and finding a pair of pink frilly pants, they looked at each other in horror. But there was nothing to be done except keep quiet and hope nothing ever came to light. Maybe they would quietly rot, or be chewed by rats.

Poppy knew that the previous day the older boy cousin had waylaid her sister and kissed her behind the milking shed. She knew it because, though no-one had accused her, Lily insisted repeatedly and vehemently that it hadn't happened. After these interesting developments, Poppy had wondered if Lily would stop being prudish; but no, she had been worse than ever.

At school, Poppy had discussed these incidents with her close friend, Nancy. Nancy, who was a thinker and liked words, said to Poppy, "Do you realise your first sexual experience has been homosexual, under-age, and incestuous?"

"Wicked," said Poppy. "All that at once, and on the first time of trying." All the same, it seemed a bit tame compared to being kissed by her cousin – a real man – behind the milking-shed, as her sister had achieved.

Mortifyingly, Dominic had barely registered Poppy's existence. She had some rites of passage yet to pass, she knew. But would a man ever want to kiss *her*? She worried that no-one ever would.

Poppy described him to Nancy. "Dominic, he's called. He's just fit and fab and… well… *gorge*. He wore his shirt open at the neck and all the hairs poked through. Really bestial. Lily says he reminds her of Tyler James, some scabby pop singer. I thought he was the image of last year's Badminton winner, William Fox-Pitt. I'm jealous – *of Lily!* I never even thought she was pretty. D'you think she's a stunner in the making?"

***

On Saturday morning, Poppy's alarm sounded at seven-thirty. She leapt out of bed and began to put on her jodhpurs and sweatshirt. Lily emerged abruptly from under the covers.

"What do you think you're doing? It's Saturday, you idiot. Get back to bed. Oh God, you're not going to that bloody stable, are you? You can't, not while we're here."

Poppy frantically searched in drawers for her socks, anxious to get away from her sister's hectoring, insistent voice.

"Daddy and Grandma know I'm getting up and going early."

"Liar. Liar, liar, liar. You never said anything last night."

This was true, and Lily sensed victory; until recently, she had always managed to dominate her sister by force of loud hectoring.

Still slightly nervous about her new rebellious self, Poppy grabbed yesterday's dirty socks from the floor and darted to the door, pausing briefly to look back at her sister.

"Why don't you just fuck off?" she invited sweetly. Closing the door quietly, she walked slowly downstairs, collected up her gear which she had left ready, and escaped into the silent, chill morning.

***

Poppy had expected a scene, but not until later that afternoon when she arrived back at Grandma's. However, mid-morning, when she was taking Solly down to the school to take the lead in the children's lesson, Mandy called her from the house. Her dad was on the phone.

Poppy had purposefully left her mobile at home, thinking it would be easier to avoid being contacted. Disgruntled, she put Solly back in his box and twisted his reins so he couldn't get his legs tangled in them.

"Hi, Dad," she said tentatively into the phone. He was in stern-but-reasonable mode. He and his mother had naturally been most concerned about her cycling all that way in the dark, on busy roads, and on her own. Why had she not said that was what she planned to do? It was not like her to be so sly and sneaky. Had she not realised they would worry? And so on.

Poppy had not thought or even rehearsed what she would say. But it all came out quite naturally, and plausibly.

"It never occurred to me to tell anyone. It's what I've been doing for months, Dad. No-one has accused me before of being sly and sneaky. Why should it suddenly become bad now? I'm being responsible. I've taken on a commitment with Solly. Mum's away, so I've got to do even more than usual. I can't just neglect him. You ought to be pleased with me. I'm managing my own affairs and not bothering you. I'll get my homework done, too; in fact, I did most of it last night."

There was a stunned silence, before he asked when she meant to come home. "Don't cycle back, I'll come and get you in the car," he said. "And tomorrow I'll take you in, too."

Poppy was astounded. Maybe adults were okay when you handled them confidently, like grasping a nettle so firmly it didn't sting.

At the appointed time, Poppy was ready waiting with her bike. Ten minutes later her dad drove up in his BMW.

"Sorry. I got a bit lost. I've never been here before." He looked at her bike. "That won't go in the back."

"Oh, I'll have the wheel off in just a jiff. No, it's okay," she assured, as he made ineffectual attempts to help.

"Don't get your clothes dirty, Dad."

She looked at the impeccably clean car, which had never before been near a stable. "Um. Have you got anything to protect the upholstery?" He had nothing, so she took off her waxed coat and put it in the boot, then hoisted the dismembered bike expertly on top. Ralph looked bemused.

"Good of you to come for me," she said, giving him a kiss.

"I can't believe your mother has let you cycle this distance on your own. How long has this been going on?"

"Oh, several weeks. But from our place I can get onto a cycle path; you know, the old railway lines? There's only early joggers and dog-walkers around. And this morning, being Saturday, the roads were quiet. I wore my riding hat."

But Ralph would not let go. Poppy perceived that he was determined to foist blame and make out her mother was irresponsible and uncaring. Her dad was so anal-retentive – words she had picked up from Nancy – and, having dug his teeth into a topic, he would not leave it alone.

"Oh come on, Dad, chill out. It wasn't like that. I had to persuade Mum to let me go to Hadley on my bike. I like to organise myself and not have to rely on you and Mum for lifts. You're both so busy. It's been absolutely great being so independent."

"But from Granny's, this is a tremendously long way for you to cycle!"

"Well, yes. I'm glad you came for me. Of course, if we were at home, it would be different."

Ralph was silent. Then he felt for her hand and squeezed it.

"It's very hard on you and Lily. We've not had much opportunity to talk. How do you feel?"

Poppy felt very emotional. There was a lump in her throat and she felt like crying. But in her new grown-up mode, she did not want to do that. Taking a big breath, she said, "Of course, we both hate what's happened. We want things to get back to normal. And we can't really see why you are quarrelling, because I know for a fact that Mum hasn't done what you think she's done!"

She hadn't meant to say that, but truly it was inspirational. She glanced sideways. Ralph looked rigidly ahead, expressionless.

After several minutes, he said, "What makes you say that?"

"It was Mrs Fraser who told me. She said, 'Don't believe for one moment that your mum's been having an affair. I happen to know for a fact it is not true.' And I believe her."

"She might just be defending your mum. She's her friend, after all."

"No. She meant it. There was no need for her to come out with it if it wasn't true."

Poppy wondered if she was wielding any influence in the incomprehensible world of grown-ups, in which the rules of engagement were bewilderingly inconsistent. She thought she would be brave, trust in her progress, and press on into the jungle.

"Dad? Can I ask you something? You know last summer, when you were off work? You and Mum had a lot of rows then, and Lily and I overheard some things. We weren't snooping, we just couldn't avoid it. It sounded awfully much as if, and Lily was convinced of it… as if *you* had been having an affair."

She held her breath, fearing an explosion of rage. But he continued driving, looking impassively ahead and studiously concentrating on driving. There was another long silence, which lasted till they drove into the gateway of their grandmother's home. Ralph pulled on the hand-brake and turned to face his daughter.

"Look. Don't breathe a word of what we've been talking about," he said. "Tomorrow, after you've done your riding, we'll go out for tea. Just the three of us. I'll take you somewhere special. We'll talk things through. It's not been easy for any of us. Maybe it would be better if we went back home?"

"All of us?"

"You, me, and Lily."

Poppy was too choked with emotion to speak. She flung her arms round his neck and squeezed hard till she had control of herself.

Chapter 19

In the distance a phone was ringing. Insistently, like part of a dream. Its persistence gradually penetrated the thick, weighty layers of Dick's sleep as he struggled as if through treacle, tuning into a niggling suggestion of alarm. His eyes snapped open. He took in the bright daylight through the flimsy, inadequate, dirty curtains.

"Fuck!" He leapt out of bed, his balance and co-ordination not quite regulated, and stumbled clumsily into the hall to grab the receiver.

"Hello!"

"Oh Dick, I'm so glad I've got you at last. I've tried everywhere. Your wife has been on the phone from Southampton, she said you weren't at home. Her plane's a bit delayed, but it's due to land in Edinburgh in an hour; about ten. She is hoping you can collect her."

Dick looked at his watch, swore under his breath, and told his PA, "Yes. Tell her I'll be there, but I might be a bit late."

Now wide awake, with a pulsing headache and a very bad temper, he rushed back to the bedroom, kicking aside a broken doll, and scrabbled around on the floor for his clothes. Sue was half sitting up in bed.

"What the fuck are you doing answering MY phone?" she spat indignantly. "It could have been anyone. It could have been Mike, for God's sake!" Her face registered agonised horror at the thought.

"I knew it was for me. Bugger! I've only got my bloody riding clothes, I'm filthy, and I've got to get to the airport in an hour, smelling of violets for my wife. I'll have to go home first and change, come hell or high water. Shit a bloody brick. I've got a monster headache, too."

The door opened and there stood Shelley, looking with big eyes at both of them. Dick, struggling into his jodphurs, turned his back on her for decency's sake. Sue got up and grabbed the little girl, not very gently, and carted her off to her room. Dick flung his clothes on, swearing copiously under his breath, looking round with profound distaste at the squalor of the room, and left without another word.

Running up the garden steps as he stuffed his arm into his jacket sleeve, he heard Rosemary's voice, pregnant with meaning, carolling, "Good morning!" He gave a curt nod. He noticed one of the farm hands – a Neanderthal with a poisonous expression – standing in the yard watching him. Dick swore again. Not usually averse to risk-taking, just at this moment the stress of the situation combined with his hangover to waken some uncomfortable Calvinistic feelings.

He had not meant to leave so late; indeed, he had not meant to stay the night at all. He'd arrived in the late afternoon for his lesson, and with Mike away on some compulsory, work-related, team-bonding weekend, had been persuaded to stay for a meal. After a glass or two of wine, his intentions had been mown down, they'd opened another bottle; then another, if his memory served him right. Finished up with some vile liqueur. God, this woman, this siren could put him on a path to perdition.

As he peremptorily started his car, cursing foully as it spluttered and did not immediately respond, he was aware of how he positively stank of stale sex. Not even very enjoyable sex, if he remembered right. Too much to drink. He skidded his way up the gravel drive, disgusted with himself, with Sue, with life in general.

He drove on auto-pilot, aware that his blood-alcohol level was still too high. He thought of everyone who now knew about him and Sue. Rosemary, and her husband, no doubt. The guy in the farm yard. Worst of all, Shelley. Would Sue manage to persuade her talkative little daddy's girl of a daughter to keep her mouth shut? Seemed unlikely. He'd been so wrapped up in his affair that up until now he hadn't cared a damn who knew. Everyone over at Leatherburn, too, of course.

God, what an idiot he'd been. He thought of waking up in that dingy, sordid bedroom, and wanted out of this thing. But he knew it was not always easy to disentangle yourself, and often that could be the danger point. He certainly wanted to keep his marriage and his family intact; he should have tried harder to isolate them from the collateral of his reckless lifestyle. He had been too prone to think of his affair as a never-never-land separated from reality, suspended in some magic, invisible ether.

Against all probabilities, he arrived home without any accidents. Glancing at his watch, he swore again then raced upstairs, ripping his clothes off, stashing them in the washing basket. His underpants reeked. Would Megan notice? He stuffed them under the smelly shirt and jodphurs, hoping the horse fumes would disguise the stench of sex. With the boys spending the weekend at their grandparents' house, there was no hot water in the taps, but thankfully the shower water was hot.

Violently pulling open drawers, he selected some clean clothes, then dashed naked down to the kitchen to put on the kettle. He was desperate for a coffee. As the water boiled, he put on pants, socks, jeans, shirt, fleece. Five minutes later, after gulping down some scalding, instant, black coffee, he was away again, checking his watch, realising the plane would have arrived – if it was on time – twenty-five minutes ago. He hoped the flight had been further delayed.

***

Lynn had dropped Megan at the airport in Southampton, said a fond farewell, and driven off back to London. They'd had a lovely few days, chatting, catching up, strolling about the forest in the early Spring, eating, drinking, sleeping. Lynn was not a rider, but had agreed to give it a go, and Megan had enjoyed having her new-found skills admired.

She phoned home as arranged, but got no answer. Bother. She tried Dick's mobile without expecting him to answer; he usually left it switched off. He was supposed to collect her, then they'd planned to pick up the boys and have the rest of Sunday together. She phoned Selena, Dick's London PA, as she usually had the best idea of where he might be even at weekends. Selena didn't, but said she would ring around a few possible places and ring back. Then the Edinburgh flight was called, and when Megan tried Selena's number again, she couldn't get through. Maybe Dick would get the message, or remember his promise, and be there to meet her. Surely he would.

Sipping orange juice and gazing out at the heavy bank of white billowing cloud below, she felt lonely in the sort of way you do when you've just spent intensively, intimate together-time with someone you love and share a deep affinity with. She was actually glad that the few days had been spent in her sister's company rather than Annabel's. Maybe the inn would not have been grand enough or the riding exciting enough for someone of her friend's privileged background.

When the plane touched down at Edinburgh Airport, Megan ambled through the various tunnels and spaces, collected her baggage, and looked around for Dick. There were not too many domestic arrivals, but she could see no sign of him. Usually she was tolerant and accepting of his erratic ways, but somehow this time – the memory of how Annabel had recently let her down still fresh in her mind – she felt annoyed. Subconsciously she knew he traded on the media-driven uncertainties of his timetable, and liked to be elusive. She waited twenty minutes before heading to the taxi rank. Sod it, she thought, I'm not wasting any more of my Sunday.

Her taxi trundled into town as she exchanged banalities with the driver, looking about her and noticing the signs of advancing Spring. Suddenly she saw Dick's car cruising along in the opposite direction; in a split second, she registered the number plate and his grimly determined expression as he hurtled through the speed limits. It was a minor comfort that he had at least tried.

Arriving home, she registered that the house felt cold and silent. She clicked on the heating and touched the kettle, which was warm. Upstairs, the bedroom looked as if it had been hit by a tornado; the drawers were half open, clothes hanging out of them. She visualised the scene here an hour or so ago, knowing how her husband in a tearing hurry brooked no obstacles in his way, and never dreamed of tidying up the chaos in his wake. She looked in the wash basket. Usually when Granny Fraser had been in residence, she took all the washing away to do herself, which could be profoundly annoying on occasions.

But only Dick's dirty riding things were there, which meant that his recent activities had involved riding and thus, inevitably, Sue. There were no business clothes, shirts and socks. Where had he spent the night? Few men realise how home-orientated women are, how finely attuned their receptors become, how they can read a room and its contents better than any detective.

She lugged her suitcase upstairs and began to unpack. Hearing the key in the front door lock, she went to the top of the stairs.

"Oh, there you are!" said Dick, in an aggrieved tone. "How did you get here?"

"Hi, darling." She came down and felt her depression lift a little in his bear-like hug. "I came by taxi."

He was rattled. He complained that he'd said he'd come for her, so why hadn't she waited? He'd gone all the way there, blah, blah… He was protesting too much. She was used to him tossing the blame back, so she waited patiently till he finished, then told him of her attempts to find him, involving his secretary, and having no success.

"How was I to know if you were coming and when? Was I just supposed to kick my heels at the airport until you eventually turned up?"

They had moved into the kitchen by this point. Megan had noted the strong smell of acetone on his breath, and that he looked rather the worse for wear. Usually he charmed her out of any close questioning of his activities. She always took his answers at face value because, as she knew deep down, she wanted to believe them. But on this occasion, she pressed the point and engaged him relentlessly in eye contact.

"You must remember we agreed you'd be here, that I would phone from Southampton and tell you which plane to meet, and you'd bring the boys. You know how they love the airport."

"Well, you know my life and its unpredictables. Things crop up. As they did yesterday."

"You obviously had a skinful last night. I can smell it on your breath."

"Sure. Again, you know my life. You can't avoid the sort of hospitality... Oh, you don't want to know."

"Yes, Dick, I DO want to know. I felt very let down. I wanted to see you and the boys. And where in God's name did you spend the night?"

The crucial question.

"As you so elegantly observed, I'd had a few over the eight. It would have been silly to drive."

"So?"

He paused. It was obvious, even to her, that he was unprepared and had no plausible story.

"I stayed at the hotel where the meeting was."

"Which hotel was that?"

Dick was not accustomed to such interrogation from his wife. Usually he was skilled in deflecting suspicion, assisted by her trusting nature.

"Oh, for God's sake. I'm damned if I can even remember its name. I'm sorry, love, I really was, candidly, quite disgustingly drunk last night. My brain is not very clear at the moment."

"Maybe you were so drunk you rode home."

He looked at her warily. She turned and ran upstairs, then came down dragging the washing basket. She fished inside and dropped the riding clothes on the floor at his feet. The underpants landed on top of the little heap.

"What's that supposed to mean?"

"Dick. I'm not stupid. These are the only dirty clothes your busybody mother hasn't washed. Therefore, you had them on yesterday. Therefore, you were with Sue."

She watched him, eagle-eyed. He was usually swift with repartee and response, but today his mind was sluggish with hangover. She could see the thoughts skating over his consciousness, how to get out of this one; would indignant denial work? Outraged innocence? But the timing of that was crucial, and he'd left it too long.

"Oh all right. I'm sorry, love. But don't get any wrong ideas. I went over for a riding lesson, meaning to come home afterwards. But Mike and Sue asked me to stay for tea. Then we had a few drinks. They just kept opening bottles, you know how hospitable they are. Then, of course, I couldn't drive home, so they offered me a bed. And then I meant to be up and back here in time for your phone call." He looked at her, then he bent down, picked up the clothes, and dropped them back into the basket.

"How very convenient for you that someone was looking after the boys," Megan struggled to bite back sarcasm. "Your parents foresaw your needs and excesses, no doubt. And why the cock and bull story about 'my life, dutiful hospitality and unpredictables'?"

Cornered, Dick grew vicious. "Because, as you are demonstrating, I knew your twisted, suspicious little mind would get worked up over trifles, would accuse me of screwing Sue and God knows what-all else!"

"I haven't accused you of anything. I never do. I am probably not suspicious enough, it seems." Megan was now totally aghast at the spiralling conflict, and even more at how easily she had penetrated his flimsy deceit. How often in the past had she given him the benefit of trust, when he had so readily deceived her? She had had plenty of grounds for suspicion on previous occasions. She almost wished she had followed her usual policy of restraint and trust. She had never seen him so mean and nasty, never been on the receiving end of his scathing attack.

To her horror, she felt the tears well up and the sobs rise in her throat. She put her hands to her face, hating to appear so vulnerable. Through her own choking misery, she heard him stalk out of the house and slam the door.

Megan had never had words like that with Dick before, and was distraught with misery. She went upstairs and lay on the bed, sobbing into the pillow, aware that some crucial boundary had been crossed. Why had she let him get away with deceiving her in the past? It had been partly to protect the boys from parental quarrels. They had never had rows within the boys' hearing.

She could still remember the agonies of anxiety she had gone through when her parents had indulged in terrible, escalating shouting matches that seemed projected to end in violence, if not murder. But now she was also aware of some personal dishonesty in herself, too. She loved to be thought of as the golden girl with the desirable and ever-adoring husband, the one on whom the gods smile. She hated to admit even to herself that maybe her life was not like that. Utterly exhausted by emotion, Megan wrapped the downie around herself and fell asleep.

***

The creak of a door gently opening and a tiny rattle of china broke into Megan's deep sleep some time about midday. She opened her eyes and there was Dick advancing with a cup of tea. He looked hang-dog and wretched. He put the cup and saucer on the bedside table and sat heavily on the bed beside her.

"Darling, I'm sorry. You've had a miserable homecoming. It was not what I'd intended. Can you ever forgive me?" Dick could do the sackcloth-and-ashes thing very convincingly.

Megan closed her eyes, trying to come to the surface of full consciousness, which required a supreme effort. She struggled to sit up, hampered by Dick sitting on the downie. She reached for her cup and sipped.

"Thanks. Sorry, I feel drugged with sleep." She rubbed her eyes. "Forgive you? Can you just... lay out for my befuddled mind, the things for which you require forgive-ness?"

"Well. Not being there to meet you. Getting drunk last night so that I wasn't here. Saying some pretty nasty things to you and storming out in a paddy."

There was a pause.

"Anything else?"

"No."

"What about lying to me?"

"Well, I knew if I told the truth you'd get the wrong idea. Which you did."

"Let me ask you again, as I've done before. Are you having an affair with Sue?"

"No, I am not."

"Dick, try if you can to look at it from my point of view. The way I see it, if there's no guilt, there is no pressure to lie. Trust is vital between us. Once it's lost, a marriage is on the skids. Like Annabel and Ralph's. You lied to me with the smoothest of ease just to protect your back. Now I ask myself, how many other times have you lied, and to what end?"

"Darling, please believe me, I've never lied to you before this, never. I was in a stupid panic because I was late and in no fit state. I couldn't think straight, I had such a pounding head. I knew appearances were against me and looked suspicious. You're the best thing that ever happened to me. I wouldn't do anything that would endanger our marriage. If you left me, I'd crack up."

Megan, the sweet tolerant pussy cat, the loyal adoring wife, looked down at the lace cover and said quietly, "If our marriage broke up, Dick my darling, you wouldn't crack up. You'd explode. The press coverage would blow you, your career, and your family to smithereens." She looked up and met his eyes.

Having let that thrust sink in, she continued, "I hope you realise that for me, having grounds for suspicion is not pleasant. Not pleasant at all. Even if there is indeed nothing going on, there is the look of the thing. There HAS been gossip. Not that I'd hear most of it, I'm sure. But over at Leatherburn, you pick up looks, nudges, innu-endoes, people in a huddle blethering away and stopping abruptly when you come up. Especially when the news came out that she was pregnant. There were some very pointed, bitchy remarks then, which were very hard to ignore. Worse still were Mrs Stark's pitying looks. That's why I've more or less stopped going there. Even at Hadley, I was aware of... something. It was eventually swamped by the gossip about Annabel."

"Darling, I'm so, so sorry. But folk will always be catty, especially about people like me in the public eye."

"They will if you give them something to be catty about, Dick. I have always assumed, perhaps naively, that two things would stop you in your tracks if you were tempted towards an affair. One is that you emphatically do not want adverse publicity. The other is that I presume you would hesitate to expose me to the risk of infection. I do think Sue is far too friendly, and it is not professional to mingle her business and social interests, as she does with you. I would appreciate it if you kept your lessons to Leatherburn, and didn't go traipsing over to Brockhol-low."

"Okay. That's not a problem. It does take up a lot of time. And of late, it's been tedious to try and get out of the pressures to stay for a drink, or a meal, or something."

"Also, I'd like to know where you are. People look at me as if I'm crazy never knowing how to get hold of you. I've had folk on the phone sometimes, implying: is there a secretary, a mistress, someone who keeps tabs on this itinerant husband of yours better than you do? Why don't you turn on your mobile sometimes, like everyone else does?"

"Ugh, I hate them. They make you too accessible."

Opportunely, the phone on the bedside table trilled, and Dick lifted the receiver. He looked at Megan, grinning and looking relieved that his *mea culpa* session was over. "There's two boys here, wanting to know when we are going to come and collect them."

Chapter 20

M egan had enough problems of her own, but as her hurt feelings and simmering doubts settled under the influence of her children's company and Dick's attention-lavishing penitence, she began to wonder how Annabel was faring. Her friend seemed so determined to have a sexual adventure, but would it stop with just one? Would she turn into a complete nympho? What would she do on her return from the Amazon?

Even though the snub she had received had been more of an oversight than a real rebuff, Megan felt it had put their growing friendship in check. Until then, Annabel had poured her heart out, sharing all her awful humiliations and revealing far too many secrets about her life than *was* really necessary. It was so inconsistent; she could not make out Annabel at all. So many contradictions. Megan had assumed her friend's marriage was on the rocks, but now she felt unqualified to predict.

The next Saturday, while Jeremy and Sam were having their riding lesson, Megan sat on the hay bales watching the eight children on ponies of assorted shapes and sizes, under Mandy's tutelage; just like a Thelwell cartoon.

Alone with her thoughts – something which happened all too rarely – she was still raw and troubled. What a delicate thing trust is, she mused, and how easily undermined. She was glad of these few moments to reflect, to allow her mind to be still in the hope that answers would present themselves. But the all too brief tranquillity was shattered by the arrival of Jackie, desperate to hear about her weekend away.

"I thought you and Annabel were going together? I must have got it wrong. So she's gone off to South America? Lord, that's adventurous. Expensive, too, I expect. Well, never mind, tell me about your weekend. New Forest, that's nice!" The questions and comments batted back and forth like an intense tennis rally, giving Megan little time to draw breath. "I expect the boys were delighted to see you back, weren't they? Were they clamouring to come, too? Who did you go with? Not even Dick? Right, well it's good to get away sometimes, isn't it? Both you and Annabel going wild without your men! Wish I could do that. You're really liberated."

Was she becoming unduly sensitive, Megan wondered, or was this probing doubly crass even by Jackie's standards? The other woman continued, asking who had looked after the boys, what had Dick done while she was away, mentioning she had seen him on TV last week on such-and-such a programme.

Wishing she had Annabel's capacity to quell such questions with a look of hauteur, Megan began, in self-defence, to ask Jackie about her home life.

"Oh, don't ask," responded Jackie, but in such tones as told Megan she wanted to talk. "Don't get me wrong.

I love my man, and appreciate all he's done for me. But it's hard living with an old 'un. Like being buried alive, ken? Or like living with my dad, except I've to go to bed with him. You know I like to blether, especially after a glass of something, but he gets irritable so I have to shut up. And he's always talking business on the phone. I get lonely. It's worse sometimes than living alone. He never wants *Coronation Street* on, or music. It's like living in a morgue sometimes. Then he hardly goes out, and I get guilty about the time I spend here.

"But I'd go nuts if I didn't. And I'm expected to do everything for him. He'll no' think of sharing the chores. I end up doing it all. Bah! What an old moan I sound. But you know, Megan, I think women can never get into the mind of a man. They're like aliens. You think you understand them and then suddenly you realise you don't. And you're always alone. Always. You have to depend on yourself, stand on your own feet. I wonder sometimes if I've given up too much."

Megan thought privately that she probably had: Jackie had married for security, but who could blame her for that?

Unthinking, she admitted she agreed with Jackie's comments on the aliens and the aloneness, only for Jackie to seize on this and demand to know what she meant. Megan paused on the brink; this woman's perceptions were like X-ray vision. Cautiously she explained that Dick was away so much, of course, and that his fame obviously had an effect on their relationship.

"Sometimes," she told Jackie, "it's as if our lives are two circles which only meet at one point. And you realise you know next to nothing about the world of the man you live with." Megan tried to keep her comments light-hearted, but Jackie was drinking it all in, eyes like saucers, hanging on every word. No doubt it would be relayed back to numerous friends and neighbours.

"If I had a man like yours, drop-dead gorgeous and famous with it, I'd wrap him up in cotton wool. I'd be so possessive, I'd scratch out the eyes of any woman who so much as looked at him. I'd probably get a private detective just to make sure no-one was trying to run away with him."

This was said with so much emphasis that Megan knew there was an undercurrent of crude warning intended. But she kept her cool and smiled as she replied, "Of course you wouldn't do any such thing. You know as well as I do, that such behaviour would drive any man away, like mosquito repellent."

This remark unfortunately acted as a trigger for another delicate subject. Moving in close – too close – Jackie whispered, "Do you think Annabel's gone away to the ends of the earth to get over the business with this Alex?"

Under the pretext of stretching her cramped limbs, Megan moved fractionally away. "I honestly don't think there was any 'business' at all. It was all a storm in a teacup. A little bit of oedipal jealousy on Fiona's part, I think, which got blown up out of all proportion in her mind. Annabel's just a friend of Alex; I am, too."

"You don't meet him every week for cosy little lunches, though, do you?" mocked Jackie, with a cynical little smirk.

"Professional people do meet for meals without there being any sexual agenda. They weren't being furtive about it. It's no big deal. There's no story. Let's talk about more interesting things. Like your cross-country event. That's coming up soon, isn't it? Is it still on?"

***

Like all business people who live "above the shop", Mandy tried to keep intrusions into her home life to a minimum. She was generous with her staff and often invited them into her homely kitchen for meals and hot drinks, especially in winter. And clients were mostly sensitive enough to respect her privacy. But there were always one or two who believed they had special privileges, were on more intimate terms than the rest, and who liked to pop in for a chat at inconvenient moments.

Like Jackie. When she'd first moved her horse, Pied Piper, into Hadley, she had been diffident and self-effacing, expecting to be out of her social depth. Everyone, including Mandy, had been at pains to show her the female freemasonry in the horse world didn't work like that. Jackie was now well-established and fairly confident, but subtle nuances of polite feminine exchange still passed her by. Although she now understood she shouldn't just go barging into the house, her behaviour tended to relapse under the pressures of gossip. Mandy sometimes wondered if Jackie would soon be moving in altogether.

There had been two reasons for them seeing a lot of each other of late. The first was Jackie's need to prepare for her first cross-country course, which loomed in her mind as the most daring equestrian challenge since the Charge of the Light Brigade. She was near to being obsessed by it, alternating enthusiasm with disabling attacks of the jitters. The second was stable gossip.

Mandy was no more immune from interest in scandal than anyone else, and lapped up the stories about Annabel and Alex, which Jackie had been the first to bring in. With that intrigue having fizzled out and Annabel away on her travels, Jackie was now eager to talk about Megan – or rather, Megan's husband. She had heard from a reliable source that he had been having an affair with one of Mrs Stark's riding teachers.

With such a juicy piece of scandal, Jackie had no compunction about asking if she could come in. She advanced into the Aga-warmed, friendly, old-fashioned kitchen as Mandy stood reluctantly back from the door. But her coolness soon evaporated at the news. "And she's pregnant!" Jackie pulled out triumphantly. Mandy was riveted, perhaps secretly hoping a scandal would harm Bridget's business.

"Everyone seems to know," said Jackie. "I heard some vague rumours a few weeks back, but now it's all over the place. Between you and me, I think Megan would have gone to the Amazon, too, but maybe can't trust Dick to be left alone! I was chatting – tactfully, you understand – to her on Saturday, and I can't make up my mind if she knows or is completely in the dark. If it hits the headlines, it's going to be AWFUL."

"Yes, quite." Mandy remembered her own share of past scandal. "Who is the lady in the case? Sue who, did you say? Sue Maxwell. Doesn't ring a bell. If she's a competitive dressage rider, I'm surprised I haven't come across her on the circuit." Mandy was one of the few competent dressage judges in the area.

"Oh now, wait a minute," she remembered suddenly. "I wonder if it's Sue Stevenson under another alias. Is she married? I bet it's her. Very, very good jockey. I might just be able to find out more from my contacts."

Seeing an opportunity for moving Jackie out of the kitchen, Mandy propelled her towards the door. "I've got to talk to you later about some cross-country practice. But why don't you go and get on with your riding, and I'll go and do some sleuthing on the phone? I'll give you a shout later."

Mandy poured a large mug of coffee, took it to the desk in her cluttered office, and picked up the phone. In no time, from her horse/dressage network, she had established that Sue Maxwell was indeed the erstwhile Sue Stevenson, that she lived at Brockhollow over towards the east, and that she occupied the basement flat in the farmhouse of Mandy's old hunting crony, Rosemary McAllister. She hadn't spoken to Rosemary in an age but her contact had even been able to give her Rosie's phone number.

The two old friends were on the phone for an hour, reminiscing, checking over mutual acquaintances both human and equine. When they vowed to meet up soon, Mandy realized she had almost forgotten what she had primarily phoned about; Sue Maxwell and her illicit love life.

"Ah yes," said Rosemary. "You've heard about that, have you? Goodness, I didn't think it had spread so far on the grapevine. I don't think there's much doubt. I've had my suspicions for months. He's always here, having riding lessons of course. But they disappear inside, and it's daytime so her husband's away at his work. But the clincher was...oh, about a couple of weeks ago. On a Sunday morning, he came out of her house at about nine – nine in the morning, in his riding clothes – in a tearing hurry, looking round furtively, and didn't look at all pleased to see me. And, of course, the husband was away for the weekend, as I knew. Between you and me, I like Sue but she's got a bit of a reputation for being fast. It's not the first rumour I've heard... And yes, there's this baby on the way. Well, one doesn't know what to think, does one?"

Mandy later shared this snippet with Jackie. They were both aware that the full horror of discovery for Megan, when it came, would be devastating. A situation that was humiliating enough would be made a million times worse on account of the publicity. And the children! It didn't bear thinking about.

"Do you think we should say anything?" asked Jackie.

"No. Definitely, no." Mandy was emphatic. "It's not our place. We could do more harm than good. Wait and see what happens. Maybe it'll fizzle out and blow over." She could see that Jackie was sorely tempted to be proactive in some way; probably with ninety per cent of good motivation at heart. But Mandy was firm.

"Promise me you won't say anything. I really feel it's terribly unwise for third parties to interfere in relationships, especially when, after all, we don't know them that well. Actually, we don't know him at all."

"I suppose you're right," admitted Jackie reluctantly.

***

Whatever her faults, Jackie always paid her livery bills promptly and was as caring as a mother over Piper's welfare. She had struggled every inch of the way in her riding career, and Mandy had supported her through numerous traumas, including the time when Piper went on strike over his jumping and decided not to play ball in her first dressage test. At each failure, Jackie plummeted the depths of woe and despair, needing reassurance administered with numerous infusions of tea.

Now Mandy had, with the help of a couple of neighbouring farmers, managed to construct a simple cross-country course in a field near the house. It included a stream at the bottom of a small valley which could be used as a water jump, and enough gentle slopes to create uphill and downhill jumps out of old timber, tyres, straw bales and hurdles. She had always intended to provide a practice course, as most riders got their first taste of cross-country jumping on an actual competition course, which could be traumatic. The new construction would be perfect for not only Jackie, but Poppy, too. With her legendary charm and excellent relations with her neighbours, Mandy's course was built in an evening, followed by convivial beer-drinking and a bite of supper in her kitchen.

The next evening, Jackie was to be the guinea pig; the first to try out the course. She was so petrified that she had begged Megan to go along and provide moral support. Keen to learn, and hopeful of doing events herself one day, Megan happily agreed and arrived with Jeremy and Sam in tow. They found Jackie in the tack-room, pale as a ghost.

She explained she'd been out and walked round the little course, and it was nice and perfectly jumpable; a real courage-booster. She'd felt good until about half an hour ago, as the time approached.

"Why in God's name am I doing this? Can you tell me? Can you explain how it is that I want to do this course at Duncanshill more than anything else in the world, yet I'm rigid with fright about the whole thing? If I could even stop quaking like a jelly, I might just cope. I told myself last night that I'd give it up; I just don't have the bottle. Then I was so bloody miserable and pissed off with myself, I had to tell myself I would give it a go. Am I mad, or what?" Jackie sounded almost bitter, and looked at Megan out of large, haunted eyes.

Megan understood. She'd felt the same way when she had lost her confidence jumping a few months back.

"I think the first thing is to get busy with something," she encouraged Jackie. "Don't just sit brooding. Is Piper ready? Why don't you get on board and we could go out and have a look at the field? You can work him in gently, get over your nerves before Mandy appears, and settle him, too. Take us round the fences and tell us all you know about how to jump them. We're dying to learn, aren't we, boys?"

Megan gave Jackie a leg up and, while the nervous rider sorted out stirrups and girth, bombarded her with questions about the special tack and clothing needed.

"You have to have colours, like a jockey; a special satin cover for the riding cap, and a shirt to match," Jackie explained, suitably distracted. "And, of course, a body protector."

"Oh, one of those things that look like a chastity belt?"

Jackie actually laughed. "Yes. I tried it on for Bill last night, and he said the same thing. It's so uncomfortable you wonder if you're going to be flexible enough to ride properly."

"Shouldn't you have it on right now, for this practice?"

"Oh cripes, course I should. Can you get it for me? In that bag on the bench there. Do you know, I feel loads better already. Thanks for your help." Jackie dismounted and they fixed the curious garment around her slim body.

Megan gave her a friendly hug. "I think if you're frightened of something, then you should put it in front of you and look at it all the way round and from every angle, examine it, and be as scared out of your wits as possible – well in advance," she advised. "Then, as it approaches and you go to tackle it, suddenly it's not so fearsome."

Piper was livelier than usual out in the field. "Oh Jesus," said Jackie, as she remounted. "Here we go! Calm down, you idiot."

Megan and the boys walked alongside rider and horse as they checked out the obstacles. The jumps didn't seem too impossible at all. Jackie explained that cross-country obstacles, unlike show jumps, were solid and didn't fall down if kicked. Horses understood that and treated them with more respect, jumping higher and more boldly

Mandy was a few minutes late, and Jackie found the delay made her impatient, but reassuringly anxious to begin. After a brief chat, she set off at a brisk trot to the first fence, which was on a level piece of ground. It was no more than a wooden cross pole adorned with some bits of greenery.

"Keep it steady first time," instructed Mandy. Then came a turn downhill, towards the stream at the bottom of the valley. "Keep to trot. Keep him straight at it, legs on hard."

Some wooden sleepers marked the best place to jump across. Piper looked hard at the water and gave a rather awkward deer-leap, which unbalanced his rider.

"Don't worry about that, at least he's not water-shy," called Mandy. "If you have a bit more impulsion, maybe a couple of canter strides, he'll do it more smoothly next time."

Next the course ran obliquely uphill, to a wattle fence sloping away from the approach. Piper took that easily in his stride. Along the straight ground, he began to canter, but his rider checked him back as the course turned downhill again. The valley had a flatter bottom here, and Mandy had arranged a coffin-type fence in which a log on the ground led to the stream, then to another log, with one stride between the elements. Again, Piper took it like a pro.

After this it was uphill again, and aware that he was on the way back home, the horse began to canter. "Hey, come back!" shouted Jackie, checking him fiercely as she realised they'd overshot the last fence. A pole on the ground with some tyres piled up behind it, the jump wasn't high, but quite wide. Cross with herself, she looped round and brought him back. He cantered into it and cleared it beautifully, with Jackie giving a whoop of delight, before having to sit down hard and apply her brakes. She looked thrilled and glowing.

"Remember, he'll always know exactly on a circular course when he's turning back for home. And coming back will be easier in one way. You'll have loads of impulsion," Mandy told her. "But you must be in charge with the steering, and think well ahead where to point him. Put him right at the fence and he'll jump anything. Didn't he do the coffin nicely? Now come and have another go."

Next time, they went round with more confidence and panache. Mandy looked pleased. Jackie was ecstatic.

"Just remember to walk your course really thoroughly, at least twice. Are you going to walk it the night before? They'll have it open for that purpose."

"Hadn't thought about that."

"Well you should. For one thing, your nerves will be calmer."

Megan listened to the exchanges, quietly longing and yearning for a horse of her own and to be taking part herself.

***

As Megan drove home – the boys absorbed with some interactive game in the back – she was deep in thought; this time pondering the question of horse ownership, and whether or when she might be able to take the plunge. Money was not a problem, they could afford – no, SHE could afford it. She had a healthy income from her job, but was aware that she could not be complacent. There was no security of tenure in cut-throat managerial roles. All the same, she had an excellent record and did not foresee problems.

If she chose to, she could stop working altogether. Dick's income was astronomical, although his security was less assured in the fickle media world. But she knew nothing would persuade her to do that. She had always felt happier being financially independent.

In the earlier years of their marriage, she had been the chief breadwinner, with Dick only intermittently employed before he became famous and in great demand. In those days she had borne all the household expenses, and there had been a certain reluctance on his part to take on some of these when he was able. She had persuaded him to take charge of the telephone bill and council tax. After the phone had been cut off a few times and he'd received a few terse final demands, he eventually got the hang of it.

He had never been a house-husband, even in the early days of his career, and was supremely inept around the house. He had resolutely avoided learning to iron, had never done a hand's turn in the garden, and would get grumpy if he had to wash dishes. She had learned not to resent his incompetence; he seemed like a brilliant but wayward child, someone whose genius could not be tamed by ordinary disciplines. Or at least, that was how he liked to present himself, and she had accepted this image.

But now she felt a twinge of resentment. His lifestyle, which took him away from home so much, gave him the perfect opportunity to escape duties, and she was increasingly aware of how creatively he exploited it. She was well supported, being able to employ a nanny-housekeeper and a once-a-week gardener, but she did not want her children to have two absentee parents. The onus of parenthood fell predominantly on her, certainly all the hard work and the disciplining side. There was no way she could take on the

added time-factor a horse would require. She would just
have to wait until the boys were older.

Chapter 21

Annabel and her travelling companion, Izzy, flew into Heathrow early, jet-lagged and weary. As their route had taken them through Bogota, they were kept for an hour waiting for their luggage.

"They'll be giving it a thorough going over with sniffer dogs, looking for cocaine," said Izzy. "That's what happened to Rory last year. Well, we've enjoyed every vice but that, haven't we?" She gave a throaty, bronchial chuckle.

Izzy was going to stay with friends in London for a few days shopping and beautifying before travelling north. She'd pressed Annabel to join her, but she was keen to be moving on. She missed home, her horse, her girls, the clean, chill Scottish air. And Ralph?

Oddly, she missed him, too. And Izzy's company had palled rather – Annabel had not realised just how much drink she could pack away. Maybe it was just as well, as it had meant the other woman had been oblivious to some of the things that had gone on...

Annabel needed space to think through the changes she had effected. Was she a butterfly emerging from the chrysalis? Or a fallen woman, tarnished, to be despised and rejected from now on like a leper? For all her grace and background, Annabel had little stand-alone self-confidence. She would need to reassure herself with a detached opinion, someone outwith her own class who had none of its ridiculous atavistic prejudices.

At first, when she had flown off into the void, Annabel had felt wounded and resentful. Izzy was not one to confide in; her gin-fuelled attention span was too short for that. But she was comforting in a mindless sort of way; someone who had found a way of numbing herself to life's vicissitudes, who offered blanket sympathy.

Annabel had found herself thinking and talking about Ralph; always Ralph. His censure and reproach, when she had not even been unfaithful – well, not in deed, at least. He didn't seem to think his own behaviour should be weighed in the same balance. He had even had the gall to talk of her betrayal of *him*, and conveyed that he was being generously forgiving by not advertising her shame to the world at large. And his mother had adopted the same attitude, looking down her nose with moral sternness and cold politeness. Even Lily had been distant on parting. Thank goodness for loyal, stable little Poppy.

And where was Alex in all this? Had her grieving mechanism simply had too much to cope with? Maybe she could not manage to mourn more than one subject at a time. First there had been the almost intolerable tragedy of Mimi; her utter indifference to Ralph and his misdemeanours may have meant that she was simply putting him on hold until such time as she could deal with him. She was perhaps not really as terminally fed up with him as she had thought. But was she now similarly just screening off the agony of Alex's defection by convincing herself she was heartsore over Ralph?

Examining her feelings, she could not restore any reaction when she summoned Alex to the front of her mind. One does not get over a passionate love-object in such short order. "Why can't I be straightforward and selfish?" Annabel had groaned silently to herself, as her companion fell noisily asleep beside her.

During the home flight, Annabel realized she was amazed that those had been the last negative thoughts she'd had in the entire trip. It was as if she had shed one persona almost as soon as she left UK airspace, and taken on another one entirely within the exotic Amazon delta. She had flashbacks of scorching beaches, sun and remorseless humid heat, tangled, green, dripping trees and creepers; intense natural beauties interspersed with areas of dreadful depredation, felled trees, muddy swamps, pipes, diggers and ugly machinery. The dug-out canoe on the broad river, the campsites, the glorious fried food in the open air, the mosquitoes. The Secoya people, their amulets, beads and charms. The piranhas, dolphins, caymans, macaws, egrets, kingfishers. Purple and saffron sunsets. The incredible orchestra of sounds as night fell.

And above all, there was Pablo. Their Ecuadorian guide, he was fifteen years her junior, burly and paunchy, olive-skinned and heavy-lidded, with an abundance of dark curly hair. And on the first evening in their platformed, thatched campsite, when they'd all got more or less guttered and let their hair down very thoroughly, she had seduced him. She had not even waited for everyone to leave the table before her hands were down the front of his trousers, encountering the most enormous erection. When everyone else had staggered off to their hammocks, she and Pablo had made love right there on the bench with a degree of imagination, adventure, and gymnastics Annabel had never known she was capable of.

Afterwards she glowed for days with newly-discovered womanhood, feeling sexy, complete, powerful. Desirable. She could still provoke lust in a man; one fifteen years younger than herself, too. How did that rate in the siren stakes? She wished her daughters could know how potently alluring their mother was. Then she wondered at such a scandalous thought.

For the rest of the holiday, she'd slept with him at night under canvas and learned the universal language of love.

On their return to the ugly little shanty town from where they'd started, they had to sleep apart. Pablo was risking his job by sleeping with a passenger, and it was too public there. He told her they'd had something much more valuable than sex. You can get that anywhere, he said. And later he proved it by sloping off to a brothel with a couple of the young lads on the trip.

Annabel found she had become fonder of him than she'd intended, but had no illusions. She quietly accepted their ways of life had briefly met and would now permanently diverge. He had proved to her that she was still lustworthy, and had renewed her sense of power through her sex. He had vanquished her demons and she was grateful. There had been romance, too, but it came from the ambience of the wild forest, not from him.

But what now awaited her at home? She had accepted that she and Ralph might be finished, but somehow when she thought of home, he was part of the picture. She would just have to learn to manage alone. She phoned home from Heathrow, expecting no-one would answer as they were all at his mother's. But to her surprise, the phone was lifted and it was Ralph who answered.

"Angel!" he exclaimed with apparent delight. Annabel's heart turned over. He wanted to know when she would arrive. He would come and meet her; she must be exhausted. He explained that the communal visit to his mother's had lasted all of three days. Lily had been absolutely right for once. He and the girls had managed to survive at home between them, with some creative cooking, a number of burned offerings, and many carry-outs. He spoke as if no quarrel had ever existed between them.

Annabel quailed as she put the receiver down. She felt panic-stricken. Had she been guilty of the most egregious folly? Had she ruined her chances of restoring her marriage? She was dizzy and trembling. If only Megan – clear-headed, ethically-minded, compassionate Megan – were here for support. Annabel wished momentarily she had escaped into London with Izzy. She prayed: if there is a God, please help me to be a complete hypocrite, to deceive for once with perfect *sang froid*.

***

In the Arrivals area of the airport, Annabel walked towards her husband as if in slow motion. The rest of my life revolves around the next few moments, she thought, still feeling shaky. He was looking resolutely in every direction except the right one. Then suddenly, as if he had received a jolt, he saw her and his expression transformed. He hastened forward with astonishing speed and eagerness, homing in as if he would sweep her up and swallow her whole. Almost, she was intimidated.

Enveloping her, he hugged her close, whispered in her hair, her neck, her mouth, everywhere it seemed but her ear, "Darling, darling, I love you so much, I'm so sorry, sorry, sorry. I'll never desert you, you are my very soul, where would I be without you? Oh thank God I've got you back, my love, my life…" and a profusion of other banalities that brought joy surging into her throat as if she was a conventional woman, rather than an adventuress of the steamy jungle. The world swirled around them as they made their passionate statement, quite oblivious of the glances of amusement, sympathy, sentiment, cynicism, or mere indifference, of scurrying, trolley-pushing passersby.

When the tension in the embrace eased and he held back a little to look at her, the flood of emotion was still far from over.

"My God, you are beautiful. There is no other woman to match you. You looked like Athene walking towards me. Don't ever let's quarrel again, Annabel, I mean it. Life has been unmitigated hell for these past weeks. I'm sorry I suspected you. I brought you down to the level of a mere man's morality. I should have known better. Can you ever forgive me?"

"Ralph, of course I can. Do you think we could do all this swearing and forgiving somewhere a bit more private?"

"Give me a kiss and say you love me, Angel!"

She kissed him lightly on the nose, then seeing this would not suffice, a fuller embrace on the mouth. "I love you, Ralph, okay? And I'm glad to be home; very glad you are here."

After a number of such reassurances, and gentle nudging of him and her trolley towards the exit, Ralph floated down to something resembling earth-contact. He put his arm possessively around her, and squinted about him.

"What have you done with Izzy?"

"She decided to stay for a few days in London. Just as well, she would have felt a bit spare, watching our passionate reunion!"

Annabel tolerated his unbridled devotion all the way home. She remembered him being like this many years ago, in the first stages of their love. It was perhaps histrionic and wildly overdone, but she knew he would become more moderate reasonably soon. Meanwhile… well, there was something to be said for being worshipped and adored. She lapped it up like a queen.

They had not had the opportunity for any pragmatic exchange even by the time they arrived home, where the two girls awaited her arrival with gratifying enthusiasm. Bemused at the attention, she let them take her luggage, carry it upstairs, make her some tea, then ask about her adventures as if they really wanted to know. What a difference a week can make. And what a week. Instinctively she glanced around, and found the place spotless and tidy. Probably mainly due to Eva, but the family must have made some effort, too.

Eventually she was able to describe the exotic life of

the Amazon, including a bit of civic disturbance they had witnessed, wondering if it had been in the news and if they had heard snippets about it. But no; nothing had been in the news about South America at all. Ralph sat listening, while clutching her hand and gazing at her in rapt admiration. Even the girls were transfixed.

"I was a bit concerned you hadn't contacted us."

"Ralph, we were in the middle of the rain forest. No telephone lines, no post, no embassies! Nothing. Not even semaphore flags or carrier pigeons."

"Mum, how cool is that? Fancy you of all people coping with hammocks and campfires and washing in the river. Wait till I tell my friends. No-one will be able to match this story. "

Annabel felt she had got away with it so far, but her conscience proved a continuing irritant. Or was it that she wanted to share her triumphs with someone? Part of her did want to scream from the housetops: do you respectable folk know what I've been up to? She was half ashamed, half proud.

But there was only one person she could talk frankly to, and that was Megan.

***

When Megan met Annabel at Hadley, she was still puzzled at her friend's previous behaviour and treated her with amicable but cool reserve. As cats concentrate on washing when embarrassed, so women fixate on their children when they feel ill at ease. They stood together, watching Poppy hoist Jeremy onto Solly's back while Sam looked on longingly.

How nicely Poppy is growing up, thought Megan; like a fair version of her mother, but with more natural warmth. And how she has shot up in the last few weeks. "She's growing out of Solly already, isn't she?" she asked.

Annabel answered, "Yes, I fear she is. It's such a pity. They'll have the summer together, but if she goes on at this rate…"

While Poppy was now reassuring Sam that he could have a little ride after his brother, Annabel put her hand on Megan's arm and gently guided her away out of earshot to the mounting block, where they could sit in the sun. Megan was astonished. It was clear she was to be the recipient of more confidences. Not wanting another put-down, she merely looked questioningly and waited.

When Annabel hesitated, Megan – kind as always – helped her.

"Is all well with you?"

"Don't know, really. Yes, I guess it's all right, maybe even very all right. I'm in a bit of a fix, though. Would love your advice."

And in matter-of-fact tones, Annabel related her affair with a hot Latin lover, two-thirds her age, in the depths of the Amazon rain-forest. Megan was suitably flabbergasted. "You never cease to amaze me!" she said with feeling.

"At the end, we both walked away without a glance back," Annabel explained, with more artistic licence than accuracy. "I'd tossed caution to the wind. I had only myself to think of, or so I believed. And then, when I got home, there was Ralph waiting to receive me with slavish adoration. My house is filled with flowers; I've had a fresh bouquet every day. And I was delighted, utterly delighted. It was so wonderful to be received into the bosom of the family, all restored to its very heart. Even Lily's being civilised.

"Everything's amazingly all right between me and Ralph. I can't believe how happy that makes me. He's apologetic, attentive, forgiving-stroke-forgetting. But I have terrible qualms that he might get to hear about – you know? That would be in the last degree dreadful. And some dreadful gremlin wakes me at three in the morning and tells me I ought to tell him. Not only the morality thing, you understand, but…"

"HIV?" Megan whispered. Annabel nodded. "What about those condoms?" Megan asked carefully.

"Still in my bag. He wouldn't use them. I didn't give a damn. In my place now, what would you do?"

Megan was aghast at having to pass an opinion. She could hardly imagine herself being in that position. But one thing was certain, the continuing survival of Annabel's marriage hung on her NOT telling.

After a long time in thought, wrestling with the conflicts of loyalty and rectitude, Megan said carefully, "You can get an HIV test. But if you do, you must be fully aware of the consequences. There are implications for insurance, even if you just get a test. Even if it's negative. But more than that, you would have to be fully prepared to face the possibility, the slight chance of being positive. You'd have to think what you'd do then. Indeed, you'd be thoroughly counselled if they agreed to test you. You could tell Ralph that his own infidelities persuaded you to take a test.

"But only you can decide whether or not to go down that road. If I were in your position, I might argue that you have only betrayed Ralph as far as he has betrayed you; arguably not even as far. And maybe it's best for all concerned that you draw a blanket over the past."

"Do you honestly think that?"

"I don't know. It's difficult to put myself where you are. I only say, it's a reasonable point of view. Are you at all concerned that someone who was there could let the cat out of the bag? What about this friend, Izzy?"

"No, I'm not worried about her. She was sozzled most of the time, and didn't have a clue what was happening around her. Besides, she's a ferocious man-hater. No-one else knew who I was. Didn't even know my surname. You aren't disgusted with me for what I did, are you?"

"Oh no, certainly not. Don't think it. I'm not guilty of double standards in judging male and female behaviour."

Megan dropped her gaze. It hadn't yet occurred to Annabel – so absorbed had she been in her own affairs – that Megan might be facing the same stormy marital waters she had already passed through.

"Well," said Annabel, with an air of finality. "Survival is my watchword. Survival of the fittest. I'll let bygones be just that." She stood up, watching Poppy and the boys fooling about.

"Poppy wants to go to Duncanshill to do her first cross-country event next month. You're going with Jackie, aren't you? It should be good fun. Jackie will be nervous, you know. Take a good supply of Valium! Or maybe gin would be better."

Engrossed in their chat, they could not help seeing Fiona emerge from the tack-room and walk briskly across the yard. Her whole demeanour screamed self-consciousness, and the teenager deliberately did not look their way. However, that meant she was forced to look in Poppy's direction.

The two girls nodded at each other and muttered, "Hi." They had not fallen out, but relations were strained. It seemed there were few behavioural ground rules for youngsters whose parents misbehaved.

Chapter 22

Sue was in the stable tack-room at Brockhollow, vigorously cleaning and polishing saddles and bridles. It was a necessary chore which ought to be done every time tack was used; a counsel of perfection that she found impossible to attain. It was part of her tenancy agreement that Rosemary's horses' equipment should be immaculate, and Sue did her best to comply with that.

It was a glorious morning, bright sunshine illuminating the suspended straw dust in the doorway. She had already taken two of the horses out for a hack – mostly walking – with a brisk pipe-opener on a mossy track up on the moors among the gorse bushes. Luckily she felt very fit, with no hint of squeamishness in the early weeks of her pregnancy. She planned to ride for as long as she possibly could, after which she would have to exercise the horses by lunging them. Rosemary's hunters could be given a rest in the summer, but could not go without formal exercise altogether for three or four months, even though they would spend a lot of time outside.

She planned to work her own horses in the dressage arena next. What a shame she would miss a lot of the summer competitions. Thankfully, she was now in increasing demand as a dressage judge, if only for riding club competitions. Pity one didn't get paid for that, although she usually received a bottle of something nice, which was never unwelcome.

She glanced out of the door, craning her neck to see what Shelley was up to in the garden. The little girl was playing happily by herself, with her dolls. Sue frequently panicked at the thought of coping with two children, but pushed the thought away into the recesses of her mind; it troubled her chiefly by popping up in her dreams. The usual one was that the helpless infant had arrived early, putting her into a frantic panic as she had nothing prepared; no food or clothing for the naked scrap of fragile pink person. She remembered one such dream vividly from last night. Maybe it was partly guilt, for she had neither time nor inclination for knitting and the standard maternal pursuits.

Her thoughts were interrupted by the phone jangling. The tack-room phone was an extension from the farmhouse, so when it continued to ring, Sue – supposing Rosemary must be out – sighed, got up from her stool and went to lift the receiver.

"Hello, Brockhollow Farm? Hello?"

A male voice replied, "Hi, good morning. Could you tell me, please, how I can get hold of Mrs Sue Maxwell?"

Sue almost said, "Speaking," but stopped herself just in time. Why would anyone call her on Rosemary's phone? Unless they didn't know the set-up?

"Who's calling?"

"This is Sebastian McMichael, I'm a reporter from the *Scrutineer* newspaper. I'm writing a piece on horse-riding and who does it nowadays. Is it an elitist activity still, or open to anyone? That sort of thing. I've heard from a contact that Sue would be a good person to speak to. Excuse me, but are you Sue Maxwell?"

Recovering from what felt like a punch in the solar plexus when she heard the word "reporter", Sue became aware of the infant kicking like mad in her belly. She knew she should say he'd got the wrong number, and maybe the sprog was telling her the same thing. But her self-esteem was tickled, and she could not just put the phone down without finding out if this really was the start of her fame as a horsewoman spreading far and wide. Caution battled with vanity. Don't tell him who you are quite yet, it said.

"Can you tell me a bit more? What sort of things would you be asking? Would you want to visit, to interview? Take photographs? Would it be for a sports section?"

"Yes, probably all of those, Mrs Maxwell. Might you be interested? I'm planning a full page spread; could be good for a bit of free advertising for you. You might be interested? Good, excellent. We're also keen to find out if you have any celebrity riders on your books. I'd heard, for instance, that Dick Fraser is one of your clients. We'd like to know what sort of horseman he is, maybe persuade him to–"

"Er, no, sorry. I don't think so. Clients expect confidentiality."

"Oh come!" She heard a sardonic, disbelieving laugh. "No showbiz person would turn up their nose at publicity! Why should he want to keep his riding lessons secret?"

She was shaking now. Oh Lord. She had walked into a trap. Like most ordinary people, she thought of press reporters as new age inquisitors. She said, "No thanks, goodbye," and put the phone down hurriedly, then stared at it mesmerised, as if it was a scorpion. After a moment, it rang again. She lifted the receiver a fraction, then slammed it down and pulled the connection out of its socket. She stood, thinking of Dick. She had not seen him or spoken to him since the drunken over-sleeping episode, when they had not parted on the best of terms.

She sat down on her low stool, hunched up and staring into the murky, scummy depths of the bucket between her knees, feeling wobbly. A cat strolled up and rubbed against her, but she pushed it roughly away. She had planned to make a great catch with Dick, but he had made it absolutely clear that she was just a bit on the side. At first she hadn't appreciated just how well-known he was. Why should she? She never had time to watch trashy television programmes. She began to wonder if she had been pitching her stakes just a little too high, and the outcome for her might be total disaster.

She was prepared to settle for mistress rather than wife, but she had no intention of losing her own support systems, and did not want her marriage to crash until there was something ready to replace it. She would speak to Dick, he would need to be warned that... what was his name? Sebastian Mcwhatsit from the *Scrutineer* had got wind of something. And in her naivety, she had handled it soooo badly. She had pulled back sharply as if she had been burned as soon as Dick's name was mentioned. And put the phone down... twice. Disconnected it. If that didn't scream guilt, what did? He would not be pleased at her ham-fisted response.

Sue's cheerful, energetic morning mood had evaporated. She gloomily foresaw that before this baby popped out, she might have lost both husband and lover. How would she cope if Mike walked out? Of course, he'd still have to provide for both children, and also to take his share in looking after them. And she was earning money with teaching. She would manage somehow, she supposed. But what a life!

Unaware that she had been sitting idle in a posture of anxious distress, Sue was startled by a shadow falling over the open door. It was Rosemary, looking surprised and concerned.

"Sue, my dear, are you all right? Good heavens, you look pale as death. You haven't been overdoing it, have you? I came looking for you because Shelley's there on her own. Look, I can't have you knocking yourself up on my account. I'd never forgive myself if something happened. Leave the tack just now, come in and have a cup of coffee and a breather."

Sue got up, aware that she was still severely shaken by the phone call. She felt weepy, in need of someone to confide in, and on the verge of confessing all. She followed Rosemary, who collected up Shelley as they went, promising her some fizzy pop.

They went into the vast, well-appointed farmhouse kitchen, Rosemary keeping up a flow of banter directed mainly at the child. Sue sank down in a chair with her elbows on the table. If reporters came scratching round here, Rosemary would have to know. And in all probability they would follow up, and ring again.

At that moment, as if prompted by her thoughts, the phone rang. Rosemary answered while Sue's heart pounded.

"Yes, she's here." Rosemary looked over at Sue with her eyebrows raised. Sue thought quickly, and in getting up, she rallied. Don't do anything before discussing it with *him,* she told herself. She would only do something stupidly naïve and incriminate them further.

"Hello." It was him again. Slimy Sebastian. "No. No thanks. No. I've thought better of it. Just take no for an answer, will you?" She put the phone down, and looked over at Rosemary.

"I'm not ill, I was upset by this fellow. He phoned earlier. It's a bloody reporter. He's been harassing me. Came all sweet-talking, interested in horse-riding as a sport, all that, then it transpires that he's really interested in… Dick's activities. I didn't know how to handle it."

Rosemary paused, her expression inscrutable, examining Sue. "I see," she said, the two words heavy with significance. She probably saw considerably more than Sue had divulged. She stood, immobile, leaning against the sink holding the kettle, staring down at Shelley playing quietly with a collie on the floor, as if intensely interested in the spectacle.

"What are you going to do?"

"I guess I'll have to get hold of Dick, to warn him. He's used to the press, he'll know how to deal with them."

There was another heavy silence. Rosemary filled the kettle and put it on to boil. Then she took a deep breath, as if making up her mind.

"Sue, dear. You've got yourself tangled up with this man, haven't you?"

"Who d'you mean?"

"I mean Dick. I saw him coming out of the house early one morning when I knew Mike was away. So there's only one logical interpretation."

Sue was silent in reluctant acknowledgement. She was uneasy that Rosemary's attitude seemed one of gentle accusation rather than commiseration.

"Now it's none of my business, of course. None whatsoever. You and I rub along very nicely, and you're one hundred percent with the horses. I like having the flat occupied, too. But I don't want any hassle. I don't want reporters hiding in the bushes, ambushing us at the gate, prying and leaving gates open, photographing us unawares. It would be a nightmare. It's quiet here at Brockhollow, and that's the way I'd like to keep it. I don't want to see this place on the front pages of the gutter press, complete with lurid stories. I've got my own reputation to think of. We don't want to fall out, dear, do we? It might be better if Dick didn't come here for lessons in the future."

"Yes. Of course. I'm sorry. You won't be hassled, I'm sure. I'll go now and… contact him."

Severely crestfallen, Sue went to take Shelley's hand and lead her away, but the child resisted. She was happy playing with the dog.

Rosemary smiled indulgently at the child. "Oh, she can stay with me. I'm not going out again. She can help me make some cakes." Shelley looked up and nodded enthusiastically, avoiding looking at her mother.

Sue felt again that there was covert criticism in this, an attack on her competence as a mother. It was almost insult added to injury; rejected even by her own daughter. But she dared not make a scene, so she left the child, telling her to be good, and went off downstairs without another word. She had not even got her promised coffee.

When she had phoned Dick in the past, she had usually gone through his PA, who was clearly well versed in the ways of the media world. Sue seldom rang his home number. But today was an emergency. Mel, the nanny, answered. No, no-one was at home except Mel herself, but she'd let Mrs Fraser know when she came in this evening. Fat lot of good that'll do, thought Sue savagely.

Eventually, amazingly, she managed to track him down, but the location was too public for him to talk. He'd phone back in half an hour, all right? That meant she had to hang about waiting. Her morning's plans had gone by the board, her own horses left unexercised. It was over an hour of fretting before he got back to her, and she was in no sweet temper. She related the story of Sebastian of *The Scrutineer.*

"Yes, I know him. Muck-raker *par excellence.* Well, my dear, you must have known it might happen. We may be in for a rough ride, but I've survived this sort of thing before."

"*You've* survived! How about me?" she asked tearfully. "Already Rosemary has given me a covert warning that she doesn't want press intrusion, and that our ways might need to part. How are you going to protect *me?*"

"Well, I can't wave a magic wand. You must learn to keep your cool. Just be polite and don't say a thing. I'll need to think. Probably the best thing would be to do nothing. I could ring him, make a joke out of it, find out what he really wants to know. Anyway, so what if Rosemary knows about us? We already knew that. How about Shelley? How did you handle her unexpected entrance on that last occasion?"

"I told her some stupid tale that you had left your jodhpurs behind, and had to come back for them. It was the first thing that came into my head. She seemed to accept it. If I told her not to tell her Dad about you and me in the bedroom in a state of undress, she'd be bound to go and blurt it out. Might still do, of course. What a mess."

"Would you be sorry? If he knew, I mean? You don't seem all that madly in love with him."

"Of course I don't want him to know. Do you want *your* wife to know? Like you, I want to have my cake – or in your case, your banquet – and eat it. *You're* not going to make an honest woman of me, are you?"

Knowing as she said the words that she laid herself open to misogynist insult, she heard him say with a laugh, "Nothing will do that, my sweet!" She ground her teeth, but swallowed her rage. She would not destroy what little hold she had.

"Look, if he or any other reporter rings again, just say you've nothing to say. Or why don't you suggest they contact me, if they want to know about me? Keep your cool, as I said. They're not devils incarnate. They're quite ordinary guys, trying to make a living."

"So that's it? Will you phone me and let me know if you do contact him?" Sue did not want him to go off into his carefully encapsulated void, as inaccessible as a man on the moon. She thought desperately of something to detain him. "You know, Rosemary doesn't want you to come here for lessons any more? She doesn't want the place contaminated by vile press intrusion. When are we going to meet again?"

"Ah yes, I forgot to tell you about *my* fall-out from that disastrous last occasion. I came in for a tremendous row from Megan. She doesn't want me to come over, either. She only just stopped short of accusing me of an affair with you. Deep down, I suppose she knows but can't quite accept it. I'm walking on perilously thin ice there, so for the present, we keep a low profile, you and me. I've got to dance attendance, be around, be domestic, curtail my freedom for a bit."

"I tell you what we might do, if you're up for it," Sue interjected hurriedly. "I've just remembered. My kid sister has a new youngster – a five-year-old that she wants to bring on as an eventer. She's talking about taking it to a very nice small-time trial over in the west, near Glasgow. Very pretty estate. It's a couple of weeks away, on a Saturday. We could go along together. The whole family gang will be there, so we can take a picnic. We don't need to be furtive, we can mingle with the crowd. My family doesn't worry who I appear with. They're used to me having a man in tow. And in a crowd, no-one will start connecting us with each other."

"Okay. Sounds good. What date is that? Might be better to take two cars, then it would look as if we'd met by chance."

"Oh, no need for that. Don't be such a cautious sissy. What do you think? Are you free?"

"Actually that might work out quite nicely." Dick's voice grew muffled as he held the phone with his chin, checking his diary. "I'm away that week up till the Friday; a long-standing thing. Megan's got something on, so the boys will be at the grandparents on the Saturday. Yes, let's do it. We'll work out where to *rendezvous* nearer the time."

"Great, Dick. So I'll hear from you later?"

As soon as he rang off, Sue contacted her sister and talked her into doing the cross-country event.

***

Dick was irritated, but not as worried as Sue. He knew the press pretty well and thought he could handle them. He was slightly amused at Sue's panic, but maybe it wasn't surprising in an unsophisticated rustic living in a rural backwater. She had certainly encouraged any grounds for suspicion they might have by her terrified *volte-face*.

Deciding to ring Seb and treat it all as a joke, he got the receptionist to make contact, so it was as public – and thus, as innocent-seeming – as possible.

"Hi there, Seb! How goes it?" Dick was in his most hearty man-to-man mode as they exchanged the usual male banalities.

"Good, good. What's all this I hear about you terrifying the wits out of a good friend of mine? Yes, that's the one. Poor soul has her work cut out trying to make a horseman out of me. She thinks you're doing some underhand sleuthing, digging for dirt. Maybe wanting to catch me in an undignified tumble off a horse? Set the anti-hunt mafia on me, perhaps? Oh come on, man! Are you serious? Good Lord, have you seen her? Pure peasant stock; hard-faced besom, like all these horsey types. Bulging muscles where she should have curves. Bit long in the tooth for me, too. Rolling in the hay isn't at all my style. I like a bit more sophistication, and comfort; women who smell of violets rather than manure. Well, sorry not to be the subject of scandal, but I'll get out there and see what I can do for you. But let me choose my own totty, okay? I've got my street cred to think of! Yes, good to talk. Cheers. Happy hunting!"

***

Predictably, Dick didn't phone Sue back. But Megan did, later that evening. Sue had forgotten about ringing the Fraser home in her earlier panic.

"Oh, sorry to bother you. I eventually managed to get hold of him." Sue thought rapidly and the glib fibs came to her rescue. "It was to check up on a long-standing arrangement for a lesson. I wanted to find out if it was still on."

"Was that at Leatherburn, or your place?"

Sly bitch, thought Sue. Remembering Dick's remarks, she replied, "Leatherburn."

"And is the lesson still on?"

"No. It's not." Safer to lie as little as possible. Odd to be having this conversation, when each of them knew that the other knew what was going on. She didn't suppose Megan would check up on her story. If she did, she was a prying, jealous old nosey-parker; if she didn't, she was a naïve airhead.

Chapter 23

Megan sat by herself at the conference table near the door as around thirty people drifted in, helped themselves to coffee or tea from catering flasks on a corner table, then took their places. There were some committee meetings that she resented; time-consuming affairs in which too many people liked to hear the sound of their own voices. All the really hard graft she did was out on the shop floor, mainly on a one-to-one basis. But needs must.

This was the Hospital Pharmaceutical Services Committee, efficiently chaired by Alex Temple, and a group that did a lot of good work in keeping drug-related costs down. He usually called meetings at lunchtime, on the principle that you had to wind up business in one hour flat to let people away for other commitments. But this one was at five o'clock – a last resort at gathering key people together.

Announcing that he had to rush off at six, Alex fixed the most verbose members with his stern gaze, willing them to keep discussions succinct. Megan was relieved, keen to be home promptly. The following evening, she,

Jackie, Jeremy and Sam would drive over to Duncanshill to inspect the cross-country course. Tonight she needed to look out their country clothes, boots and waterproofs, and make sure Mel knew what to prepare for a packed supper for them all.

She also wanted to spend some time with the boys before they went to bed, then get ahead of the game with some paperwork. Fixing her mind on the agenda and the points where she had to make some contribution, she could not help noticing how unusually drawn and tired Alex looked. He was normally the essence of enthusiasm, good health, and vigour. Like the prototype surgeon, he had been a rugby fanatic in his youth, and now played golf – a useful way of networking out of hours. But he didn't completely fit the mould; Megan had exchanged recipes with him and knew he was an enthusiastic cook.

Her intention to nip out the door as soon as matters drew to a close must have been expressed in her body language, as Alex scribbled a few words on a scrap of paper, folded it, and passed it along to her. It said: "Do you mind not rushing away at the end? I'd very much like to talk to you. Alex." How odd. She looked up and caught his gaze then nodded briefly, somewhat bemused.

The business ground on in its lumbering manner. Alex was in no mood to tolerate long-winded meanderings, and these were nipped tetchily in the bud before they even got underway. Some frustrated glances were covertly exchanged around the table. Must have been a bad day in Theatre Three, was the verdict.

At the end, as usual, people tended to gather in little knots, talking intently. Megan could never understand why they didn't want to escape to their out-of-work lives. Alex came over, gathering his files together, and ushered her to the door. Was there something unpleasant he had to say to her? she wondered. His manner was formal, almost brusque. "Shall we go to my office?" she offered, leading the way along the corridor. He merely grunted in reply, looking distracted.

In the office, he sank down into a chair and rested his chin on his hand, looking down at the floor with no attempt at small talk. He was the picture of restrained unhappiness. What could it be? she thought in rising alarm. What have I done?

As the silence stretched on, she saw that it was nothing to do with her; he wanted to unburden himself but was finding it difficult to start. She perched on the edge of the desk.

"Alex, what is it?" Her tone was gentle and sympathetic. He looked ghastly, she realized; a man in deep trouble. "Are you all right?" Instinctively she reached forward. He smiled, a pale, grim smile, and took her hand.

"No. Megan, I'm sorry to inflict this on you. I'm in trouble. You may have guessed, it's my marriage. On the rocks. It's all been so miserable, so bitter, so hurtful, so bloody primitive in its viciousness. I've not slept properly for… God knows how long. I'm struggling to keep my mind on my work. I have to tell someone or I'll go mad."

"Alex, I'm so sorry." It sounded banal but she meant it sincerely. "Has this happened because of the Annabel episode?"

Again the tired, thin smile. "Oh no. That was a mere symptom of the problem. That was why Fiona was so anxious to keep me out of an entanglement. We were struggling then to get things together. I just so much needed a kind word, a bit of affection and warmth. Annabel was a tonic. Rachel doesn't even know about the Annabel thing.

"But she's made it clear she wants out. Maybe I shouldn't blame her. It's not easy being married to a workaholic surgeon. She can't organise her social life as she would like; I'm never there to show off to her friends. Or if I am, I probably get called away to some emergency. She can't understand why I can't just go into private practice and make a whole lot more money with much less grind. Or why I'm not a jet-setting professor from the Edinburgh Royal. She can't understand there's more to it than that." He made a hopeless gesture with his hands..

"She's never worked herself since we got married, and the gulf between us, the total failure of understanding of each other's lives… well, it's eaten away at the love we once had."

"Look, do you need some time off, Alex? Might it be better to do that rather than risk some mishap or other? You look awfully tired and stressed. I thought that when I first saw you this afternoon."

"I don't want to if I can avoid it. You know what men are. We don't want to admit we're not coping." He managed the hint of a smile. "But I am desperate to talk to someone – a friend, a sympathetic, unjudging friend. My wife seems to revel in arguments and verbal onslaughts, she attacks me with words till I feel I'm the worst kind of bastard that's ever walked this earth. Have I been that awful? I've really tried to be good to her. I've never been unfaithful, ever."

"Has she?"

"Maybe in the past, but not right now. Maybe I'm naïve, but she says there's no-one else. It's all my fault for failing as a husband. If – when – she leaves me, she hopes to find someone better, someone more congenial."

Megan looked at him. Alex was adored by his patients, and half the nursing staff were said to be in love with him. His colleagues liked and approved of him. His reputation as a surgeon was deservedly high. He'd shown in committee work that he was capable of a feminine degree of tolerance and mediation – qualities not usually found in egotistical consultant surgeons, who were often a quarrelsome bunch. What crazy woman was this who thought she deserved, or could find, something better? Privately Megan wondered if there was another man, and that the ruthless Rachel was keeping him quiet in the hopes of a better divorce settlement. Or was she just becoming cynical?

"I suppose I may as well tell you the worst. Rachel has had affairs in the past. Or so she now tells me. It seems I've failed in that department, too. Now she says we have to think of Fiona first, and as she will naturally want to stay with her mother, Rachel thinks I should leave the family home to disrupt my daughter's studies and life as little as possible." Alex became restless, gesticulating and shifting with anxiety. "But I'm not prepared to do that. I've always paid the mortgage payments, of course, but that's neither here nor there.

"I was so angry at this summary dismissal, without any thought for the demands of my work, quite apart from anything else, so I suggested we ask Fiona if that was her wish. And, bless her loyal little heart, she wants to stay with me. So on the basis of Rachel's argument, I announced that it should be her who walks out – and there's the door.

"That went down like a lead balloon, of course. I can see her ferocious face even now, turning on me like a ferret with its teeth bared. And she delivered the *coup de grace*; the knock-out blow." Alex buried his head in his hands again. His voice shook. "She told me that… Fiona is not my daughter."

Megan, the experienced consoler of many lacerated hearts, was so aghast she hardly knew how to react. Quietly, she got up and turned the lock on the door. They did not want someone bursting in at such a delicate moment. Then she knelt down and put her arms round him. Tears were running down between his fingers. Megan's heart twisted agonisingly. Who was this woman that she could treat such a treasure of a man so callously?

She held him close, caressed his neck, gave him time. After what seemed like an eternity, she got up and he mopped his face with a hanky. She hated to see him so exposed, as if she had come across him naked in a public place, and tactfully turned away.

"Alex. Is she not just lashing out in spite and hurt pride, saying the thing calculated to hurt the most? I can't believe it. For one thing, Fiona's so like you. Not just her flaxen hair, that Scandinavian ice-blond that's actually quite rare, but her features, too. They just shriek of you. I've remarked on it before."

"I don't know, Megan, but it wouldn't make any difference. I love Fiona and she's my daughter, come what may. In my heart, I know you're right. But I'm glad to hear you say so. What's unforgivable is that Rachel brought this out in front of Fiona, as if to punish both of us for ganging up on her. How could Rachel be such a Godalmighty–" He clenched his teeth.

"Bitch, is the word," Megan interrupted. "To do that to her own child? I don't understand that. What will she do now?"

"So far, she's taken no steps to pack her bags. It seems as if she wants me out of her life with minimal trouble to herself. If *she's* got to do anything, be uncomfortable, have her life disrupted, then it's not going to happen. I wouldn't put her out on the street, don't think it. Anyway, Rachel has her own money as well as a claim on my earnings, so she knows she'll not go short. She has family up in Wester Ross, and we have a second home up there; a lovely country cottage. I suggested she move there while we sort things out, but she doesn't want to leave her cronies who meet for lunch and shopping in town most days. They probably get a blow-by-blow account of the state of our union. But life's not comfortable for any of us at the moment."

"I can imagine. She's been incredibly heartless, Alex. After all, you are the breadwinner. She lives a life of leisure and yet expects you to abandon your home at her whim!"

"I don't want to demonise her, Megan. I think we've been rubbing along in a loveless marriage for some years," he admitted. "But I thought I was still doing my duty, keeping her content if not happy. And for the sake of Fiona, it seemed the right thing to do. I suppose I was unwise in my choice all those years ago. I knew she was well-heeled, with no ambitions other than social jousting and frivolous pastimes. Not ideal for a soul-mate. But blame Cupid; I loved her to distraction… a long time ago."

Megan did not want to glance at her watch, but knew she would have to phone home soon and explain the delay. Alex must have picked up her momentary hesitation, and he stood up.

"Thanks, Megan, you are a gem. I really just needed a shoulder to cry on. You are a tower of strength, as always. I'm sorry for burdening you, holding you back and all that, when you've got your own family to see to."

Megan swept his thanks aside and asked him to consider taking some compassionate leave; she offered to smooth the way for him that very night. But he protested that working at least kept his self-esteem intact and gave him other things to think about.

"Fair enough but please use me if you need to let off steam or want a female perspective, advice or whatever, Alex. Or a drink somewhere," Megan offered. "And don't forget about the leave. On mature reflection, you may decide it's a good move. I won't, of course, breathe a word to a soul until you give me the say-so."

Alex gave her a grateful hug. "Take care," she said, watching him go, aching on his behalf.

***

Megan drove home, her heart full of her friend and his sad, sad tale. We humans are not a nice species, she thought. Why do men and women entrust themselves so passionately to each other when they have such a limitless capacity to wound? Do I know any couple who are happy together? Well, yes, my parents, after their stormy past; and Dick's parents come to that. Some folk seem to scull through life's deeps and shallows, white waters and meanders, and come to sheltered mill-ponds of contentment at last. It's always lovely to see an elderly couple walking out together hand-in-hand. Who knows what they have been through to get there? But my immediate friends! Alex and Rachel seemed to be the exceptions to the rule that so many men were shits and so many women sublimated their disappointment – with a horse, or some other comforter.

And that's what I'll do, Megan determined. Somehow. It's possible to find novel ways, maybe to share the care and the riding, as well as the livery costs. Then she drew herself up sharply. How one's mind wandered. Her thoughts were straying to her own concerns when she should be thinking with compassion about Alex. In his case, it was the woman who had been selfish and brutal. Megan wondered if she had responded adequately to his cry for help. She promised herself she would follow up, to make sure he was aware of her support.

***

The next day – a Friday – unrolled into a beautiful April evening and Megan drove herself, her boys, and Jackie over to Duncanshill Estate, in the west country towards Glasgow. It was a drive of about an hour-and-a-half in the rush-hour traffic – part motorway and convoluted urban rabbit-warren, then out into the countryside. Jackie had the map on her lap and gave directions.

"Have you ever been to a cross-country before?" Jackie asked.

"Oh yes," answered Jeremy airily from the back seat. "We've been to Badminton. Twice!"

"Badminton!" Jackie gasped. She knew that was the Mecca of the eventing world. "You didn't tell me that!"

Megan laughed. "My husband has a genius for turning up at the most fashionable horsey events. Ascot, Kempton, Aintree, the Beaulieu Hunt. You name it. To tell the truth, I was the moving force behind the Badminton trip, and it was amazing – about as far removed from what we do as it's possible to be. I imagine you have to be fabulously wealthy, born to magnificent estates, or brought up with acres of land and access to the finest horses to end up competing there. It was terrific to watch. All the ceremony, the tails and top hats for dressage, the magnificent thoroughbreds, the flunkeys, royalty arriving to present the prizes. To say nothing of the incredible jumps.

"We had become members of the British Horse Society. Dick wanted to rub shoulders with the great and the good, you understand. And sitting in their enclosure, watching the dressage, this young man," still keeping her eyes on the road, Megan indicated Jeremy with a slight movement of her head, "announced in his penetrating voice, 'Daddy, that person's just done a RUBBISH dressage test!' Everyone turned and stared at this knowledgeable infant prodigy! He'd been watching the scores flash up, of course."

Jeremy grinned and looked foolish.

Megan continued, "The jumps are awesome. When you see them when everything's quiet, they look impossibly huge. You wonder how any animal could leap over those with a person on its back. And yet, in action, they make it look so easy; most of the time."

"Well I never," said Jackie. "I think it's you who ought to be doing this, Megan."

They eventually turned off the road, joining with a string of Land Rovers, four-byfours, and other rural vehicles, obviously bent on the same destination and purpose. A gate with a cattle grid stood open, and a relay of passengers indicated to the one behind that the last in line was expected to close it. All the cars were full of adults, children, and dogs.

"Looks like we're going to a gypsy fair!" laughed Megan, as Jeremy jumped out to hold the gate and hand over to a youngster who emerged from the following car.

The dirt-track drive took them to the brow of a hill, and spread before them was the most breathtaking view. Gently sloping hills interweaved and fell away into the distance, partly covered with the fresh green verdure of Springtime and profusions of blossoms, especially on the many horse chestnuts. In the middle distance shone the mildly ruffled waters of a river or lake, coloured violet and pink with the setting sun's reflection. Sheep grazed here and there, and beyond the lake they could pick out a small herd of deer.

"Imagine owning a gorgeous estate like this and letting riff-raff like us stomp about all over it!" joked Megan.

She drove down the hill, where a widening of the track and various branches gave ample parking and turning space. Jackie was relieved, as she was already anticipating manoeuvring her horse trailer the next day – a tricky art she had only part-mastered.

They joined the groups of people in the uniform of waxed coats and green Wellington boots, with their dogs on leads, striding purposefully over the uneven tussocky ground until they found the starting post. Jackie was still calm and cheerful. She had spent hours mastering the course at home, and trying out variations where possible.

"Remind me of all the valuable bits of advice Mandy gave me," she asked Megan. "I should have written it all down. It'll all go screaming out of my head tomorrow in the heat of the moment."

Megan dutifully went through all the gems of wisdom Mandy had offered about steady speed, firm legs, balance, riding at the fence and looking beyond, walking and planning alternative routes…

"You've got a great memory. It really should be you doing this, Megan."

"I'm good at the theory; nowhere near you on the practical side." Megan was amazed at herself for keeping up a constant flow of patter. It served several purposes, she supposed. First it gave Jackie something to keep her mind off her nerves, whose jangling could be triggered by too much thought. Secondly, it kept her from the embarrassing probing to which her friend's conversation usually veered, given half a chance. Thirdly, it kept Megan's own mind from dwelling too much not only on Alex, but on her own personal problems. She saw no solution to either, so her concerns were best kept at bay.

She had been beset by a weird series of dreams the previous night, aware of a swirling, cacophonous upheaval in her subconscious mind. Initially, there had been an impressionistic confusion of sorrows, like something from scary modern art. Then she had been trying to catch a train in some foreign land – a child under each arm and dragging their spilling luggage, in a terrible panic. And lastly – just before waking – she had been alone in a huge house which was coming apart, letting in water, streaking down the walls, doors which would not close, beset by hooligans trying to get in.

They were just dreams. A way of cleansing anxiety from the mind, she rationalised. She gave herself a mental shake and looked over at her two sons, fresh-faced from the novelty and the exercise, seemingly carefree. Her need to protect them was so insistent it was painful. All these things flowed like an underground current in her mind, only glimpsed fleetingly between the multitude of other concerns.

As they talked, they walked from the start position to the first fence. It was very easy and inviting-looking – a low wooden board with green vegetation piled up over the ends, which positively pushed you into jumping the middle.

"I wonder if we'll meet Annabel and Poppy today," said Megan. "We must certainly look out for them tomorrow. Poppy's in a younger age group, so she'll be earlier than you, won't she?"

They picked their way round the course, pausing to discuss and examine. It all seemed welcoming – wide solid jumps, built of timber or brushwood; old tyres, barrels, and other agricultural paraphernalia.

"Presenting the horse right at the fence seems to be the key," mused Jackie. "Getting the line right. So far, height is not the issue at all."

The track took them into a woodland area, and round the corner, quite suddenly, there was a quarry. Jackie stopped, her jaw dropping in horror. It looked as if you were walking to the edge of an abyss. Then down below were three wide steps to drop, after which the track fell away for two or three strides, then turned uphill.

"No! There's no way I'm doing that," she said, eyes dark with panic. "My God, he'd never stop. Just think how that drop would look when you're sitting up on the back of a horse, peering down!"

"No, hang on," said Megan. "I think this is a rider-frightener. I really do. I think you'll find Piper doesn't turn a hair. The thing is, even if he goes fast down that bit beyond the steps, the upward turn will have its own braking effect. You obviously trot before the drop, and the corner back there will be a good chance, and a good reminder, to do that. I know from being carted off by a horse how good a brake a steep upward hill is." Megan thought back to her experience on runaway Lucinda the previous Christmas.

Eventually, Jackie was persuaded. "Anyway, you can always bale out when you get here, if you must," said Megan. "You know you can't chuck in the towel altogether." She reckoned that if Jackie got this far, her blood would be up and she would certainly give it a go.

The water-jump was just halfway round, after which the course turned back for home.

"Is that all there is to it?" Jeremy asked snootily. "You should see the one at Badminton."

"All you have to do here is drop into the little pond, one stride and out again," added Sam.

"All very well for you," Megan reproved them. "Plenty horses just freak out at water. Half the battle is to get them to cross it at all."

"From here," observed Jackie, "it's full speed for home. We'll probably go up a gear or two." They found a nicely measured coffin, just like the one back at Hadley. "He'll pop that easily enough." Just before the end, there was also a ski fence in which the landing side was a good bit lower than the take-off. Jackie showed signs of turning to jelly again.

"Look," said Megan. "If you get this far, you'll be so thrilled you'll not think twice about this one. Just point him at it and close your eyes!"

And the last jump was a solid couple of bars with a roof high over it, called the gallows fence. "How cheery," said Jeremy. "Where's the graveyard?"

They sat on the grass next to the car and discussed the various jumps as they tucked into the picnic Mel had organised. When they'd finished and cleared up, Megan made the boys promise not to stray while she and Jackie briskly walked round the course one more time. Then they all piled into the car and set off for home.

Chapter 24

Duncanshill Estate, the following morning, was scarcely recognizable; it was a veritable hive of activity. Much of the available space at the sides of the tracks had been taken up by horse boxes, four-wheel drive vehicles, and trailers. Horses of all shapes, colours, breeds, and sizes, were either tethered to their vehicles, munching on hay nets, or being walked around clad in rugs, ridden to and from the course, or being tacked up by a nervous competitor. There were hairy native ponies, chunky cobs, fine slender classy ponies, huge, bony, man-sized horses, sleek Arabs, and elegant thoroughbreds.

Each animal seemed to have a personal team of humans in attendance. One or two competitors – mostly women – had come on their own, competently and quietly managing a biddable animal. But mostly it was a family affair. Riders, in their bright, electric-coloured shirts and hat covers, stood out among the helpers in green wellies, quilted or waxed jackets in muted country colours, and holding Labradors on leads. Excitement was in the air as groups of friends chattered like starlings, clutched each other, and shrieked with hysterical merriment. A rather primitive tannoy system crackled in the background and projected information in a strident voice about riders on the course, pleas to competitors who had not arrived at the appointed starting times, and reminders to keep dogs on the leash and not lock them in cars. Periodically there would be bellows of "loose horse" spreading like a chain reaction, after some mishap had parted horse and rider.

Annabel, Poppy, and Suleiman Shah had arrived very early, giving themselves plenty of time to park, unload and tack up, remove Poppy's outer garments and don her smartly polished boots, body protector, shiny, silky, matching yellow shirt and helmet cover. The youngster slid her bib, with her number on front and back, over her head and tied it round her waist then mounted Solly and took him for a brisk walk around the perimeter of the lake.

It was good not to have to rush; a relief to have dry weather. They'd already walked the course, so Annabel knew that Poppy was happy and that Solly was coping with the party atmosphere extremely well and wasn't too hyped up. Poppy rode so well. She had good seat and excellent posture; the only problem was that she was sprouting so fast her legs already looked miles too long on him. Luckily she was slim and light as a feather. But she'd grow out of the horse within months, that much was sure. What a pity. Still, he was always meant to be a stop-gap.

I wonder if Megan might like to buy him? Annabel mused, thinking ahead. Megan was petite enough, he'd be a super ride for her. The more she thought of that plan, the more she liked it. It could be a partnership of years, decades even. He would bring Megan's boys on, too. And she felt she owed her friend, for taking her in hand when she was in despair, and helping to turn her life around.

Poppy walked back to base. In another ten minutes or so they would make their way over towards the start box.

"I wouldn't dismount," said Annabel, surprised to see Poppy slither off Solly's back. "It's nearly time to start."

"I must go spend a penny," muttered her daughter. "Sorry, Mum, it's my nerves. I'll have to find a tree, there don't seem to be any bogs."

"Well, buck up. You'll have to dash a fair distance to get away from the crowds."

Poppy duly dashed, while Annabel held the pony and watched anxiously, fretting and looking at her watch. Eventually her daughter reappeared and nimbly remounted.

"Do you know who I saw?" she asked.

"Jackie and Megan? Good, I've been looking out for them."

"No. It was Megan's husband, Richard Fraser. I'm sure it was him; I've seen him on the box often enough. He's such a show-off, with his sexy charm and his loud voice." They chatted as they made their way up the grassy slopes to the starting area.

"Maybe he's come with Megan, although I thought she said he was to be away in London."

"Well, I didn't see Mrs Fraser or the boys. And he's with another crowd, all fussing over a horse that definitely wasn't Piper."

Annabel raised her eyebrows; she had heard the rumours about Dick. She hadn't explored the subject with her friend, but maybe the couple had a mutually agreed open marriage. Megan was broad-minded; and not everyone liked to parade eccentric morals even if they held them.

Annabel had other things on her mind right now, giving Poppy last minute reminders.

"Don't go like the clappers. Remember it's your first try. The optimum time is neither too fast nor too slow, so just go at a pace you can manage. Watch your approaches. The essential is to get round clear." Poppy had gone quiet and Annabel knew this was one way of coping with those horrendous, last minute nerves. She remembered only too well how the wait seemed to concertina into those interminable seconds before the off; agonising units of frozen time that seemed never to advance. She also knew that Poppy's nerves would evaporate with the first stride.

There was a short queue of entrants ahead. An official checked tack and clothing, ticked off Poppy's name, and explained about starting and timing. Then they were in the box, and the starting steward shouted, "Go! Good luck!"

Annabel watched, her stomach churning as the pair streaked off, heading straight and true for the first fence. Then she set off at a trot into the countryside at the centre of the loop, where she knew she could follow progress at most of the jumps.

Poppy was sailing over the obstacles, covering the ground, already heading for the fourth, through a gate where she would have to turn sharply and straighten quickly to get only two or three strides before the woodpile; no problem to this agile little horse as long as his jockey didn't mess up. She didn't. Annabel had to scamper to keep up. She climbed a little hill, where she could see the pair intermittently and watch as they turned the corner into the quarry. A couple of first-aiders were visible on the corner. Hope that doesn't put her off, Annabel thought.

There were some anxious moments as she waited for her daughter to appear out of the woods and head for the water-jump. Solly leapt in as if he adored water, and out again without putting an extra stride in, a bounce, an incredible leap. Poppy's steering would be put to the test now, but she seemed to be in charge, taking all the short routes with lovely accurate riding. The tricky ones – the coffin, the ski-jump – Solly made them look so easy, finally galloping up to the gallows and sailing over in superb style.

Annabel hugged herself, so proud of them both. She saw the official photographer catching the image of the pair over the last fence, before she ran to greet and praise them both. Poppy was elated, panting, glowing, ecstatic, hugging first Solly, then her mother. Just five minutes before, so tense – and now so joyful. This was what life should be all about!

Poppy dismounted and they walked happily back to base, analysing the course and the jumps. "You were very fast," Annabel said. "Might get penalised if it was under the optimum time limit."

"It just felt right for him. It was so easy, well within his capability. He was brilliant at the quarry. Gosh, I did love that, Mum. It was amazing! When can I do another?"

They untacked Solly and put his sweat rug back on. Poppy opened a bottle of Coke and took great gulps to quench her thirst, then took her horse a little walk in hand to cool him off a bit. Annabel stacked the saddle and bridle in the boot, gathered the muddy leg bandages into a bag, and began to look out the picnic basket and coffee flask.

A car and trailer drew up beside her. When she heard her name called, she turned to greet Jackie and Megan who had just arrived, as the adult classes were later.

Delighted to hear Poppy had successfully tackled the course, Jackie wished it was all over for her, too. "Oh my God, how lucky you are!" she said morosely. "It's like a damn great river in spate that I have to cross, and there you are waving from the other side!"

"It rode like a dream," Annabel said encouragingly. "Seriously, you'll enjoy it. Piper will sail over everything. No nasty or serious questions."

"Hmm. We'll see," replied Jackie fatalistically. "But I'll give it a go. Whether I finish is another matter."

Annabel watched them slowly roll down the hill to park near the lake. Thankfully, the usual nightmare of turning and parking your trailer was simplified by the super circular track round the lake.

Turning back to her own car, she suddenly remembered what Poppy had said earlier about seeing Dick. Had she been mistaken? Dick was indeed flamboyant; Poppy's description had been all too accurate. Annabel had met him on a few social occasions, and he had even tried to flirt with her.

Strangely, Megan rarely spoke about her marriage; she didn't even talk much about Dick. Most women married to a TV personality would be name-dropping the whole

time, "Dick says this, or thinks that; according to Dick..."
But not Megan. Annabel had assumed that this was
evidence of the strength of the relationship. But maybe it
indicated something else.

She sat on a canvas chair in the delicious Spring
sunshine, eyes closed, dozing, feeling so contented with
her own life that someone else's problems seemed remote
and irrelevant.

Hearing crunching on the gravelly track, a footstep
with some urgency in it, she opened her eyes to find Jackie
hastening towards her, looking haggard with stress.

"Annabel! You'll never guess. Megan's husband is
here! Just round the corner, look – you can see through
the trees, that big blue horse box. And she doesn't know. I
thought I'd have a heart attack when I saw him, just yards
away as we drove past. Luckily, she was looking the other
way, she didn't see him. Do you suppose he's with that Sue
woman?"

Annabel stood up and peered through the trees where
Jackie indicated. "Good God, it *is* him. And that's Sue.
That's definitely her. They seem to be with a crowd."

"You know her, do you? My God, Annabel, what are
we going to do? Megan could just walk into him. We're
parked right over there on the left, round the lake. But it's
not that far and she's going to have to walk this way to the
course."

"Are you absolutely certain she doesn't know he's
here?"

"I'm positive. She said he was in London, and would
get back tonight. What a bloody swine the man is. Oh
God, I've got to go and get ready, and I'm already a bag of

nerves. Do you think you could… maybe go and tell him to piss off? It's no solution, but at least it would save face for poor Megan."

Annabel was not usually one to interfere, but maybe this was different. She gave Jackie a brief hug, turned her round, and pushed her gently away.

"Yes, of course. You go and get yourself ready. Where are you parked? Ah, yes, I can see. Go on, off you go. I'll go and confront the bastard. I don't mind embarrassing him! Hopefully he'll scarper pretty smartly."

"Bless you. Give him what-for," croaked Jackie, as she rushed away.

"Forget him, just think about your ride. And good luck, enjoy!"

Annabel looked around for her daughter. Nowhere in sight. She was probably letting Solly munch on some grass. She gave her head a little toss, straightened her tweed jacket and smoothed her hip-hugging jeans, then set off down the track to the right. She could see Dick and Sue chatting, a little removed from the activity of their group of friends. They certainly didn't seem to be helping much. They were laughing, joking and teasing with easy, playful, physical contact, in that intimate, flirtatious manner that bespoke mutual self-absorption. Annabel consciously carried herself very erect, and put on a sardonic smile as she rounded the curve in the drive. Oh brother, Dick Fraser, are you going to get a surprise.

He and Sue were so close, they were on the point of canoodling as Annabel sauntered in her best catwalk manner towards them. When she was a few yards away, Dick saw her out of the corner of his eye and looked up sharply, pulling away from his companion. Sue glanced at Annabel then turned away. The classic response to being caught-in-the-act from both of them.

Annabel stopped and raised her eyebrows, leaving her unspoken question hang in the air and in her feigned posture of surprise. Dick recovered quickly, smiled broadly, and greeted her far too heartily.

"Hello, Annabel… Didn't expect to see you! Are you competing?"

"No, it's my daughter's turn today. She's already done her round." She waited. Let him hang himself.

"How did she go? Oh, er, this is Sue Maxwell."

"Yes, I know," Annabel said curtly, with a brief glance of supremely royal disdain at Sue, who barely turned to receive it.

"Are you here with Megan?" The arched eyebrows went higher still.

"No," he said genially, still smiling. "She had something else on. Another… event…"

She looked him squarely in the eyes where, deliciously, realisation and panic were burgeoning.

"Oh no, Dick. How strange you didn't know!" Annabel gave a tinkly laugh. "Megan's here. I've just seen her, in fact. She's come to help one of the girls from Hadley stable. Look, I can show you." And, bending to point across the lake under the canopy of trees, she started to give a detailed explanation as to where Megan was encamped.

"Did you really not know?" And she gave a peel of genteel, mocking laughter. "How very odd!"

Dick looked positively grey, she was pleased to observe. Annabel was enjoying herself. "Would you like me to take you over? Both of you? Do come. Just think how surprised she'll be."

Dick's smile and pretence had sagged. Sue had moved away a little. He looked venomously at Annabel. "No, that won't be necessary. If you'll excuse us, we should be helping…"

Annabel extinguished her smile, too. She went up close to Dick, her expression intense, her affected manner dropped. She hissed, "Understand this, Mr Dick Fraser. I'm not the least bit interested in saving you embarrassment. Megan's friends are anxious to spare her the humiliation of stumbling across you with your hands all over your fancy woman. So I suggest you get the hell out of here. I suppose you know the press covers this event?"

The last sally, which she had made up on the spur of the moment, was probably lost on him, as he turned from her abruptly and stalked away.

***

Sue's sister and friends, under the pretence of busying themselves about the horse, were all surreptitious ears and eyes. When Dick left Annabel, his face was pale with fury. He stalked after Sue, grabbed her unceremoniously and roughly by the wrist, and pulled her away. He jerked his head to indicate she should follow him down the track, away from the lake and the hub of activity. As she followed, unresisting, he dropped her arm.

"I'm sorry, Sue, I'll have to go. I can't possibly hang around if my wife's here."

"I don't see that at all," argued Sue indignantly. "We've only just arrived. You can hide behind the lorry if she comes this way. Anyway, there's no reason why she should."

"Don't be stupid," he said testily. "I'm not going to spend the afternoon hiding and being furtive. I never dreamed she and her friends would be at the same event as you and your sister. Didn't even cross my mind. Look I'll have to be off. Really sorry about this."

"You mean you're just going to blow? What about me? How am I supposed to get home?"

"Well, you'll want to stay and watch your sister, won't you? You'll get someone to give you a lift. I can't take you with me. We can't be seen together. If I fall over Megan as I leave, I can say I came looking for her or something. I can hardly do that if you're sitting in the car beside me."

"You're bloody scared stiff of your wife, Dick. How manly is that? Running away with your tail between your legs. And abandoning me! Get a lift? For fuck's sake! It's sixty sodding miles!"

"Well, you'll have to cope, I'm sorry. There's always public transport." Dick turned and began to stomp back to his car parked beside the horse lorry.

She yelled after him, "It's the country. The middle of nowhere, you clown!"

Sue was beside herself with rage. Her day spoilt, her street-cred – which had been astronomical, arriving with this star in tow – shattered. How in God's name was she to get back to where she had parked in the genteel end of town near where Dick and Megan lived? She strode after him, radiating wrath. He was clambering into the driving seat, almost slamming the door in her face. She grabbed the handle and yanked it open.

Never at her wisest when she lost her temper, she snarled, "If you go now, Dick, you walk out of my life for good. Don't fucking bother to come back. I've had it up to here with you, you spineless dork." She'd meant to simply deliver an ultimatum, but she'd ruined it with her insults.

"Suits me," he said, starting the engine and beginning to roll forward so that she had to let go the door. He slammed it again, and with his hallmark skidding of tyres and spray of gravel, sped noisily away. As Sue gaped after the disappearing car, she remembered she'd left her bag with her money and keys in it on the passenger seat.

***

Quite a few heads turned, shocked and disapproving, at the hastily retreating car with its engine roaring – a flashy Jaguar going far too fast on the narrow track, with all these animals and children around! Annabel saw him go with relief. But it was only a temporary reprieve for poor Megan, she knew.

Poppy wanted to wait for her result, which would take at least an hour. The runners – kids from the local pony club – ran round the fence judges, collecting up the lists of results more or less continuously. Then the stewards had to collate the start and finish times for each horse and rider pair. It all took time.

Mother and daughter relaxed and enjoyed their picnic, watching the world go by. When Jackie came by on Piper with Megan in attendance, Annabel gave a discrete thumbs up to Jackie, and a wink, which could easily have meant, "Go for it, girl!" Leaving Poppy in charge of Solly, trailer and car, Annabel went along to watch Jackie and Piper perform.

***

Hours later, as Megan drove from Hadley to collect her sons, she felt completely exhausted. Thank heaven it was Sunday tomorrow. Horses were harder work than children, she thought. But perhaps the stress had come from Jackie, coping with her terror, keeping her calm enough to be rational. What a strange contradictory person the woman was, for sure. In some ways so tough and brave, in others so frail.

Jackie had completed the course, though with a cricket score of penalties. She'd almost been eliminated at fence three – a little wall built at right angles to a gentle slope, so that one end was much lower than the other. Forgetting her instruction to go for the middle of the fence, she had tried the low end, only to discover that Piper thought it logical to run out to the side. Perplexed, she put him at it again, with the same result. Three refusals would be elimination, and Megan's heart had been in her mouth. But then Jackie had remembered, and booted him firmly at the middle.

She didn't make that error again. She had taken it slowly, even being overtaken by the following competitor; but she had been safe. To her amazement, she'd even coped well with the quarry. After the water, Piper got really strong so that they missed a fence and had to go back to it.

Jackie said later that he felt a completely different animal on the way home. He'd surged forward with a sense of going places, and they'd eaten up the fences, even the terrifying ski jump and the mighty gallows. Megan had listened to her detailed account on the drive back, and stored it all away for the future.

Chapter 25

After a day of over-stimulation and over-indulgence with their grandparents, Jeremy and Sam were fractious and a little difficult when Megan collected them that evening. Jeremy, in particular, was keen to take her to task for not letting them go along to watch the event.

"It was a really long day," she reasoned. "If you'd got tired or bored, I wouldn't have been able to abandon Jackie to take you home. I really needed to concentrate on her."

"We'd have been in the way, you mean," Jeremy said sulkily.

"That would have been up to you. I didn't realise you were so keen to come."

"I'd love to jump round a course like that one day. It's all so exciting. If I don't watch others doing it, how will I learn? I think I'd like to be a jump-jockey when I grow up. Anyway, how did Solly and Piper got on?"

"Solly was fifth in his class; a terrific result. Ideal, in fact. Annabel didn't want Poppy to be first, because too many wins and you have to move up too quickly to the more advanced classes. And Jackie bravely managed to get round, but with lots of penalties."

They wanted a blow-by-blow account, and practically remembered the sequence of all the fences. "Will we ever get a horse of our own, Mum?" asked Sam, sucking his thumb. He'd mostly grown out of this habit, but it recurred at moments of stress or tiredness. Then he would suddenly remember and pull it out sharply with a noise like a cork being pulled from a bottle.

Megan was pleased at their enthusiasm, but gave them a little pep talk about the commitment and hard work of looking after a horse. With the Easter holidays coming up, Mandy's "Own a Pony for the Day" classes would soon be starting. She thought it might test their yearning for the whole horse experience, but wondered if they would find it too much like hard work. They were, however, wildly enthusiastic.

"You'll be fine at Hadley with Lady Mandy," said Megan. "I wouldn't trust you to Mrs Stark. She'd probably sell you off as slaves to some horse dealer."

As they pulled up in the drive, they saw Dick's car. The house, however, was quiet when they went in, which usually meant he was in his study. Megan put her head round his door, saw he was on the phone – looking ill at ease at her interruption – so waved and quickly withdrew. Later, when he came to greet them all, he seemed subdued. Megan guessed something was amiss and sensed trouble, but they were all tired from their various activities, so she pressed on with preparing their meal and easing the boys up to bed.

Afterwards, she sat down with a book, but kept dozing off. Dick had disappeared again to his study and didn't appear until just after ten when Megan was about to head up to bed.

As he sat down beside her, looking grim, Megan knew something unpleasant was coming.

"Darling. I've got something very serious to discuss." Pausing for effect, and to gain full attention, he perched on the edge of the chair and looked at her searchingly. "This past week, doing this new series down in London, it's been made very clear to me that if my career is to progress, I need to be there more. I really need to be based there. Everywhere outside London is seen to be provincial; silly, I know, but I have to go with the flow. I can't see any other alternative, we'll have to up sticks and live in London." He fixed her with his steely grey gaze.

They'd had this discussion many times before, but he had never been so dictatorial. Previously, he had graciously given in to the family's needs, as well as the wish to be close to both sets of grandparents. Now he was speaking as though her job, the boys' schooling, everything was deemed to be a minor matter and that they would easily adapt to change. His career, it appeared, was the lynchpin on which everything else turned.

"You'll find a job. Heavens, there are plenty of hospitals down there to be managed. There are hundreds of hospital manager positions, you know. But there's only one Richard Fraser," he smiled self indulgently. "We'll need to discuss where we want to live, but I've got a few possibles in mind. Then we can look at schools and so on."

"You're talking as if it's agreed, cut and dried."

"My love, it has to be. There isn't any room for discussion. Look, I hate seeing so little of you and the boys. I worry about what it will do to us in the long term. It doesn't help with you being at work and always at that stable."

Megan looked at him in amazement. Was he serious? "Those aren't the reasons we don't see much of each other, Dick, as you very well know. Look, I'm so tired I can hardly muster the energy to go upstairs. Let's leave the topic till the morning. We can think about it then, with my brain properly awake."

"Well, I want you to realise that there isn't going to be any discussion. I don't want to twist arms or anything. But in my world, you either go forward and up, or you vanish without trace. And I've no intention of doing that. I shall live in London and I hope very much that you will see your way to coming and living with me."

Again, she looked at him in total astonishment. Was this her husband speaking? Or had his body been taken over by an alien?

"I can't cope with such heavy things right now, Dick. I'm away to bed." Megan felt giddy. Was this a ham-fisted attempt at getting his own way? He could not be working towards a separation, could he? What exactly was going on in his mind? God alone knew.

***

Expecting to lie awake troubled, Megan's day in the open air worked its own magic and she dropped off in seconds, unaware even of Dick settling down beside her. But she woke early – about six-thirty – and immediately the London problem was foremost in her mind.

Her baseline was that she and the boys would stay put. The boys were happy at their primary school, and if they were to stay in the State system – their original intention, as both she and Dick leaned leftward in their politics – the local secondary school was highly regarded and suitable. Her own job was a real plum, and she was extremely settled and contented. There was an excellent working atmosphere and she was building her own reputation, whereas the London hospital scene was tribal – even for the managerial class – and difficult to penetrate.

Dick seemed to think simply being his wife would open doors for her but she knew things didn't work like that. His world was a different planet, another solar system altogether. Then there were family connections. They relied enormously on both sets of grandparents, of course, but she felt viscerally that it was so beneficial for the children to regularly mingle in an extended family. And, of course, it was good for the older generation, too. Should Dick's needs be allowed to break up this idyllic arrangement?

But then, what if she and Dick broke up? The whole network would unravel. They were the epicentre of the family. Was she being selfish, too? Obstructive? Stuck in a rut? What would the children think? Dick had delivered an ultimatum in objectionably autocratic terms, but what if this was code-speak for "Help me, I'm lonely, I'm desperate. Listen to me, please!" She liked to think she was emancipated, but she knew that you had to be a little pliant to allow for the inflexible yet vulnerable male ego.

One thing was clear: she must not draw battle lines. She must do him the favour of listening to his case, and not getting in a fury because of his tactics. Maybe he had been aware of Sue's siren call and his own vulnerability to temptation, and this was his way of trying to protect them all from such dangers in the future.

Dick was still sound asleep when she eventually slipped gently out of bed, put on her robe, and padded downstairs. It was a beautiful morning. No sound yet from the boys' room. She put on the kettle, meaning to make some tea, then go and wander round the garden amid the glorious colours of flowering shrubs, bursting buds, fresh green leaves, the smell of the earth and the ecstatic bird-song. These would put her in a rational frame of mind.

Waiting for the kettle to boil, she took out her feelings for Dick and gave them a close looking-over. She loved him, always would. She knew his faults, of course, and was alive to the tarnishing her love-image of him had received in recent weeks. Yet he and she were inextricably bound. She didn't believe he meant to move out, as he had said. It was no more than manipulation. How many times had he said to her that he loved her to distraction, that she was the best thing that had ever happened to him? He often bought her flowers and well-chosen presents to prove it.

The ring of the front doorbell abruptly interrupted her thoughts. Who could it be at seven-thirty on a Sunday morning? Megan went to the intercom system in the hall – installed more as a way of dealing with press intrusion than for safety reasons – and lifted the receiver, which turned on the screen. Standing outside was a young man holding his ear to the speaker; so close he appeared distorted. Further away she could see a figure holding what looked like a camera.

"Hello? Who's this?"

"Good morning. Mrs Fraser?"

"Yes. Who is it?"

"It's Bob Tooby, of the *Sunday Scrutineer*, Mrs Fraser. Sorry to trouble you so early. I wondered if you'd seen the *Scrutineer* this morning?"

"No. Why do you ask?"

"There's something in it that might be of interest to you."

"Oh? What about?"

"It's about your husband. Do you know where he was yesterday?"

"Just tell me your business and go away. This is intrusive and unwelcome."

"Well, I'm sorry about this. If you would come to the door, I could show you the paper."

"I'll do no such thing."

"Did you know your husband was seeing a lady called... Sue Maxwell?"

"Please don't try to question me. I have no comment to make. Goodbye."

Megan put down the receiver. My God, what now? Had Dick lied again and deceived her more outrageously than she had ever believed possible? As she stood there, a paper rattled through the letterbox and landed on top of their usual Sunday broadsheet, already lying on the mat. She paused before switching on the screen again to see if the two were moving away; they were hanging about in the courtyard in front. She switched it off and went to pick up the paper.

On the front page was a large picture of a rural scene with two figures, unmistakably Dick and Sue. They were not touching, but the body language was explicit. A child could see they were coquetting and leading each other on. The familiarity of the scenery tapped at Megan's stunned memory.

Looking at the caption, she double-read the line, convinced she must be mistaken. Duncanshill! Yesterday! There must be some mistake. *More pictures inside*, it said. Shaking and scrabbling, she took the paper to the kitchen table and found the rest of the article. One picture of the pair – from a different angle – showed the lake in the background, and them so close together they looked about to embrace. The second showed a slim, dark woman facing them with a mock gesture of surprise, a brilliantly captured shot of the discovery and guilty parting of the couple. Then another showed Dick and Sue facing each other with angry faces and arms akimbo. And finally, the parting shot of Dick's car speeding off leaving an enraged Sue in its wake.

Megan looked closely. Annabel! The slim, dark woman was Annabel! Dizzy with incomprehension, wondering what the devil it was all about, Megan tried to steady herself. As people do when they have received a terrible shock, she resorted to the mundane. She made herself a mug of tea. Then she returned to the paper, sat down, and tried to read in a coherent manner.

It required several readings, accompanied by soft moans and head-clutching, but she picked up the threads. Dick had been rumoured to be involved in a romantic liaison with Sue for some months. Several unnamed witnesses at Brockhollow Farm, Leatherburn stable, and the Pie and Pint pub nearby, had observed their togetherness; there was a general understanding that the two were an item. They had both denied such a thing when challenged. Mention of Sue's pregnancy was made, with the innuendo that this was Dick's baby, although this part was carefully worded and ambiguous.

Then the whole story of yesterday was detailed. How they had arrived together and joined the party of a competitor. They had drunk some whisky in plastic cups and seemed very jolly and affectionate. Until the dark lady appeared. The reporter had not identified her. Then the stark change in mood had been dramatic, and the pictures told the story of a tempestuous parting.

Megan realized that Annabel must have stumbled across the pair and told them that his wife was only a few hundred yards away. And he had done a bunk. How humiliating! Everyone seeing her husband in company with this siren, this vixen; and out of pity, her friends trying to stop her from finding out.

Megan moved on auto-pilot, preparing another cup of tea, climbing the stairs, then sitting down heavily on the bed beside her husband, who was now awake.

"Oh thanks," he said, as she put down the tea.

As he drank it, presumably assuming her sombre, silent mood was due to their previous night's conversation, Megan tried hard to control her voice.

"Dick, this sudden decision to live in London. When did you come to that conclusion?"

"Last week, really, when I was down there. Though, as you know, I've been thinking about it for long enough."

"What brought matters to a head?"

"Oh, missing you all so much. The boys growing up, and me not being there. So much travelling. Missing out on your weekend activities."

Megan said quietly, "Well, you could have come with me yesterday. The boys could have come then, too, instead of going to their granny's."

Dick replied impatiently, "Now don't nag. I had to stay down in London yesterday to finish everything off. Lots of pressure just now. You know I always come home as soon as I can."

Megan looked at him for a few minutes before speaking, her tone one of sadness rather than anger or accusation, and placed the paper – front page up – on his lap. "I'm afraid, dear, you've got some explaining to do."

***

That Sunday, the story and pictures in the *Scutineer* caused widespread consternation. Many people in the horse world are too busy for current affairs and reading newspapers, but the news still spread rapidly around the bush telegraph. Sue was treated to the same treatment as Megan, from another lowly journalist working his novitiate in door-stepping. And when she saw the pictures, she knew the game was up for her. In no very sweet temper with Dick after the terrible time she'd had yesterday, she now saw him as the blackest of cold-hearted villains.

She had tried to borrow money to get home the previous day, but neither her sister nor anyone else in her entourage had more than small change. In the end, she had been forced to wait until her sister had finished her competition, then go back to her house and phone Mike from there. He had not been pleased to have his afternoon of sloth in front of the football on the box disrupted by a three hour drive to come and collect her. She had lied to him about her handbag being stolen, then had to change her story when he made a fuss about reporting it to the police. She'd also had to explain why her car was parked in the middle of town. He must have smelled a rat; her story was so shot full of holes.

Sod Dick, he's not worth all this deception, she'd told herself. He doesn't give a toss for me or anyone except himself.

And now, here it all was on the front page of the gutter press. Sue supposed that the official event photographer had recognised Dick and sold the pictures to a colleague. Or maybe he was actually employed at the *Scrutineer*. That was more than probable. Rosemary upstairs took the *Scrutineer*, she would know all about it by now.

Sue, ever courageous, decided to face the music. She took the paper in to Mike, and confessed it all. She had half assumed he knew what was going on, but his reaction was so extreme that it was clear she had been mistaken. He sobbed and screamed, shook with anguish, uttering the most horrible threats to Dick, shaking his fist in his rival's imagined face and acting in so demented a manner that Sue feared for her safety and his sanity. His oaths were so violent that Rosemary came to rescue Shelley from the mayhem.

Sue tried to soothe and calm him, and intermittently succeeded before he would explode again. She had never seen anything like it before, and was terrified at the immensity of his wrath and the extremity of his sorrow.

Eventually, she called her doctor, who came and gave the now distraught and exhausted Mike a sedative.

She had managed to speak briefly to Dick on the phone the previous night and arranged to meet him to collect her handbag, but that was not going to be possible now. She couldn't leave Mike, and no doubt the press would be watching them to get more stories.

Eventually Mike fell into a troubled sleep, leaving her thinking bitterly about how payment for her little fling was being exacted with compound interest. God knew how Rosemary would react. They'd probably be given notice to quit.

***

Jackie was up and about early, planning to take Piper out for a short gentle ambling hack, then have a relaxing day. Her husband – always a light sleeper – was up, too. Bill went to pick up the paper and perused it.

"Have you seen this?" he asked, waving the front page at her. "Isn't this where you were yesterday?"

Jackie snatched it from him. "Oh my God! My God! No! Oh poor Megan! What will she do? Oh Bill… look, this is what we were trying to prevent. I was telling you all about it, him appearing and her being there."

She had related the whole saga last night, conscious that he was barely listening, not taking it seriously, not realising it was front-page dynamite.

"What on earth should I do, Bill?" She gazed at him in distress, tears welling up.

"Silly woman, you can't do anything. It's nothing to do with you. Let these flashy folks sort out their own affairs."

"But she's my friend! I wonder how the paper got hold of it. Maybe I should phone Annabel. Look, that's her, she went and warned him and he cleared off sharpish."

"Leave well alone. You can't do any good, that's for sure. Just mind your business and let them mind theirs."

Still upset, Jackie sped off to Hadley, taking the paper with her in case Mandy hadn't seen it. They were deep in earnest discussion in the house when they saw Annabel and Poppy come into the yard. Jackie waved frantically through the window, then went to the door and called Annabel to come in.

She had not seen the paper. But as they were leaving home, they had been stopped by a journalist who had asked her some very strange questions. Annabel was appalled, as most people are, to see herself in the paper.

"They obviously didn't know who I was at the time this went to print," she said. "How did they find out my address?" Then she remembered the official photographer taking pictures of all the competitors at the last fence.

"That was just up on the hill above where they were parked. He must have recognised Dick and seen a chance to make a scoop," Jackie suggested.

"That's right," said Annabel, realising the photographer would have a list of names and numbers, and would have seen her with Poppy and Solly. He might even have known her from previous events. "I wonder if poor Megan has the press camped on her doorstep."

"This is crunch time for her, isn't it?" said Jackie sombrely. "Aren't men total shits and bastards?"

Chapter 26

Bridget Stark pored over the photographs in her *Sunday Scrutineer*, bitterly regretting that they hadn't been the ones to break the story. She knew Ned had tried to interest a reporter, but his innuendoes and attempts to make an anonymous deal over the phone had only planted suspicions about the parties concerned without getting anything out of the journalist in return. She wished now she had seized the initiative. Ned never did have a head for business; that was her department. Ned might be a guru when it came to horseflesh and dogs, but striking a bargain? Forget it. Too surly and impatient by half. He still lived in his past, suspicious of authority and as shy of officialdom as a wild animal. He never could quite realise that he was now affluent and respectable, a home-owner, a success story.

Only interested in gossip if it could serve her own purpose, Bridget pondered how the news story would affect Leatherburn, which was named in the paper as the place where Sue worked and where she had met Dick Fraser. It was unlikely to put off customers; rather the reverse. Ghoulish people would come just to gawp and be where it had all happened. The association of her stable with a name like Dick Fraser could only be beneficial. What was the phrase? No publicity is bad publicity.

She glanced out of the window into the yard, her attention caught by a knot of people huddled together in a state of visible tension. There was a fellow with a notebook and, yes, another with a camera. Instantly fiercely possessive over her yard and all that happened in it, she gave a little squawk of outrage and rushed outside. As she appeared, the group of Sunday clients fell back and the two journalists looked hungrily towards her. She stalked towards the group – an untidy, skinny, shabbily-dressed woman, strangely the centre of attention. The clients glanced at each other with covert smiles and stayed within earshot.

"Ah, good morning. Mrs Stark, is it? We're from the *Lothian Times*. Have you seen the story about one of your clients, Dick Fraser?" The question needed no answer, for she was still clutching the *Sunday Scrutineer*.

"How does it feel to be the scandal centre of the horse world?" The reporter laughed, as if to tone down any offence conveyed in his words. But he had misread her downtrodden appearance.

Her eyes blazed. "Scandal centre!" she spat. "Scandal centre! This is a respectable business. We can't be held responsible for what our clients get up to."

The cameraman began quietly and surreptitiously snapping away, while the onlookers hung on, electrified.

"Staff as well as clients, isn't it? Sue Maxwell works here, doesn't she?"

"Part time only. But I can tell you, young man, that this place is like a convent compared with some other riding centres not too far from here." She nodded and folded her arms defiantly, visited by a wicked little idea.

"What other centres would those be?" asked the reporter softly, his journalistic antennae sensing a story with a capital S.

"How much?" whispered Bridget, bending close, making money-massaging movements with her fingers.

"I can't promise anything until I've got a flavour... should we go somewhere private to discuss this?"

"No. No, I don't think so." Bridget thought quickly, feeling excited and inspired. "Will you print the story if I tell you?"

"Is it something that's not yet appeared in print?" He gestured towards her paper.

"Yes. And it's scandalous. Outrageous. And it concerns Hadley Riding Stable."

"The clientele or staff?"

"No. The owner." Bridget nodded for emphasis. "Lady Miranda Morton-Merrydew. She sets herself up as being so respectable, but she's no better than she should be."

As Bridget got onto her bugbear, her voice rose in volume and shrillness, and the audience edged in, ears flapping. But she wanted them to hear. The reporter affected to look deeply shocked, encouraging her with his attention.

"She's lived all her life on immoral earnings, and she's doing that right now. Lived in brothels after walking out on her husband and kids. Then she moved in with some high heid-yin, a Governor I think, and stole all his money. Now she's got a bidie-in and lives off him. She should be in jail. Everyone knows the money for her property wasn't honestly come by." Bridget was briefly visited by a glimmer of an idea that she was getting herself into dangerous waters. "So don't call *this* the scandal centre. You go and ask her if it isn't all true. What paper did you say you wrote for? *Lothian Times*?"

Bridget knew she had spilled the beans without making a deal. But the thought of destroying Miranda's reputation at a stroke, of spreading the story she had heard from Dick only a few months ago, and with a journalist in attendance, had been too much for her prudence. She took a deep breath, swept them all with a look of fierce defiance, turned on her heel, and walked away. She found she was shaking from head to foot.

***

The press camped on Megan's doorstep in large numbers and stayed for two or three days until the story became stale and was displaced on the front pages by the next scandal. But that was the least of her troubles. How to protect the children, how to tell them about their father's betrayal without undermining their filial affection, how to answer their bewildered questions, how to manage their difficulties at school and other people's casual crassness and insensitivity; those were the things she faced in the coming days. And her own disorientation in finding so cruelly and abruptly that the man to whom she had committed herself and been unfailingly loyal, whose love she had rejoiced in, was not even a carbon copy of the man she imagined; this was tragedy beyond describing.

Her initial, rather passive and gentle sorrow that Sunday morning was soon replaced by contempt and distaste when she saw him with no remaining stock of plausible lies or excuses to cover his naked duplicity. He seemed to shrink and cower in the full glare of her icy scorn.

Megan found she could not even bear him to be near her, and asked him to leave, to go and live somewhere else; his well-favoured London, perhaps. He need not worry about her raising any more objections to him living there. He discovered, to his apparent dismay, that she really did want him out.

"That's all very well," he said petulantly. "But how the devil am I to get out of here without having a trail of journalists on my track, like a hive of disturbed hornets?"

"Just get in your car and drive away!" she said, surprised at his reluctance.

"Oh, come on. They'd just stick like flies till they ran me to earth. Don't be naïve."

In the end, it was left to Megan to solve the problem. She phoned her neighbour – a good friend – and explained the situation, amazed at how cold and clinical she was able to be. The neighbour braved the pack, deflecting questions, was admitted to the house then left with Dick's car key. The pack looked hopeful – cameras poised – each time the door opened, but fell back into inertia when neither Megan nor Dick appeared.

Half an hour later, the neighbour's husband strolled nonchalantly across the courtyard and drove Dick's car away. The car was taken to a cul-de-sac, accessible from the Frasers' house by a garden gate, and fortunately no-one thought to follow. He then came through the garden to the back of the house, handed Megan the key and gave her an encouraging hug with some awkward muttering about help if she needed it, then left.

Dick later slipped out of the family house by the back exit, his tail firmly between his legs. His sons were not even awake, which Megan felt was a mercy. He had briefly looked in on them, innocently asleep, and walked away.

When the boys eventually awoke, she told them that Dad had had a spot of bother with some journalists and needed to go away. With the cameras waiting to pounce at the front of the house, she explained that for the time being they would be better going out the back. Children accept things so trustingly, she thought sadly. Perhaps it was simpler to ease them into a gradual realisation that their father was no longer going to be around. He had been a good dad during the times when he was there for them; when things were eventually sorted out, he would have plentiful access to them.

Megan seemed to have a million things to think about. That evening, she telephoned her General Manager at home to ask for compassionate leave, remembering her own recent advice to Alex.

Presuming Dick would not think to phone his parents, she then took that unpleasant duty upon herself, as well as breaking the news to her own. Her mother sobbed as if her heart would break. "I thought you had such a strong marriage!" she wailed.

Megan thought it highly probable that Mel would not turn up that evening, and worried the nanny might even hand in her notice. But, bless the sturdy, sweet girl, she braved the press pack, ignoring them as she stalked past them, head held high. Then she drove Megan's car round to the cul-de-sac at the back of the house, rather enjoying outwitting the forlorn group of reporters who were unaware of this escape route.

The following morning, Megan took the boys to school by car and waited to see the headmaster. She wanted to warn him that if Jeremy or Sam faced any trouble – bullying or teasing – she would not hesitate to take them out of school. He was quietly understanding and undertook to speak to the various teachers before classes began. Later that day, she collected them from school, too. She didn't want to become over-protective, but was keen to shield them from the worst effects of a family breaking up under public gaze.

Annabel was the first friend to visit, fully aware that Megan's marital disaster had been sweeping in like a tsunami even as she had been acting out her supportive role herself. Immediately she owned up to the subversive, though well-intentioned, interference at Duncanshill.

After the first day or two of frenzied activity, Megan collapsed in grief, and Annabel was there to hold her together and console as best she could. It was a new role for her, and she helped her younger friend through those days when somehow the least little task seemed to take an age to complete, when concentration and planning were beyond reach.

Megan discovered that when she was in company she longed to be alone, and when alone she yearned for someone to talk to. The loneliness yawned like an eternal emptiness, never to be refilled. She learned at first hand the phantom-limb anomaly of pain from something that wasn't there.

Eventually, Annabel persuaded her to come round for supper and they had a few glasses of wine and talked about horses and riding. Ralph was there, too; kind and attentive. Megan was aware of the irony of the exchange in their respective marital fortunes. But she was also amazed at how she could enjoy such a happy little oasis in the midst of the void of her grief.

The most pressing factor that made Megan keep going was the need to keep life as normal as possible for her children. After dropping the boys off at school each morning, she would buy papers at a corner newsagent, keeping an eye open for followers. The Monday's press had picked up on the story at great length, and Annabel – the mystery woman – had been identified and photographed leaving her home and arriving at Megan's.

Brockhollow was featured the next day, and Dick's career given a good going over. Megan's secretary and one or two close colleagues telephoned and reported that a few journalists had been hanging out at the entrance to the hospital. But as the principal actors had all gone to ground, Megan fervently hoped the news would dwindle for lack of material to feed on.

***

That week Lady Mandy received a strange phone call from the *Lothian Times*, from a well-spoken man who announced himself as the Editor-in-Chief. He asked if he could meet her to discuss some extraordinary allegations made against her by a certain Mrs Bridget Stark. He duly came, dressed in a suit and tie, and was taken into her study where they remained for more than an hour. After he had left, she was ensconced there for another hour with Hamish.

"I don't know whether to be elated or devastated," she said, after she had told him the torrent of vitriol Bridget had allegedly poured out. "I'm sure it's libellous. Except that it's maybe near enough the truth to be defensible."

Hamish was incandescent at the very suggestion. "In this day and age! Men and women live together all the time. Is *she* married to that villain she lives with? I bet she isn't. You and I have a business arrangement, from which we both benefit to an equal degree. I am sure it was exactly the same with your previous… situations. That's not living on immoral earnings! What a poisonous shrew she is."

"Well, I certainly did pinch the dinner plates."

"You had a right to them, after all you'd done. But in any case, can she prove it? I think you hold the whip hand, my dear. Look, ring your lawyer and discuss it. What is the *Lothian Times* going to do meantime?"

"They're going to put the story on hold, of course. They don't want to offend me, and – even more – they don't want to offend my son, the current Lord Morton-Merrydew." She thought for a moment, leaning her chin on her hand. "I suppose that I must at least threaten the Starks with an action for libel. Stupid woman. She's trying to damage my business through my reputation, but no-one gives a damn about such things nowadays." All the same, Mandy couldn't deny she was upset.

***

Megan found herself strongly opposed to any suggestion from Dick that she would forgive him and take him back, even when he generously offered to forget the London plan. He phoned every night as he had always done, and tried to insinuate himself back into her favour. He chatted and called her "darling", as if only a minor crisis had been encountered and which, with patience, they could work through. She was surprised at her own resistance, perhaps finally realising that she had habitually looked the other way and ignored the blatant evidence of his skirt-chasing, and that this was no one-off weakness he had fallen into.

When he eventually accepted that she really meant to divorce him, he became mean and nasty and tried to drive a hard bargain. The situation became so stressful that Megan dreaded speaking to him. Thankfully, by this time, Annabel had found her a good divorce lawyer, and she realised that she held all the strong cards. As his position dawned on him, Dick shouted and raged, leaving her no alternative but to put the phone down on him mid-tantrum. Feeling a little fearful of what he might do, she had the locks changed on all the doors, and made a point of telling him so.

After two weeks in which she had only left the house for brief forays to the school and shops, and one to visit her new lawyer, Megan decided she must try to get her life on track and return to work. Mentally, she was still at sixes and sevens, but she hoped that routine would help to sort things out.

Annabel had suggested she return to Hadley, that horses were excellent therapy, but Megan felt she could only cope with one thing at a time. On her first morning back, she arrived at her office early to find an enormous bunch of flowers on her desk – a glorious range of colours, the gentle perfume sweetening the air. She felt a tightening of her throat, and tore open the card. It was from Alex.

Only a few minutes later, as she was arranging the lovely blooms in a vase, there was a tap on the door and Alex himself appeared. He looked slightly ill at ease, but Megan was touched, knowing how difficult men found dealing with such highly-charged emotional situations. She thanked him profusely for the flowers.

Taking both her hands, he told her how sorry he was for her situation, and apologised for burdening her with his problems when she must have been battling with her own.

"Oh, I didn't even know then, although I suppose I had suspicions," she assured him. "I think, to be honest, I've been wilfully blind. How are things with you?"

But he dismissed talk of his own affairs, just saying that things were getting sorted out. And he did look much better than the last time they had talked in her office. He told her not to shut herself away; her friends were all around and wanted to see her again, and he would be there for her any time she needed anything. Then he gave her a quick hug and brotherly kiss, and left.

He can't know it, thought Megan, but he's done wonders for my morale already. And then the phone went, the business of the day began, and soon she was in the middle of it, almost... *almost* forgetting herself. Most people made no reference to her absence and its cause, and just interacted as normal. But one or two gave her a warm smile or squeeze of the arm, and a couple of the nurses whom she knew well popped their heads round the door, said, "We're all thinking of you!" and vanished again. Her close colleagues visited and expressed their sympathy in various ways, including an offer to take her out and get gloriously drunk.

With the reappearance of Sue, Dick and Megan in their respective ordinary lives, the press had another flurry of stories, accompanied by photographs of each of them. Sue was now visibly pregnant, and naturally there was open speculation as to the father. When challenged, Dick announced publicly and firmly that the child was not his, and continued to deny that their friendship had ever been an affair. He had obviously got at Sue, as she also publicly stated that the baby was her husband's.

It wasn't long before the first of a series of photographs appeared, showing Dick in some fashionable London nightspot with a glamorous, expensive lovely on his arm. When he was asked if he had left his wife, he admitted they had separated. Without making accusations, he managed to convey the impression that she had neglected him, was more interested in her work and her love affair with horses, and that she refused to live in London. No wonder he was lonely.

Some newspapers managed to catch Megan looking severe and solitary in her dark working suit and sensible shoes, and ran articles on the folly of career women who failed to support their husbands. Agony aunts were wheeled out to say how foolish she had been not to cherish and keep tabs on her husband. There were plenty of right-minded women out there who knew how to look after a man, and she only had herself to blame if other women took his fancy.

Megan kept the newspapers out of Jeremy and Sam's sight but was aware that they heard things at school. They seemed to be coping, but inevitably wanted to know when Dad was coming home. When they eventually asked not when but if, she sat them down and tried to explain that though he was still their dad – and always would be – he was no longer her husband, and would not be living with them.

Dick had not yet made any move to visit them, but once the divorce conditions were agreed and the exchanges between them were less fraught, she suggested that he come and take them out for a day. Hopefully, once that difficult milestone was past, at least the parents would feel better. Megan tried hard to talk to her sons in simple, non-judgemental terms about the situation, and to get them to talk freely, too.

When Dick did finally visit, he had a woman in tow – a soignee glamour-puss – which made things tense. When her sons went off in the company of this other woman, Megan was filled with passionate anger; a fury she had never experienced ever before. But when they returned home, Sam put things right by hugging her and saying, "Don't worry, Mum, no-one will ever replace you."

And the next time Dick came, he had a different woman. Megan got the impression he preferred not to be exposed to the children's probing questions, and that a companion – any companion – was a bulwark, a bizarre kind of chaperone.

Chapter 27

It was unfortunate for Bridget that her husband picked up the post the morning the lawyer's letter arrived. She had been out in the yard early to check over a horse who was suffering from intermittent colic. Although he was virtually illiterate, Ned had an uncanny knack of recognising a missive or an official envelope that spelt trouble. He could pick out bills and final demands with the best of them.

He unerringly homed in on the thick, textured, creamy envelope, ripped it open, and tried to make out the details. Glaring out the window at the yard, he then wrenched open the door and bellowed, "Bridget!" at the top of his coarse voice. Seeing a terrified young girl standing nearby like a rabbit in the headlights, he roared, "Go get her!" The child bolted.

Bridget came in breathless haste, not knowing what to expect but fully aware it would be painful. "What is it? What is it?"

He thrust the letter into her hand and loomed over her while she read it. She shook her head and read again, her stomach dropping with terror, then sank down on a stool, trembling.

"Read it out loud!" he ordered roughly.

In a faltering voice she read from the lawyer's intimation – couched in official language – that on such and such a date, at Leatherburn Equitation Centre, she, Mrs Bridget Stark, had uttered accusations against Lady Miranda Morton-Merrydew of Hadley Farm, West Lothian, which had been witnessed by (and here followed a list of names, including the *Lothian Times* reporter and several of her clients); accusations that Her Ladyship construed as libellous. Furthermore, there was every possibility that these would be published in the press, and further damage Her Ladyship's reputation, on which she depended for her self-esteem and her good name in business. The letter wished to know what steps Mrs Bridget Stark might consider taking to reverse the damage she had done. If no such steps were forthcoming, they would have no other option than to take Her Ladyship's instructions, and to sue for very considerable damages.

Ned glowered at Bridget with an expression of incredulity and outrage. She had always verged on the mad in her hatred of Miranda, but this time it seemed as though she had flipped. He seemed to double in size as she cowered before him.

"What the de'il did ye say about her? Whit? Were ye out o' yer mind? Whit fer did ye say that? D'ye no ken the power they folks hae to squash the likes o' you? They snap their fingers an' the polis come runnin." He clicked his fingers in her face. "Ye'll be the wan behind bars this time, woman, I'm telling ye." He raged on until she was a cowering wreck, sobbing flat out on the counter. For once he did not lash out and hit her, but prowled like an animal to and fro across the kitchen floor, periodically bending and roaring an insult in her ear, when she would wince away from him with terror.

As storms come in waves before they run their course, this one eventually simmered down. The staff in the yard, who had heard every word, were frozen with fright, half wondering if she would get out alive. Bridget had seldom seen Ned so angry, and lifted her head very gingerly to see if the lull was temporary. She wiped her streaming eyes on her sleeve. Best to be humble. She knew better than to meet his eyes but she was almost as terrified of the letter's threats as his, and was ready – eager indeed – to back down.

"What do you think I should do?" she mumbled into her hands.

"DO!" he growled. "Ye'll have to eat humble pie, won't ye? Ye'll have to grovel and ask pardon. Ye've got too far above yersel', woman. Wan thing's sure. I'll see ye in clink afore I'll pay anything out fer yer stupid tongue runnin' awa' wi' ye. And ye'll have to gie them a sight more than words, for sure."

Bridget knew he liked to rub her nose in the muck on the rare occasions when she made a mistake, and that he was relishing tearing her apart. She would just have to take it.

"Ruined!" he snarled. "We could be ruined. After all we've built aroon' oorselves. And all becos' ye're a stupid, bletherin' bitch. Ye needna' think I'll go doon wi' ye."

"I suppose I should ring them." Bridget saw he was pondering, and feared he had some nefarious purpose. He was quite capable of clearing out and leaving her to face the music alone. And clearing out with as much of value as he could, too. She felt extremely vulnerable. "You won't leave me Ned, will you?" she whined.

He stood chewing his lip, looking through her as if she had ceased to exist. Bridget looked into the abyss, and imagined herself carted away in a police van, deserted by her man and everyone else, all her remaining assets seized, and shoved in jail for an indefinite period. Ned turned his back, hunched-up shoulders, hands in pockets, and moved to the door. He turned back.

"Dinna do onything. Ye've done enough damage. Leave me to sort it."

Bridget gazed after him in surprise. Tentatively she tried to go after him, asking what he meant, what he was going to do. But he had vanished, and she did not see him again that day. She remained a bag of nerves, nauseous and distracted, half expecting the police to appear at any minute, handcuff her, and drag her away to a terrible fate.

***

After a busy morning, Mandy bustled into her kitchen and found Hamish setting the table, broth heating in a saucepan on the Aga, and fresh, brown crusty rolls in the oven.

"Curious thing," she said casually, as he began ladling the soup into large earthenware bowls. "We seem to have a stalker."

Hamish looked up sharply, his dripping ladle poised over the savoury-smelling broth. "What do you mean, dear?"

"Claire mentioned she saw a strange man lurking in the field to the right as you come along the drive. He was keeping near the hedge, but easily seen. Looked very suspicious, she said. And yesterday morning the postman said he'd seen a stranger in the woods over beyond the stream. Just hanging about. He thought I ought to know because of the girls who work here."

"Have you informed the police?"

"No, not yet. Don't want to over-react. No-one goes out riding alone in the week anyway. And you're less vulnerable on a horse. Just keep an eye open, will you, love? Are you going out this afternoon?"

"Yes, I'm golfing later so I'll keep my eyes peeled. Perhaps you should report it, though. Could be someone planning a burglary."

That evening, Mandy came in from lessons about ten o'clock and found Hamish standing in a state of agitation at the sitting room window, peering out into the late evening twilight. "I've seen him. He was out there on the horizon; actually in your own field. Looked like one of those tinker chappies. He was quite brazen, very peculiar; almost as if he wanted to be seen. But he's away now. I really do think you should report it, my dear. Seriously."

"Mmmmm. Hamish, I have an idea who it might be, though it's quite bizarre. I'm not sure what it means, or how threatening it is. I'm inclined to think, not very. My instincts may be wrong, but trust me on this. Maybe I should go and look."

Hamish glanced at her quizzically. He was accustomed to her eccentricities. "Not on your own, you're not. Let me come, too."

They walked out across the field in the balmy summer evening breeze, encountering a few rabbits and birds, a fox, and plenty of insects, but no humans. Mandy looked around rather uneasily. "It might just be me, but I have a feeling we're being watched," she said, holding firmly onto Hamish's arm.

Next day there were no reported sightings. After her evening activities in the indoor school, Mandy popped her head inside the house to check if Hamish had seen the stranger, but he reported nothing untoward.

Heading back out to the yard to do her late night checks, Mandy went round the boxes, locked the tack and feed room doors, and the gate into the yard, then crossed to her front door. Something made her look back – and there he was, standing at the gate in silhouette. It was Ned, she knew, though she had not seen him for almost fifty years. She should really alert Hamish, but knew that if she did Ned would vanish. Let's get it over, she thought, slowly walking back towards him. She had no idea what to expect and warily stopped a few feet from the gate.

As she stood peering at him in the gathering dusk, he didn't bear much physical resemblance to the slender, black-haired stable lad she had once known. But his expectant stance, his sullen, bovine look and the way he deferentially removed his cap and bowed his head, brought memories trickling back. He was now thickset, his hair was grey and sparse, and he had a dark growth of several days' stubble on his chin. He looked obsequious rather than threatening.

"Well, Ned," she said sternly. "What can I do for you?"

"Good evening, ilady. I hope I see you well?" No-one back at Leatherburn would have recognised his voice, it was so servile and oily.

"Did you want something?" she asked crisply, not trusting the cringeing act.

He clutched his cap in one hand and held the top bar of the gate with the other.

"Yes, ma'am. I'm sorry about all this…" he waved his hand vaguely to indicate his manner of approach, "but I wanted to see ye alone."

She waited, her head slightly inclined, inviting him to continue.

"My wife said some stupid things. She's no' a bad woman, ye ken. But lately she's got ideas above her station. She didna mean the half o' whit she said. Folk ken she wis in a passion and winna take her words serious like. I'm asking ye… to call these lawyers aff. Please. Ye ken I've aeways admired you, ilady. I've never forgotten ye. But Bridget. She blamed ye, she never forgave ye. It jes' all came boilin' out, like. She's really sorry, ma'am. Really sorry. I know ye've a good heart, ye willnae punish her."

Ned had probably never made such a long speech in his entire life. Mandy could hardly believe her ears at such pleading, but did her utmost to keep looking severe.

"Well, Ned, that's all very well, but things have been said that cannot be unsaid. How do you think I feel, having such things said of me in public? That I'm no better than a thief and a fallen woman?"

"Oh milady, she wis wicked, very wicked, and I'll punish her for it. See if I dinna."

"I hope you'll do no such thing. Don't use violence on her, ever, Ned. What I meant was that until these words have been taken back, people might believe them. They may even appear in the papers. Bridget will have to speak to my lawyers and the *Lothian Times;* take back everything she said – everything; state it was totally untrue, said out of spite; and apologise to me. I want to see that in print, mind."

Ned stood in an attitude of deference, anxiously nodding his head.

"And while we're having this chat," she continued, "I'd like some assurance that this silly vendetta, trying to steal my clients, my ideas, and my business, will stop forthwith. There's enough work for both of us, goodness knows."

Ned was almost going down on his knees in his abject desire to please and to agree to her terms.

"Milady, she'll speak to all they folk, I'll see to it. And ye need never worry aboot her again. I'll promise ye, she'll never undercut ye again ever."

"What guarantee do I have about that, Ned?"

"Milady, I canna gie ye onything in writing. I never wis much good wi' a pen. But I'll gie ye a token o' my truth, and ye'll know it's frae me and that I'm a man o' ma word. An' ye'll call aff these lawyers, ma'am, will ye? Bridget will go oot o' her mind wi' worry, else."

"I daresay," said Mandy drily. "Once she's made amends through the paper and the lawyer, and I've heard from both of them, then – and only then – I'll let them know that they don't need to proceed against Bridget."

Ned bowed and backed away as if from the presence of royalty, holding his cap in both hands, and saying with each step, "Oh, thank ye, ma'am, thank ye. God bless ye now for a gracious lady, thank ye, thank ye..." until Mandy, fearing for her composure, turned and went off into the house.

The following morning both the editor of the *Lothian Times* and her lawyer rang Mandy to say that Bridget Stark had been on the phone first thing, apologising profusely for her outburst, and saying there was no substance in what she'd said; she claimed she didn't know what had come over her. The editor wanted to know if Her Ladyship wanted anything to appear at all. He was inclined to let it go, and she agreed.

The lawyer suggested Bridget should be required to put a notice in her stable office for the clients who had heard her wild words. Mandy thought about that, but said no. People forget; best leave it alone. If this signalled an end to the ridiculous rivalry, she thought, she would have gained more than redress. Instead, she instructed the lawyer to tell Mrs Stark in writing that, on the basis of Ned's personal assurances, she would let the matter drop.

Hamish felt she'd let them off too lightly. "People like that need to be left in agonising suspense for a while," he said. "To have their noses rubbed in their folly." But Mandy just smiled enigmatically at him.

Later that week, Mandy learned what Ned had meant by "a token of his truth". Leaving the house early on a fine summer's morning, with slight early chill and mist on the fields, she saw a vision in the yard. Perhaps the most exquisitely beautiful mare she had ever seen was standing quietly, tied by a scrubby head-collar and rope to a piece of twine where the farrier usually did his shoeing.

An elegant, bright chestnut filly, with faultless conformation, a thoroughbred probably or maybe three-quarter bred. She was awed at the mirage, hardly believing it until her hands made contact with the creature's head and neck and flank.

Mandy stood back, delighted at the calmness of temperament; many a horse would have become hysterical tied up alone in a strange yard. Head like a lady's maid, backside like a cook's, Mandy mused; just perfect. She untied the horse and walked her round the yard, then ran ahead to elicit an effortless, floating trot.

Where did he get her from? Will I find the police on my doorstep, looking for somebody's priceless treasure stolen from a field? Should I make enquiries? Mandy mused, but she could hardly take her eyes of the mare. She was falling in love already.

***

Some weeks later, a freelance photographer snapped a picture which prompted renewed interest in the stable scandal. Megan was caught on camera looking beautiful in a low-cut, elegant, figure-hugging, black velvet dress and sparkly jewellery, dining with a tall, blond man in one of Edinburgh's most exclusive, expensive, and atmospheric restaurants. The newspaper identified him as Alexander Temple, consultant surgeon at the hospital where Megan worked. Both parties, according to the report, refused to comment on their relationship. But to anyone studying the photograph, their body language and joy made the question redundant.

Epilogue

One year later

Annabel and her family had sailed into more harmonious waters. There had been one or two choppy stretches, but the family had learned to pull together rather than apart, so these were less disruptive than before. Lily had fully embraced her angst-ridden, hormone-driven adolescence and, paradoxically enough, this was something of a relief for the family. She got herself pregnant, and was duly conducted through an abortion plus counselling, which centred attention on her, gave an outlet for her histrionics, and made her feel she had endured one of life's profound experiences.

Lily sublimated by writing about it, concentrating her mind on self-expression, and seemed to have found her metier. She joined a literary group at school and this occupied her emotional energies, introduced her to some interesting friends, and provoked some constructive thoughts about a career pathway. She treated Poppy with even more older-sisterly disdain than before.

Annabel now worried more about Poppy, who had become completely horse-mad. Might the promising,

academic future they had mapped out for her be sacrificed for this enthrallment, low as it was in its capacity for
a rewarding career? But Poppy was too well-balanced and
eclectic in her interests for that to happen. It was unclear
which of her many school interests would direct her choice
of university studies, as she was so extraordinarily good at
everything. But her riding activities, demanding as they
were, in no way distracted her from her school work, and
indeed seemed to fill her with delight and contentment
and spur her on to greater efforts. Annabel could only
marvel and thank her lucky stars.

She and Ralph had, against all the odds, renewed their
mutual affection and trust, and moved on from the sexu-
ally turbulent phase of their lives. They had learned the
hard way how much they needed each other, and hopefully the lesson would not be forgotten. "Think of me as a
comfortable armchair you sink into at the end of the day,"
said Ralph.

Annabel had found herself horse-hunting again sooner
than she intended, but with so much lighter a heart this
time that she enjoyed the routine of checking adverts,
enquiring, visiting, trying out. When she could not
decide which to choose of two lovely mares who answered
all her hopes and dreams, the solution was simple. And it
was Ralph who pointed it out. "Buy both," he said. "You're
going to have to sell Suleiman Shah, since Poppy has
grown out of him, so there's one for each of you."

Annabel suggested to Megan that she might be interested in taking over Solly, but the offer left her friend with
a plethora of conflicting emotions.

"Not sure if I can quite cope with a horse on top of
everything," she protested. But she really wanted to agree.

"Think it over," said Annabel. "No rush. I'd love you to have him."

Megan and Alex had found mutual comfort together, especially since they were both recovering from the same kind of bereavement and on a similar timescale. Megan tried very hard to slow the pace, protesting that they must not be blinded by love on the rebound; they needed space to mourn their lost loves first.

"No problem for me," said Alex. "I've fancied you for ages." He wanted them to get engaged, and marry as soon as their respective divorces were accomplished.

In spite of Megan's prudence and protests, she found she was too deeply, exhilaratingly happy to resist. Thinking back, knowing that it was invidious to make comparisons, she remembered the doubts she'd had about Dick. But she had none about Alex; he was a gentleman in every respect.

They decided to sell both of their houses and buy a new larger home for their combined family. And the plan became slightly more urgent when Megan found she was pregnant.

"My God! We shall have four children between us! And a nanny!" exclaimed Megan, subconsciously viewing her life in terms of her previous partner, who had given her no help at all.

Alex positively glowed with the prospect of his enlarged family. He seemed to revel in the idea. Megan had rescued him from loneliness and neglect, and could see that he was going to be a very different sort of helpmate indeed.

When Megan told him that Annabel had broached the idea of her buying Solly, it was Alex who suddenly made it possible.

"Look, I'm under some pressure to buy Fiona a horse," he reasoned. "She's been such a great support to me that she deserves it. Why not share Solly between you, to start with? With a new baby, you won't want to do too much at first, but Fiona just about lives at the stable already. She'll have exams and school work, so it should be ideal for you to share. And Jeremy and Sam look as if they're getting very keen. There will be no shortage of riders for the poor beggar."

It was a brilliant idea, and Megan loved it.

"The boys certainly love riding and messing about. I'm not sure they'll be as committed as girls like Fiona and Poppy are," she admitted. "But still, they'll do their bit."

"In no time at all, we'll be buying them ponies, too."

"Alex! Give me a break! There's a limit to what even this superwoman can cope with."

"Listen, you've got me to help now. I'm not like your ex, always rushing off and leaving you in the lurch. I'll be here for all the family activities."

Alex was so courteous and considerate that Megan was repeatedly reminded what she had previously put up with. All her reservations were cerebral, and all her instincts told her to go ahead and be happy. Fiona was a delightful girl, who doted on her father and any fears Megan had harboured of jealousy and rivalry between them had not happened. The girl had already been accepted as a fantastic big sister for Jeremy and Sam, who quite suddenly found themselves with an extended family; a stabilising influence to mitigate their bewilderment over their father's defection.

Megan's one concern was how Annabel and Alex would cope with each other, as the newfound relationships meant they were bound to meet frequently. But if there was any awkwardness, nobody noticed. Annabel did whisper to Megan that she would have to be sure never to quarrel with her, as she knew so many of Annabel's guilty secrets. But she seemed content simply to harbour those secrets, and not to go in search of any more wild adventures.

Jackie's situation remained much the same but, with her friends' extended equine families, she had more chance to improve and stretch her own capacity.

Dick's career did not take off as astronomically as he had expected on his move to London. Maybe he missed the stabilising influence of family life, or perhaps the publicity of his infidelity had stirred some resentment amongst his female fans. His expectations that gorgeous young women would continue to fall into his arms and his bed, though, were not disappointed. And if that was the motivating force behind being famous and successful, maybe he did not need to work at it any more.

His partners were too ephemeral – or too savvy – to give him much domestic support, and all his cleaning and laundry had to be organised and paid for. He seemed in no hurry to remarry, and was photographed in trendy nightspots partying with minor royalty and stars of sport and screen. He joined the ranks of well-known faces who don't do much, just turn up at chat shows and other venues, famous for being famous. He put on weight and sometimes appeared rather raddled.

His riding was now carried out in fashionable places like Windsor Park and Rotten Row, on hired horses; with an escort, of course. Above all things, he liked to be seen, so he would stop and hail some acquaintance with hearty badinage, hoping that his horse would curvet and prance a bit – but not too much. He wanted to be admired for his horsemanship, as long as it wasn't tested too far. He didn't want another Barney episode. His escort would smile indulgently on these occasions, for she was discretely in charge however much he might flaunt himself. He was typical of her clients – semi-skilled riders who paid a huge sum for an hour or two on a showy horse, which was well-trained, docile, and virtually bomb-proof.

Dick had not seen Sue again, nor had he ever made contact. Perhaps if fate threw them together again, he might renew the affair. Who knew? Meanwhile, he had other fish to fry.

Sue had endured a terrible spell with Mike. For several months he had been off work and on mind-bending medication, and she was terrified that he would lose his job and their main income. She nursed him as devotedly as if she really was a detached professional, and managed at last to convince him that he had exaggerated the extent of her waywardness. She had only had a mild flirtation with Dick, and the baby was Mike's, of course it was. Did he ever seriously believe otherwise? Didn't he know how the gutter press made up these stories? Really, what did he think she was?

By the time he was living in the real world again, the fuss was over, the media stories forgotten. It was like a bad dream. So they drifted back to normal. Sue's baby duly arrived – another girl, as co-operative as Shelley. Soon after the birth, she got back into the swing of teaching, competing, exercising, mucking out, and all the multifarious activities that keep the horse world on track. But with two young children, she was far too busy to even yearn for sexual adventures, which was just as well. Even her farmyard cockerel had avoided her since… that time. Her hormones were just too occupied to cause trouble – for a while at least.

She regularly needed to reinforce the message of her devotion to Mike, babying him through his periodic nightmares about her leaving him. It seemed a small price to pay, as otherwise he was as trusting as before. One or two of her dressage associates were inclined to look down their noses at her, as if she had just crawled out from under a stone. But these were known to be strait-laced old virgins, Mary Whitehouse clones, and she could brush aside their rudeness.

Sue's belongings which she'd left in Dick's car, had been returned by post about a month after the Duncanshill episode, with a note saying, "Sorry for the delay. I guess I wanted to keep some reminder of our time together." Oh right, Sue had thought, her lip curling; how bloody typical, to do it at my expense. Selfish bastard.

Her pride had been scarified by his abrupt desertion and subsequent public repudiation of her. He had used the most unflattering terms to the press, implying she was some rustic simpleton. She would certainly not fall for his empty charm again. Looking back, she realised she had become too emotionally involved with him, when she should have used him as callously as he had used her. Why could women not skim happily on the surface of emotions as most men do so sublimely? Sue was determined she would not make that mistake again, oh no. If she needed extra sex in future, she would remember her adage; the one she had explained to Dick. Though mildly insulting in the context, he'd managed to take it as complimentary; that good riders tend to make good lovers, and vice versa.

Standing pondering such philosophy at her kitchen door, sipping her mug of coffee, she felt passingly content. From now on she would stick to horses for her significant relationships.

Bridget continued to flourish in her business, and whether it was the fright of nearly losing everything or Ned's curbing influence, she was never heard to denigrate Lady Mandy ever again. She quietly allowed her children's classes and activities to dwindle, gave up on trying to do liveries, and did not even think about opening a saddlery. And perhaps Mandy's words to Ned had also made an impression; he never struck Bridget again.

Mandy's precarious finances stabilised enough to keep her solvent. She gradually built up the stock in her saddlery, with Hamish's help, and people coming to buy stayed to admire her well-run yard. The word got around and, with a waiting list for liveries, she began to plan to build more loose boxes.

After much soul-searching, she kept the chestnut mare. She decided if she heard anything to suggest it was stolen or belonged to someone else, she would willingly hand it over. Well, maybe not willingly. Could there ever have been a more exquisitely beautiful horse? Her paces were heavenly, poetry in motion, absolutely designed for dressage. The girls called her Marigold. Time enough to think up a fancy name when she was ready to compete.

Mandy soon slipped into regular riding, and dreamed of taking to the arena herself. In all her bonding and delight in her new acquisition, she was sublimely unaware of a presence. It was no more than a shadow slinking around the hedgerows and the woodlands around Hadley – and even further afield, as time went on – just keeping a distant worshipful eye on the duo he had forged; the perfectly matched woman and horse.

About The Author

Margaret Cook was born in South Africa, brought up in Somerset, and studied medicine at Edinburgh University where she met and later married fellow student, Robin Cook. While bringing up their two sons, she continued to work full-time in NHS hospitals, taking a  consultant haematology post at St John's Hospital Livingston.

When Robin was UK Foreign Secretary, the couple famously split as a result of the press "outing" his affair with his secretary. Margaret wrote her memoir, "A Slight and Delicate Creature", and followed this with a study of the effect of power on personality, "Lords of Creation". She also combined a number of years of freelance journalism with her day job.

"A Bit on the Side" is her first novel, and her first self-published work. She lives in active retirement in Edinburgh, with her second husband Robin Howie.

Lightning Source UK Ltd.
Milton Keynes UK
UKOW07f1830250115

245101UK00001B/1/P